SOJOURNING
with
ANGELS

The Rise of Zazriel

a novel

R. LEO OLSON

Grand Rapids, Michigan is a real place but the characters, faith communities and businesses in this story are fictitious. Any resemblance to any real person, faith community or business should be dismissed as coincidence due to the commonness of such things.

To Emily, my love—floating you like a cloud

"But he was angry and would not go in. Therefore his father came out and pleaded with him."

-The prodigal son's elder brother- Luke 15:28

PROLOGUE

I am a watcher. Therefore, I watch.

And I have watched it rain for four straight days and the flowers can drink no more! You remember to water the wild crocuses of the field but have forgotten me. Haven't you had enough to drink, my little purple friends? Here we sit in the desert. You are drowned by the rain, and I am downcast with the heavy clouds of memories.

They're not here anymore, my little crocuses, but I can still envision them. Twenty watchers, my brothers, slowly orbited each other, looked into each other's eyes and shared unspeakable lustful thoughts. They devised a most evil plan in the lunar light, above Mount Sinai that night. It was an evening much like this one. Why did they do it, you ask? Oh, I don't know why, my flowering friends, but they did.

"Come, let us make a pact together. United we will stand," Semjaza said. At first, he was hesitant in speech but gained confidence as they all joined him, assuming the risk of judgment.

Of course, I interjected at their unholy communion!— As you would have, if a patch of your kind spoke such things against the Creator. "No, we cannot go against the Most High!" I told them.

Azazel, my friend, came close to my face. 'The Almighty One has left us to do what we want," he said. "Lucifer gained a kingdom for his rebellion and so will we. We will add to their knowledge of good and evil, and they will think they are like the Most High." He smiled. "Then we can take their daughters, satisfy our lusts, subdue the earth, and multiply it with our own seed!"

"Disgusting, isn't it? Why did they not listen to me? I constantly think about those days, and how I should've done more. But I am left here to watch, disgraced by association. At least I have you. Yes, a field of crocuses to keep me company. Oh, woe is me!

I watched as they divided their knowledge, taught men all the secrets of angelic culture, and then ravished the daughters of men. What could I do to stop them?

I just watched like a flower of the field when they bore the giants, Nephilim, evil hybrids, fashioned in neither the image of God nor man. Think of them like ravenous vines violently sprouting in your field, strangling your kind, the lilies, the wild tulips even the tufts of grass. They destroyed all things created 'good' by the Ancient of Days. They subdued the whole earth with reckless abandon and defiled it. I watched it all.

I should have begged for mercy when Michael, Uriel, Raphael, and Gabriel came to execute the most terrible judgment on my brothers. "His ways are sovereign and just, but is the punishment too severe?" I dared to ask. Why didn't I say more?

Michael stared at me, thinking something. I can still see his eyes filled with tears as he held his mighty fiery sword of death. But he offered me no response. He and Raphael spoke for a moment. I still wonder what they discussed. It doesn't matter, though. For with the same force as Lucifer was cast down from the highest heavens, they cast some of my brother watchers into dark caverns deep in the earth. One cavern is just over that mountain range to the North, probably covered with crocuses, like you.

Azazel's plea for help still echoes in my memory even now. I watched Raphael bind his hands and feet and encompass him with jagged rocks on every side. He is still entombed in total darkness.

I watched as the four mighty angels hunted down the rest of my brothers, uprooting them like trees and imprisoning them in the nether regions. Who can fight against them? Who can reason with Divine judgment? Surely not I, nor you.

"I watched time pass until it was the six hundredth year of Noah's life, in the second month, the seventeenth day, in the evening. I was sitting among the flowers, like I am now, when the rain began. The land mass split apart and the waters of the deep were angry with the wrath of the Most High. I hovered in the firmament begging for mercy. Leviathan devoured most of the Nephilim in their attempts to withstand the torrents. Some survived, as well as the ark of image bearers, sealed by the Almighty. That is mercy, I guess?

Yet I am left here, mournful with memory, watching as generations upon generations pass. They pick you to decorate their homes but cannot see me. No one sees me anymore. The creatures that bear the Image of the Divine are so similar, yet as different as their names: the Hattians, the Akkadians, the Hittites, the Assyrians, the Greeks and the Romans. To this day, my little friends, I do not fully understand them. The last to make use of this rubble were the Laodiceans. But that clan has long been spat out by the Almighty, and now this land is forgotten by the Turks, a lonely place covered with you. Yes, I am a watcher and I have watched for millennia.

ENTRY 1

"Thru the intercessions of the Bodiless Powers, Lord, save us."

- Eastern Orthodox Monday prayers honoring divine angels

"Who's here? Reveal yourself!" I shouted. The Archangel Raphael revealed himself and stood before me in his full angelic splendor. I bowed down, in the field of crocuses before him, but could not take my weary eyes off him. He was one of the most beautiful creatures in the heavens. He was magnificent to behold up close, holy, powerful and dangerous, but good. As he stood before me his transformational beauty radiated divine energy into my being and enlivened my dull purple feathers. I knew from this that he had come from the presence of the seraphim who continuously adore the Ancient of Days on the throne.

His wings were half opened, cupped around him, inviting me closer. As I approached I noticed the ornate name crest around his neck. He bore scars, injuries from past battles, and the most curious weaponry was girded about his belt, pouches of powder and fishery instruments. I wondered why the angel in charge of all guardian angels would call on my kind, after the Nephilim, whose spirits torment the image bearers to this day. I had long been resigned to my fate of watching over this region of ruins.

"Master, bless," I said.

"Rise," he spoke in my mind. "You have been found faithful in watching this region."

"It's in ruins and forgotten. Only the stones cry out now."

"Glory to God in the highest, watcher, for He has watched you and not forgotten your faithful obedience, as was not shown by your kind in ages past."

I was silent before him.

"He has another message for you. You are to be a guardian of a yet-to-be-born image bearer. He will be like an anointed one, and the aerial demons will try to destroy him and trap him in their terrible toll houses."

"Master, may His will be done on earth as it is in heaven, but I lack knowledge concerning guardianship of an individual image bearer. I have been here among the rocks for so long, I confess, I am unfamiliar with those tortuous nether regions of the aerial demons, and the ways they pervert the cultures of the children of the Resurrection."

"I am sending you to learn under Savlo and Kallistos, in the northern region of earth, until the babe is born. Learn from them. Make a record of all you see and hear. Obey only them. The aerial demons are cunning and your presence will spark curiosity and inquiry into the movements of the Almighty."

I bowed my head in acceptance.

"Master, I will obey, but even I've heard the demons tell stories of this Savlo and his failures."

His wings unfurled to their full expanse. A rushing wind engulfed me as he moved closer.

"You admit a lack of knowledge, and now you question His wisdom? You are too quick to speak. Guard your tongue first, watcher. His ways are not ours to question."

I fell to my knees again and could not look up. I trembled before him and said, "I'm unworthy, but here am I, send me as He wills."

"Take strength, for you have been given a new name. Names are sacred in the terrestrial dimension. Your name is a gift and establishes you in His eternal memory. Names also have the power to summon or rebuke. Tell no one and guard yours."

I nodded and looked down at my name crest. My old name faded and the new name appeared as if the finger of God was writing it.

"Arise, Zazriel, strength of God, and depart in peace."

— • —

I traveled to the northern region and found the Christopoulos family in a place called Grand Rapids, Michigan.

As I walked down the street in the darkness of night, I saw hundreds of demons, grotesque creatures. Some were dancing in the shadows. Small winged bat faced demons were swarming around the light post. They were all working themselves into frenzies, mimicking bestial sexual acts, cursing, laughing, singing and talking about an image bearer named Milo.

"Look, a watcher," a small black faced one yelled, causing the hordes to press in around me.

"I thought all the purple winged ones were in the prisons," another said as they stroked my feathered cloak.

"They really do have viper eyes," another said as it hovered in front of my face.

"What is your name?" another asked.

They continued to dance around me, poking me, pinching and tripping me. I stamped my staff against the ground. The fiery bladed tip ignited and I postured in attack formation. The demons scattered and laughed, making way for a dark figure that did not want to be seen, and thus remained just outside the rays of the street light. "Watcher, are you for us or against us?" he asked in a guttural voice.

I remained silent and poised to strike.

"Speak, before we devour you like your giants of old."

"I come in the name of the Lord," I said, and all the demons shrieked.

Through the roof of a nearby house two guardian angels arose, wings extended and showing a great light from within, almost unbearable to look at. One of them motioned me to enter the house as the demons ran from their light.

Soon, I cautiously appeared in the bedroom of the sleeping image bearers. It was a large room with windows in the roof. Moon light reflected off the white carpet and white laced bed coverings. Savlo and Kallistos were meditating, lightly vibrating with wings embraced. The strong communion between them was obvious. I fell to one knee.

"Greetings in the name of the Most High, Savlo-El. I have been sent by the Archangel Raphael to be your humble apprentice."

"Rise. What is your name?"

I slowly surveyed the room in search of other creatures. Finding none, I whispered, "Zazriel."

Savlo smiled at my caution. "Greetings, Zazriel. Where do you come from? Are you a true watcher, or just appearing as one?"

"Oh most gracious Savlo, I have been appointed to be the guardian for the babe when he is baptized. I lack experience, having only watched a region long laid desolate by an earthquake from a most powerful demon. I am a watcher, the last of my kind not imprisoned. I was told that you have much experience. Will you take me under your wing and teach me?"

He faced me straight on. I was taller than him. He had large gray wings with red tips and a pale translucent appearance. His face was sad, as if troubled from a heavy burden, but the zeal in his eyes was endearing. He welcomed me under his wing. I trusted him immediately. He turned to Kallistos, the guardian of the wife, and said, "This is unusual."

"Divine intrigue has come to us. The heavens are moving again." Kallistos smiled at me. "Zazriel, the watcher, welcome."

I looked at the three image bearers lying in bed, a husband, a wife with child, and another small child sleeping between them. I went to look at the woman and knelt down close enough to take in her maternal effervescence.

"Her name is Natalie," Kallistos said.

She was fair skinned, with delicate facial features, light brown wavy hair, strong but petite in frame, marked on the forehead with the seal of the Holy Spirit and magnificently pregnant.

"She has a pure soul."

Kallistos nodded.

I looked at the child nestled close to her. "Where's the child's seal?"

Neither answered.

"Unbaptized?"

Savlo affirmed, with a nod.

I rose and looked at Milo, one leg hung off the bed. He was a Grecian man with a fair build, square jaw, curly black hair and olive skin. He too was marked with a seal.

"Milo is soul sick and has excommunicated himself from the Holy Church. He thinks the Almighty One has abandoned him and he has become a double minded man, unstable in all his ways. Do you know this feeling?"

Our eyes met. I knew Savlo was familiar with the sadness that comes from serving a silent God.

"Go look out the window and tell me what you see," Savlo said.

"Why is there such dark interest for the image bearer, Milo?" I asked looking at demons lounging in the trees.

"They have been mounting attacks. The dark energy engulfs his every interaction. Now you are sent to us. I am even more concerned for him, young guardian. Is there anything else Raphael told you?"

"He told me you have valuable experience concerning the aerial toll houses of the fallen, and I should watch, and keep a record of everything I see and hear."

He and Kallistos wrapped in their wings and were silent, eyes closed. I remained silent, watching the demons dance for almost a quarter turn of the planet before I was emboldened and asked, "Mighty Savlo, being the lone watcher of deserted Laodicea for centuries, I must know how the aerial toll houses grew so strong after the destruction of hades."

Savlo and Kallistos opened their wings. Both were attentive to me now.

Kallistos who was more beautiful than Savlo, with deep golden hued wings, muscular, glowing a tint of pink from an almost transparent bodily form, said, "The simple answer is, His permissive will must allow it to exist and, secondly, the free will of His creatures must choose it."

"Why would the image bearers choose such terrible dwellings?"

Savlo interrupted, "Why did Eve choose to eat from the tree of knowledge of good and evil? Why did the watchers of old corrupt the image bearers, teaching them to use that knowledge of good and evil? Why did they impregnate the image-bearing women creating the evil Nephilim? Why did the son of perdition choose to betray the Christ with a kiss? Why does He not scatter His enemies and why is He delaying their judgment? There are many questions that remain unanswered to this moment."

I bowed my head, for I knew my zealousness for knowledge had been mistaken for idle inquiry.

Kallistos spoke to just my mind. "There are still many mysteries long to be understood. We still are amazed how the Uncreated One became one of them and entered the mystery of death. Lucifer had been baited like a fish with a hook when he swallowed the Incarnate One. Hades was destroyed by that most divine deception. The armies of the aerial demons, enraged by this, waged even fiercer a battle, since now hades can only yawn, keeping no one against their will. They invaded the second heaven and now battle with our general, Raphael. They set up the aerial toll houses to torment and ensnare the baptized image bearers, keeping them deceived and in despair until the end of days."

Milo stirred awake and stumbled to the bathroom.

"Are you okay, honey?" Natalie asked as the light from their adjoined bathroom shone on her.

"Yeah, I'm fine. God, I hate getting old. Can't even sleep through the night." He stumbled around. "Shit, I missed the toilet. Damn it."

He got back into bed, scooted his daughter over to the middle and exhaled.

"Did you clean it up?"

"Huh?"

"Milo, that's disgusting."

He laughed. "I'll do it in the morning." He pulled the covers over him. "Still love me?"

"Kind of."

"Good, because you're the only person who does."

We all looked at each other, as they drifted back into the murky sleep of indolence.

"If you are to learn from me you must obey three rules," Savlo said.

"Forgive my zealousness. I will trust in your wisdom."

"First, you must only observe. Do not enter a battle or a conversation with any demon unless we permit you. Secondly, you must record everything you see and review it carefully, for Raphael will hold me accountable for such a unique apprentice as you. And finally, and most importantly, one question per day, so ask wisely."

"I understand and accept. Thanks be to God for such a wise mentor."

"All thanks be to God for His long suffering," he said.

"One question for each of you, each day?" I asked Kallistos.

"Can you hear the monks on Mount Athos?" he asked.

"Yes."

"Pray with them. Monday is our day."

"One question per day," Savlo said. And so we communed in silence the rest of the lunar light.

ENTRY 2

The Last Tuesday of Milo's Life

At 6:01 a.m., the red lit clock clicked on and buzzed. Milo reached up and hit the device. "God, I hate that sound." He got up, stepped on a piece of paper he had laid on the floor the previous night, bent down, picked it up and read it. He walked into the bathroom, disrobed, turned the shower on, and faced the mirror. He placed the paper next to the sink and paused for a moment. I positioned behind him. After several deep breaths with his eyes closed, he opened them and spoke with great conviction:

"I am an amazing real estate agent—
I give others positive energy—
I am powerful—
I claim riches. Money flows to me every day and every way—
I am resourceful beyond measure—
I find solutions to every obstacle—
I am healthy and beyond sickness—
I have all I need to be successful—

I am the captain of my own soul and I claim the universal law of attraction to help me realize wealth, success and happiness—

I am the captain of my own soul. I am the master of my own fate. I am the captain."

He took a few more deep breaths and looked down at the paper where the question was written, 'How do I make thirty thousand dollars this week?'

He smiled in the mirror and said, "Thank you, subconscious." Then he took his shower and finished his morning ritual. Soon Savlo and I were en route to his office.

It was a sunny spring morning. We travelled hovering over the vehicle's rooftop as Milo suddenly pulled over and parked on a red bricked street named Wealthy. Savlo told me he didn't usually drive in this part of town. A young bearded image bearer with tattoos and several piercings about his face was scraping the window stencil, *The Eagle and Child*, off the door and was going to install a new stencil which lay on the ground, *The Rabbit Room Café*.

"New ownership?" Milo asked as he approached the door.

"No, copyright issues. The lawyers are being a pain in the ass."

"I like the new name better anyway."

"Thanks, go on in," he said as he slid the stool out of the doorway.

"I'll have the 'shot in the dark'," Milo told the barista. "What's in that, by the way?" he asked.

"This is our bold dark roast, fair trade coffee with a shot of espresso. It's a real kicker," the barista said.

"Just one shot of expresso?"

"Yes sir, and it's pronounced *espresso*," he enunciated slowly.

"Just give it to me." Milo jingled his hand of change over the tip jar but pocketed the money instead and walked to sit in the back corner of the café. The small table sat on the hardwood floor and wobbled. He sighed as his drink spilled. The walls were cream painted wood paneling featuring pieces from local artists. Milo pulled out a note pad and a pen. He was dressed in a modern business suit. He sat for a while without writing a word, just holding the pen in a writing position. Savlo said this was the first time in months he had sat in silence with nothing occupying him.

Soon, The Rabbit Room Café filled up with young people and their computers. Milo sipped his drink and watched them. He was the oldest person in the room.

A young female image bearer walked in and caught his eye. She was full breasted and wore a low collar t-shirt and a scarf tight around her neck. Her head was covered with a béret. She sat near him. They smiled at each other. By uncontrolled habit he glanced at her chest and winked. She moved to another table.

In walked a vagabond. He was dressed in an old sweater and camouflage cargo pants, and was cloaked in a black coat. His hair was disheveled; forehead bore heavy creases, unshaven with jowled cheeks. He mumbled an ancient language. We recognized it immediately. It was an angelic dialect.

He walked past the barista, who was just finishing a drink order. Most everyone in the café noticed him. Milo had not taken his eyes off him since he entered the building. He walked straight to the back and stood four paces from Milo. He stared straight ahead at a painting on the wall, mumbling. Milo looked up at the art piece, then at the man, and then waved the barista over. The man snapped his head to the right, mumbling faster. He was looking at Savlo.

"I know your reputation, Savlo and the Wolf of Souls is ready for him."

"He is baptized, sealed with the Holy Spirit. It is not for you or the Wolf to require his soul," Savlo said.

"His heart is dark. He will never make it through the toll houses. He is my greatest work."

The man took two steps toward Milo, made eye contact, and smiled at him. Milo shifted in his chair as if to defend himself. He then looked me over from head to toe and smiled. Milo folded the pad shut and was about to confront the man when the barista approached.

"Excuse me sir, we have a one-drink minimum and a free table up front."

The man turned to face the barista, mumbled in our language a most vile accusation of some secret sin, and then shuffled out the door. He stood outside the window and looked in.

Milo looked at the barista. "Who the hell was that?"

"I don't know. I haven't seen him before. He's probably mentally ill, but he'll leave soon."

"You thought I was creepy, huh?" Milo said to the image bearer who had moved away from his lustful glance.

"Enjoy your coffee, sir. It's no biggie. They wander in every now and then," the barista said.

Milo stood, looked toward the front of the café, and watched him through the steamed glass, staring back at him.

We went to the front of the café and faced the demon. "Be gone," Savlo said.

The demon walked down the street, cursing the air.

I looked back at Milo in the rear of the café. There he stood alone, dressed in a suit, encased by wood floors, wood walls and a wood ceiling. He was in a coffin. "That was a personal hindering demon. I've watched some of them. Milo is going to die soon," I said.

I looked at Savlo who was looking at Milo and now I knew his heavy burden. "Yes, after the hinderer confronts its image bearer, they die within seven days. He is too soul-sick to make it through even the first terrible and dreaded toll house. This is most vexing," Savlo said.

Milo finished his drink and left for the office.

— • —

Milo entered the entryway of the Open Door Realty office, greeted his clients, who were early for their meeting, and escorted them to a glass-walled room. He then went to the office where the name, Lilly Maneyu, was on the door.

"Hey gorgeous, my clients are here. You ready? Whoa—look at you. I'm not sure that's business casual or even legal in the Midwest."

She looked at him with her deep green eyes and his heart beat faster.

"What? Oh, this. Well, they say leather is the new cotton and only certain types of women can pull off these boots. I'm one of those women, sugar," she said with a slight drawl. He blushed.

"What type of woman is that?" he asked.

"Obviously not the type of woman y'all know up here."

"I might want to get to know one."

"Really? Even though you're happily married?"

"Who said 'happily'?" He winked.

"Oh, I'm not sure you could handle all this, honey." She went back to organizing a file.

"I may surprise you."

"Well, this is all fun talk, but I'm into action. So you let me know when you're ready."

She walked towards him and rubbed her breasts against him as she passed through the doorway. "Excuse me, I have to make some copies."

He smirked, gaining great energy from her. "Back-to-back closings, right?"

"Bang-bang, baby, just like we always do it." I noticed her meretricious way caused him to smile a covetous and lustful smile. I had seen that kind of smile before from my brother watchers. I saw no seal and I saw no guardian for Lilly.

— • —

After Milo and Lilly had executed the transactions, he walked to the break room where a group of agents had gathered to congratulate a young image bearer on his betrothal to a maiden.

Milo poured himself a cup of coffee. "Wait, wait, I know the real truth about marriage."

"Oh great, marriage counseling from Milo, that's all he needs," someone said from the back of the room. Everyone laughed.

"No, really, I got it figured out. Marriage is the constant renegotiation of double standards," he said. The break room clamored with laughter and gaffs from the other married men. The women just shook their heads.

"Robert, let me tell you a thing about sex. It will be great for a while but after some time, sex is like a B minus in college; not always your best work, but never bad." Everyone laughed again except for the newly betrothed who looked embarrassed, but smiled. Milo slapped him on the back. "I know you don't believe me, and you shouldn't really, but let's talk again in a few months. Wisdom must be proven to the young. Enjoy your wedding, my man." He walked out of the break room and sat in his cubicle, sipped his coffee and interacted with a device named Facebook.

We stood away from him. I watched the business of the office and the other guardian angels prompting their image bearers. I looked down at his desk and saw his name plate read, Milo Chris. He went by a name other than his given one.

His phone rang.

"It's a great day at Open Door Realty. This is Milo Chris. How can I help you?

"Hi, Bill. I'm glad you called, because selling houses is exactly what I do. Sometimes I even buy them if I can't sell them…Foreclosure may be an option for you and hey, thanks for being up front about that. Going through foreclosure is a bitch. But since 2006, when the market tanked, it's very common, and I am an expert in dealing with banks…Yeah, that's right, sometimes I buy them or I'll guarantee a sale…Interviewing other agents? Why would you want to do that? …Oh, of course, I'm married too." Milo laughed.

"What's your wife's name? …Monica, that's a good name, sounds like she's taking this pretty serious to be interviewing agents. Maybe you should interview other agents—for her sake. Do you have anyone lined up? …Amber Lightfoot? Yeah, I know her, she's just down the hall…No, there's no conflict of interest. You choose an agent to sell your house, not a company. The trick is to find the right agent. You do want to choose the right agent, an aggressive agent, like me, don't you? …Yeah, I can make it tonight but I want to go after Amber, is that cool with you? …I'll tell you what. Let me give you a couple of questions so you can be sure to choose the right agent. Would that be okay?"

Milo continued the conversation for several more moments. I assessed he had mastered the art of manipulation by asking questions to which 'yes' was the only answer.

He hung up, walked to a large white board, and wrote his appointment on the listing agent of the month contest, 'Dinner for the Winner'. As he walked past Amber's cubicle he mockingly rubbed his belly, alluding to the prize. He was tied with Amber for this month. He smiled at her. She did not smile back.

While he sat at his desk, I was careful not to ask my question, obeying Savlo's rules, but uttered, "Savlo, based on all I have observed so far, I am unfamiliar with this modern type of economy."

Savlo waited for a moment, and then spoke, "There once was a farmer who owed a debt of a hundred denarii to a wicked money lender who purchased the land for him. The farmer was working on the land producing grains, selling them at the markets to pay the debt on the land. A sickness overtook the regions' livestock. The farmer's mules died and he could no longer collect and transport his harvest in the fields. The wicked money lender was going to imprison the farmer for nonpayment and take back ownership of the land.

"Another man who worked in the markets, full of opportunistic thinking, learned of the farmer's trouble. He offered to talk to the wicked money lender for the farmer. He offered to buy the land for seventy five denarii, because seventy five denarii was better than zero denarii, a farmer in prison, and dead crops in a field. The wicked money lender agreed to this plan, as did the farmer. What neither of them knew was that the man who worked in the markets offered to sell the land to a foreigner for a hundred and twenty denarii. Once the foreigner paid the hundred and twenty denarii, the man of the markets paid the wicked money lender for land and told the farmer he saved him from prison but that he must move immediately and work as a hired hand on a different farm."

"Milo's work is a opportunistic deception," I said.

"Yes, unjust and exploits the ignorant."

"I noticed Lilly helps him with this deception."

"He needs her to enforce the laws of the banks, but she under-stands it's about the deception of timing and shielding of knowledge."

"I sense she is dangerous to his soul."

"He may gain the whole world, and lose his soul because of her."

Lilly had made her way around the office and walked past Milo's cubicle. "You're a very funny man, but I expect more than a B minus."

She stood behind him, leaned down and whispered in his ear, "I have to work late tonight and the next night and the next." She sauntered away.

He leaned back to look upon her. An image bearer across the walkway, a man of considerable girth but cheerful in demeanor, as was his guardian, looked over at Milo. His name was Ricky. "Don't be so obvious, my man, you're married and your wife's pregnant. You can hold out."

"Hey, I can still look at the menu, can't I?"

"I don't know about you, big M."

"Maybe a taste test, a sample, ya know? Is that so bad?"

"Whatever. You're the craziest Greek dude I know."

"Yeah, whatever, I wouldn't know what to do with all that, any-way."

They both laughed and continued about their work for the rest of the day. I watched everything and learned much of the present culture. Milo headed out for the appointment, moments after Amber left for the same appointment.

— • —

Milo pulled up to the house knowing that Amber was still inside. He got out and knocked on the door. "Hi, I'm Milo. We talked on the phone today. I know I'm a little early, but I wanted to take some outside pictures while the sun was still up. Is that okay?"

"Um, yeah, I guess, feel free to take some pictures." Bill looked at Monica and raised his eyebrows, signaling for her approval.

Amber looked at Milo with a clenched jaw.

"Great." Milo smiled at the husband. He walked around the house, taking photos, and I followed. He was now visible from the sliders to the back deck. He zoomed in to the dining area and could see Amber inside, talking quickly and with animation. Milo laughed as his premeditated plan was having its effect. He walked around front, leaned on his SUV, and waited.

Amber walked out the front door and glared at Milo as she passed him. She got into her car, backed out of the driveway, drove slowly around the corner, and parked.

Milo bounced up, camera in one hand and a folder in the other. He knocked on the aluminum screen door. Monica answered, welcomed him to the dinette table, and offered a glass of water.

"That would be wonderful. Thank you," Milo said and pleasantly held a smile, intentionally enunciating without ever breaking his gaze from her. Monica came back into the room and put the glass of water down on the same wet coaster Amber had used. He sipped his water and then took the presentation from his folder. He laid a script out on the table and turned it around so they could read it.

"Are you going to read us a script?" Bill asked.

"Of course I am. Didn't Amber read from a script?" he asked.

"Ah, no," Monica answered.

"So you're telling me, Amber just winged it?" He paused. "Interesting," Milo said with a voice inflection.

They looked at each other. Bill raised his eyebrows and smiled. Monica tightened her lips and looked at the glass of water in full sweat now.

"I am guessing you two are…like me." He paused and pointed to himself emphasizing the last two words. "A little embarrassed about a pending foreclosure, but still wanting to do the right thing."

They looked stunned.

"That's how I felt when I went through it, many years ago. It's a feeling you don't forget."

Savlo told me and their guardian angels, who remained silent, that Milo never went through a foreclosure, himself, but would now offer them a narrative about how they could handle this embarrassing situation with a modicum of self-respect.

"You're not choosing this, it's choosing you," Milo said, "it's just collateral damage from a hemorrhaging economy—all that subprime, toxic asset stuff you hear on the news."

They nodded in agreement.

"Now he will leverage their emotions against the bank and position himself as their mediator," Savlo said.

Monica and Bill were now listening to Milo's words and the tension in their faces lessened.

"I do real estate a little bit different than Amber. I'm very good with the bank negotiations. You know, being in foreclosure, that you cannot get any money from your house?"

They seemed to accept this statement.

"Because house values have dropped so much I'm going to offer to buy your house for a very low price." He handed them a sheet of paper detailing some neighborhood houses that had sold over the past year.

They both looked over the sheet.

"Ouch, right? So you can see it looks like the banks are losing money, but they got theirs early. Have you noticed how much you pay in interest the first years of your mortgage?"

They nodded.

"I will have to be authorized to speak on your behalf to the bank. In fact, you will not have to talk to them again. Won't that be nice?"

"Yes," Monica said, with a tone of exasperation.

"I'm going to offer, today, to buy your house for seventy five thousand dollars, in a contract that I will hold open until I can get the bank to agree with me on that price."

"Damn, we paid a hundred and twenty five for it."

"The prices don't really matter to you now. Once I get the bank to agree to my price, then you can walk away, feeling you've done everything you could to make it right. That's how I work what's known as a short sale."

They looked apprehensive.

"I know it can be confusing, so look over this flow chart while I take a look around the house, snap some pictures of the inside and make some notes for the listing description while you two think it over?"

Milo made his way through the house. He was coming up the basement stairs when he noticed a small Byzantine icon of Mary positioned high at the top of the door to the garage. He paused and almost crossed himself out of childhood habit, but resisted.

I heard a small demonic laugh and looked for it.

Milo stepped back to the maple dinette. "So, are we partners?"

"What if the bank doesn't agree to sell it to you at your price?" Bill asked.

"Well, I'm going to list the house for sale for a hundred thousand, while you live here for six months for free. That gives me time to wrangle with the bank, so we won't close on my seventy five thousand offer, right away. Once the bank sees that the house won't sell for a hundred, they'll agree to my seventy five and I'll buy the house."

"What if someone buys it for a hundred?" Monica asked.

"That doesn't matter to you, anymore. If someone buys it, whether it's me or not, you will have done all that you could've done. You need to get through this season in your life. Listen to me, Bill and Monica, you seem like a nice couple. Monica, you're pregnant. My wife is pregnant. You have an icon of the Virgin Mary, I was raised Greek Orthodox. We were meant to help each other out. You can't sell this house for what you bought it for, and you will go through foreclosure. I am offering a chance to save some face and ease the ethical conflict you feel. I'll do my best to step into your situation, and get you out of it feeling okay. If you choose not to work with me, then call Amber, and hope someone will pay top dollar for your house when the house down the street is for sale for thirty thousand less than you owe."

The husband looked defeated.

Milo raised the energy in the room by standing up. He said, "Let's do this. Sign the contracts and let me loose on your bank; those bastards. I'm giving you a chance to walk away with a clean conscience—a fresh start."

They consented and signed every form Milo passed their way.

He shook their hands and walked down the driveway. He noticed Amber's car at the end of the street. We positioned in the back of the SUV.

His phone chimed; a text from Amber.

-*theyll list with me tmrrw*
-*doubt it*
-*y*
-*i bought the house tonight*
-*what?*
-*i bought the effing house :-)*
-*how*

-w. $
-dick
-i know. luv u 2
-fu milo
-u wish

His phone rang. He pushed a button and spoke through the vehicle's speaker system.

"I don't know what the hell you're doing exactly, Milo, but it seems a little shady."

"Amber, my dear, what are you accusing me of, exactly?"

"Of cheating the system, somehow."

"See, that's just it, Amber, and this is why you will always be second to me. You work within the system, and I transform it."

"You're a crook and taking advantage of poor folks."

"By buying their house?"

"Whatever, you're still a dick, I saw the list of questions they asked me. Wonder who gave them that?"

"Well, I'd love to chat with you some more, but arguing with other agents is not a money making activity. Another way I transform the system." He laughed and hung up.

"He is very soul sick, Savlo," I said.

Milo turned up the radio. A voice announced music by Nirvana. Ironically it was disturbing music. He was going seventy seven miles an hour, north on highway 131. Milo drifted slightly right. His eyes were locked on the white line; the tires had reverberated violently as his vehicle now straddled the rumble strip. The mile marker reflector posts were flashing by.

The radio blared, "I feel stupid and contagious…" He sang along.

Savlo positioned right behind him and whispered, "You have so much to live for, why tempt death? Think of your family. Get back to the center lane. Do it now."

Milo started to rant out loud as he course corrected over the rumble strip. "Who the hell does she think she is, calling me a crook? Hell, I'm saving these schleps from the financial slaughterhouse. Crook, my ass. She can kiss my ass."

Another text chimed his phone. It was Lilly.

-*Still at work. u commin back*

-*want 2 but cant*

-*cant or wont*

She sent him a picture.

-*damn r u sexting me*

- *lol yep. if u get lucky 2nite, think bout me K?*

-*no luck tonite but will think bout u*

-*come here and u will get lucky*

I could tell he was thinking about it.

He texted back.

- *C u tmmrrw*

-*all talk. night xoxox*

-*muah*

He pulled into the driveway of his brick two-story house. He sat there for a couple of minutes, watching his family's activity. His daughter was chasing the neighbor's basset hound with a spray bottle, in the side yard, because the dog had torn open a trash bag. Natalie stepped to the front bay window holding a phone to her ear. Her hair was a mess, and she had spilled sauce all over her clothes. She aggressively motioned for him to come into the house. He dropped his head on the steering wheel, let out a sigh, and mumbled, "Should've went back to the office."

We heard demons cheer as Milo uttered this phrase. They were not visible, but they were so infested in his life that it was hard to keep track of them all.

Milo entered the house and spent the evening retelling the events of his day without asking one question about Natalie's day. After dinner, he spent hours alone in his office, planning the next day's events and flirting with many other women on Facebook. A lusty little she-demon danced outside the office window in the backyard.

He readied himself for sleep. After he set the alarm for 6:01, he wrote a question on a piece of paper, and laid it on the floor by his side of the bed. He soon was restlessly dreaming. Natalie tried to lay still, for she was sick with her pregnancy.

"We saw his hindering demon today," Savlo told Kallistos.

"He is too soul sick to make safe passage through the toll houses. He has forgotten who he is," Kallistos said.

We were all quiet for several moments.

"Savlo, my question for the day is, how did Milo get this soul sick?"

"One question per day, remember? Reflect on all you have witnessed today."

"Gracious One, I did not ask a question, simply made statements."

He thought back to our conversations and smiled, "Well done, watcher. You will do well when it comes time to defend your image bearers through the toll houses."

I smiled back.

"Laodicea was renowned for its medicines for the eyes, a knowledge you imparted to them, I would guess. Correct?"

"Yes."

"I once knew an image bearer who owned a small mirror. He was smitten with his own reflection. He was extremely handsome, doted on by his family, given every good gift to have a blessed life, and desired by many maidens. He was born with perfect eyesight, but over the years he began to squint into the mirror, drawing it ever closer. He fell in love with his reflection. His devotion to staring at himself with so much concentration eventually ruined his perfect eyesight. He no longer looked at others, only himself. He carried the mirror before his eyes always, groping about so as to not trip or bump into anything. One day he had need to go to the market. Several bandits came along-side of him. He talked with them as friends but could have known otherwise if he had looked at them, but he did not break his myopic gaze. They led him deep into the forest, down paths he did not know until they were sure he had lost his way. They beat him about the face, stepped on his mirror and robbed him, leaving him alone, penniless and disfigured. Do you know what he did?"

I shook my head.

"He bent down and put the shards of the mirror into his hand and stared at a fractured reflection of his disfigured face, forever lying to himself that he was still handsome."

He then pointed to Milo.

ENTRY 3

The Last Wednesday of Milo's Life

We were hovering over Milo's car as he was driving his mother, Helen, into town for an early coffee at Simon's Books and Café. As they reached a rural stretch of road, Helen said, "Milo, isn't that Maria in the field?" They slowed down.

"Yep, it sure is," Milo said. "Mrs. Thoma, I haven't seen her since——"

"Oh look, she's getting grape leaves. That must be where she—oh my goodness."

Milo slowed down.

"Drive Milo, drive, she'll see us."

Milo pushed the button to lower the window.

"Milo, no, please don't," Helen begged.

"Hey Maria, we know where your patch is!" Milo yelled.

She looked up to see who was yelling at her.

"We found your patch, Mrs. Thoma!" Milo laughed and sped off.

Helen broke out in laughter and blushed, covering her face with her strong but age-spotted hands. "Oh, Milo, no, no, Milo."

"What? Now you'll have a real chance at beating her at the Greek festival. You know where her grape leaf patch is, and it's all about the leaves. Right?" Milo asked smiling.

His mother laughed and smiled at her son. "I'm going to get it at church on Sunday."

"She adores her son with the same affection as Mary did," Helen's guardian angel said as we all hovered above Milo's car.

They pulled into the café, secured their usual seat by the fireplace and went to the counter to order.

"Hmm, the bacon spinach quiche looks good. I'll take that and a coffee. Leave room for cream and whatever my mother wants."

"Milo, it's Wednesday," she whispered, "Don't eat meat, get the veggie bagel. It's better for you anyway."

He ignored her comment. I heard a demon snickering that sounded like pigs snorting. They sat down and Helen crossed herself. Milo had already started eating.

"So, Milo, Father Luke was wondering if you were going to come for Holy Week this year. He sure would like to see Natalie and Sasha again."

"Aw, come on, Ma, can't we at least enjoy our meal before we get into this again?"

"Does it upset your stomach to discuss church?"

Milo shook his head and started inspecting the cleanliness of the utensils.

"Milo, you have to come back to our church and have Sasha baptized. My only granddaughter is not baptized. Do you know what this means?"

"We go to a good church now, Ma. Kids are baptized when they're older, it's really their choice. It's how it's done in this country."

"Tsk, tsk, tsk, this is not right. Children don't decide when to be baptized. It's the parents' job to raise them in the proper ways of the Church, which is to baptize after forty days. It is how we raised you, and Natalie was raised that way too. We are Greek Orthodox. It's the way we are Christian."

"See, that's just it. It's because we're Greek that we do all this stuff. We do it for old fashioned traditions. Nat and I are fine at Dogwood Bible Church. The sermons are good, nice people, they teach the Bible. Isn't that good enough?"

Helen accidentally knocked over her glass of water as she reached for some sweetener. A barista quickly came to help clean up the spill. The image bearer had piercings in her nose, ears and lip. Her dreadlocks were tied in a ponytail, and she had a large cross tattooed on her forearm and a fish symbol on her ankle. She had a seal but her guardian did appear to us.

"Thank you, dear," Helen said, and went on when she was out of earshot. "See what happens when you let children decide what to do without minding the traditions of the Church?"

"Come on, now, don't be like that."

"Be like what?"

"Old fashioned. No one cares about the old traditions anymore."

Helen looked at Milo as only a mother can look at a sick child.

"God cares, Milo. I taught you everything about our faith and now you break my heart," she said as her eyes watered.

"It's not like that, Ma. I will not be guilted into following dead church traditions just because I'm Greek. I wasn't getting anything out of going. Nothing. No nourishment." He took a bite and said with food in his mouth, "Hey, I believe in Jesus and this is America. You get to choose however you want to believe. It's all pretty much the same stuff, anyway."

Helen put down her fork and stared at Milo for an uncomfortable amount of time. Milo continued to chew loudly.

"Ma'am, here's some more water. Anything else I can get you two?" the server interrupted her stare.

"No, it's all good," Milo said with a mouth full of food.

"I'll take a box to go."

"Ma, c'mon, we do this every other time I see you. I know what I'm doing with my child."

"This is not about what's best for Sasha, this is about you. If you loved her you would baptize her."

"Oh my God, are you saying I don't love my child? Really?"

"Not more than I do, at least about their spiritual upbringing. Don't worry about it. I'll take care of the whole thing," she said and smiled at him.

"What the hell does that mean? What are you going to do? You're scheming. I can tell."

"I will not give up on you or Sasha. My love is very strong and God loves us in spite of what we think or do. So eat, my son—eat, drink, and be merry." She smiled at him.

Milo stopped eating. He put his fork down, dabbed his mouth and laid his napkin over his plate, took a sip of water and pointed his finger directly at his mother's face. "You stay the hell away from my child. I don't want anything to do with your church. I've moved on."

"My church? I thought it was God's church."

"No, your church—your precious Greek Orthodox church with all its mumbo jumbo. I read the Bible for myself now and the pastor's sermons are pretty good. I agree with most of what he says, and that's good enough for me and my family."

She continued to smile at him. Milo continued to point his finger. Demons laughed, one said, 'I'll be mumbo; you be jumbo.' I looked under the table and saw two small black bat-faced devils with wings and dull red eyes.

I looked to Savlo for permission to dismiss them but he motioned me to leave them alone.

"So my faith and love anger you, is that what they teach you, too?"

"Sheesh, enough already. This is the last conversation we're going to have about this. It really pisses me off."

"Fine. I'll talk to Natalie. I'm going to wrap this up and bring it home for your father. Take me to church. I have Canasta club."

"Fine."

They left in silence. Milo dropped her off at church. She pulled out a small box and gave it to him.

"What's this?"

"It's a cross for your next child's baptism, just like the one I gave you. It's going to be a boy, I just know it." She smiled at him, and then walked away.

He tossed it on the seat and we went to the office.

— • —

Milo was quiet, nurturing a low grade anger through the rest of the morning. We stood off to the side. Savlo meditated and I observed all the other guardians prompting their image bearers with seemingly little effect. The world had become too noisy for the image bearers to hear us. Milo made some phone calls and was playing games on his computer when Natalie called him.

"Hey babe, what's up? ...Oh, she just went on and on again about church stuff. She might call you about baptizing Sasha and certainly our bun in the oven. She bought a huge gold cross. Just be ready for it... I know she means well, but damn, she is annoying... Um, I'm not sure when I'll be home... Okay, you have a good day too. Yep, love ya too." He hung up the phone and Savlo drew close to him.

"Aw, that's sweet, Milo. A group of us are going out for lunch, want to come?" Lilly asked as she walked by his cubicle.

Milo leaned back in his chair to look at her walk away, again. "Sure, why not? Give me ten."

He retracted his lustful leaning and muttered to himself, "She has the best legs in the business."

Ricky from across the aisle asked, "Lilly?"

Neither of them looked at each other. Savlo was now whispering into Ricky's ear, with his guardian's permission, of course.

"You've got to stop looking at that," Ricky said.

"I know, I know, I'm happily married." Milo swiveled his chair to face Ricky. "Honestly, my wife is like a Corvette, and the Corvette is a great car, but so is a Porsche."

"Yeah, I hear ya, but..." Ricky swiveled around.

Milo interrupted, "Ricky, you going to lunch with us?"

"Nah, I brought mine."

"Suit yourself."

Milo tidied up and then headed down the hall to Lilly's end of the office. As we approached a darkened conference room, a hermaphroditic demon was standing inside. "Hey Savlo, I agree with Milo, a Porsche is a really good ride."

Savlo spun to face the demon and stepped in front of me.

"Pharzuph," Savlo said.

"Who's the watcher? I didn't know they were still used for anything good," he said.

"None of your concern," Savlo said.

Pharzuph disappeared, leaving an awful scent.

"Hey Lil, we all set for my closings Friday afternoon?" Milo asked.

"Yeah, I think so. We might have a slight glitch but I'll tell ya about it later. I'm waiting to hear back from the lender." Lilly looked up at Milo, and smiled, her bright red lips curving open. Milo stopped breathing for a moment.

"Gentlemen, start your engines," Pharzuph announced from behind me. I turned to confront him, but again he was gone.

"So who's all going to lunch?" Milo asked Lilly.

"Oh, Frank, Heather and Steve already left, and said to meet them at Rudy's on Cherry Street. Can you give me a ride?"

"Sure. Let me go to the bathroom first, then I'll give you a ride," Milo smirked.

Pharzuph appeared again down the hall with the same smirk on his face that Milo had. Centuries of lust and sexual perversion had made his genitals swell and pulse.

"This is gonna be easy, my old friend. She works late, you know?" He smiled. "He could be really depraved, if he let himself go. But for sure he's an adulterer, if ever I've seen one. And trust me, watcher, I've seen the best adulterers and he's got the same look in his eye. Plus just enough boredom at home and opportunity at work, easy, easy pickings." Pharzuph gargled a mucus-filled laugh.

"You must leave. Pharzuph, in the name…" Savlo said.

"You have no power over me, guardian. Milo freely chooses to indulge in my temptations," Pharzuph interrupted, "So shut the fuck up, fowl, and don't say that name to me or I'll focus all my attention on your pupil and see if we can make his loins burn like the watchers of old." He grew to a size formidable even for us to combat. "Milo's coming to our humble home soon anyway."

"What do you know about home? You have fallen so far from His gaze," Savlo replied.

"Don't try and distract me. I have orders from down low and much work to do here." Pharzuph disappeared. We met Milo in the hallway coming back from the bathroom.

"C'mon woman, I'm hungry," Milo said through Lilly's doorway. She locked her computer and said, "Yep, me too. Let's go."

As they walked to Milo's vehicle, a dirty clothed man approached them. The man stumbled closer to Lilly, so Milo hurriedly opened the car door and rushed her in.

"Hey brotha man, can I acks you an honest question? Uh honest one now? My name is Bill and I wanna know if you can spare ten bucks and seventy-fy cents. That's all I need. Ten seventy-fy."

Milo had shut the door and turned to face Bill.

"An honest question? Really? Why don't you take an honest look at your life, Bill?"

"Aw, man, why you gotta keep a brotha down? Ten bucks, isn't that much. Look at you with yo' lady friend and yo' ride. You doing awright. If you don't have the ten bucks how about the seventy fy-cent?"

"Yeah, I am doing alright, but, you know why? Because I worked for it. Listen, Bill, if that's your honest name."

"My honest name is William Oscar Washington. My friends call me, Wow," he said.

"Well, in our office, we call you 'gimme a buck Bill,' and we all try to avoid you every time we step out of the building." Milo stepped closer to him and spoke directly to his face, "So Bill, do you know the situation you're putting me in here? You're scaring my friend in the car, but I'm not afraid of you. In fact, I'm getting a little pissed off because every time I'm downtown, I have some bum asking me for a dime or in your case, ten, oh how do you say it, 'seventy-fy'." He took another step closer, William took a step back. "In fact you annoy everyone in our office. Do you want to know why?" Milo was becoming more animated.

"Brother man, please, I jus need some meds. I have diabetes and need my meds."

"Meds, huh? What, Colt 45 gone up in price, or are you an Uncle Jack guy?"

"Nah, it's not like that, man."

"I can tell you have a buzz already today, or maybe working one off from last night. If I give you ten bucks it will be like feeding the pigeons in the park. You'll keep coming back and harassing everyone in this building as they leave. Bill, do us all a favor and get a fucking job. Hell, clean yourself up and I'll interview you for a job."

"Really?"

"Well, since we're having an honest conversation here—no. I actually can't stand to look at you. I think if you took a look at yourself, you'd see what a piece of shit you've become. Take control of your life. Homelessness is a choice. You're humiliating yourself."

"No, your humiliating me, right now. You don't know what I had to go through to make it through last night. You honestly don't have ten bucks for me?"

"Oh, I have it, I'm just not going to give it you, and that's being honest. It won't make a difference in this world if I help you get your drunk on or not, and it certainly won't be helping you either, Bill."

"Aw brotha man, you crushin' me."

William Washington dropped his head and walked away, his guardian angel following in like demeanor. Milo got into the vehicle. We joined them in the back seat.

"What'd you say?" Lilly asked.

Milo sighed and put both hands on the steering wheel.

"I told him to clean up his life, get a job and stop humiliating himself."

"How much did he want?" Lilly asked.

"Ten seventy five for diabetes medicine. I laughed and asked if his meds were Colt 45 or Jack Daniels."

Lilly laughed. "He is a little freaky to look at." She exhaled. "What's with poor people being so lazy anyway?"

"I know, right? Maybe he'll leave us alone now. I was pretty firm. Tough love, ya know?"

"Ooo, tough love, sounds fun." She laughed again, in a seductive tone.

Milo turned around in his seat to back out of the parking spot. He glanced down at her legs as she crossed them and raised her skirt to mid-thigh.

"You're horrible, you know that?" he said.

Savlo and Milo were face to face as he backed out, "Remember your wife," was Savlo's prompting.

"I like to call this handout highway," Milo said as they drove past St. Isaac's Orthodox Church, the Catholic Diocese headquarters and the lines outside God's Soup Kitchen.

Lilly smiled and slid her hand down her long smooth leg as the sunlight made it shine. Milo saw it without looking directly at it. "The sun feels good," she said.

As Milo neared the restaurant, he noticed a street metered parking spot. "Sweet, I'll park here."

Milo parallel parked his SUV with precision and they both got out. They stood in front of the meter. Milo reached in his pocket for change but only had a money clip with large bills.

"Need some change to cut that thing on?" Lilly said.

"Shoot, yeah, I do."

She handed him three quarters. He opened the door for Lilly with one hand and placed his other on the small of her back. He looked across the street and saw a Red Cross tent set up with a banner reading, 'Free Diabetes Testing All Month.' He thought briefly and then entered the restaurant.

— • —

After a lunch of exotic meats and conversations seasoned with innuendoes, Milo left alone. We followed him to the Middle Eastern Market where he bought fresh ground lamb for dinner. He wanted to surprise Natalie by coming home early. He then stopped by the office to get some files to review at home and check on his closings for the end of the week.

"Hey Lil, we still looking good for Friday?

"Um, yeah, we look good." She never looked up at him.

"What, I don't get your eyes? You mad I ditched you after lunch?"

"Oh, sorry. I'm just stressed. End of month is such a mad rush and people get crazy. You know how it is."

"Yeah, but my Friday back-to-backs are okay, right?"

"Actually, the one on Silver Street has a glitch with the lender. He hasn't called me back yet."

"What?"

"Yeah, I've got to call Doug, again. He said something about not having enough in reserves for the buyer to close."

"What the hell? It's not like they haven't had access to her accounts for the last month."

"You want to call him?" Lilly asked.

"Absolutely. See ya later, babe."

Milo walked to his vehicle and I stood looking at Lilly. I walked over to her desk. The files she was handling did not appear to look formal. They were random copies of text and some were even blank. I bent down to look her in the eyes. She avoided my gaze. "Why are you stressed?" I tilted my head to try and get low enough to see in her soul.

"Come, he's in the vehicle already. Remember, rule number two," Savlo said as he appeared in the doorway. We located in Milo's backseat again.

Milo called the lender from the vehicle and put him on the speaker system, while he drove.

"Doug? It's Milo—Dude, what's up with the Ludlow file? I thought this was a zero down conventional loan?"

"Hey man, it is but she still needs to show she has money. She has to have six months reserves to close and she doesn't have it. She's screwed," Doug said.

"You didn't see this coming? You didn't check?"

"Of course I did, but the underwriter called for a reverification of funds and she spent it. I'm telling you, it's the mortgage crisis bullshit. No such thing as an easy deal nowadays. It ain't closing, buddy."

"Bullshit. Doug, come on, the power of positive thinking, think and grow rich Doug, we can do this. There's got to be a way. It's just a hurdle."

"It's a fricking wall, Milo. It's dead in the water and now she won't call me back."

"Hello, we have turn signals for a reason, butthole!" Milo raised his middle finger to another driver. "Sorry, Doug, I'm driving. Okay, so what's the problem, specifically?"

"She needs to have six months worth of payments in reserves. It has to be in a savings account and she doesn't have it."

"What about her parents?"

"Hmm, no, it can't be from a family member. Plus part of the down payment is coming from them, anyway but I'm not supposed to know about it."

"Does she know she needs, what, another six grand or so?"

"No, I told you, she won't call me back."

"There's a solution here and I'll find it. What's the minimum information you need to get it 'clear to close'?"

"I need a bank teller stamped statement on a savings account with her name on it and the money has to be at least thirty days old."

"Doug, this deal will close. We've closed harder files than Ludlow. You'll have what you need by end of biz tomorrow."

"Dude, don't get us in trouble. Maybe she shouldn't buy the house. You ever thought of that?"

"Nonsense. The universe is on my side. See ya Friday, and you'll owe me lunch for this one."

Milo hung up and called Karen Ludlow.

"Hey girl, it's Milo. How ya doing today?"

"Milo, I can't buy the house. Doug said something about not enough savings. I feel horrible and pissed and ugh, I just don't know, maybe it wasn't to be."

"Listen to me. I just talked to Doug, and it turns out we're all set."

"Really? How?"

"Just trust me. Come Friday at four, bring everything Doug told you to bring, and it'll close. You will have your house. I guarantee it."

"Really?"

"Yeah, it's all set."

"You're the greatest," she said.

"Well, just to let you know, The Steak Haus is my favorite restaurant."

She laughed. "The Steak Haus, hey?"

"Yep."

"Okay, thanks, Milo, I mean really, thanks a million."

"You're welcome, and you'll keep me in mind for all your referrals, right?"

"Of course."

"Alright, see you Friday at four."

"Okay, 'bye."

Milo hung up and exhaled. "Thirty two thousand dollars this week—it's so easy. Amber can kiss my ass."

He drove home and surprised Natalie. She greeted him with a kiss. He bent down, spoke kind words to her womb, and hugged Sasha.

"My, you're in a good mood today," Natalie said.

"Well, let's just say I am an amazing person and a real estate god."

"And so humble."

He smiled and handed her the freshly ground lamb. "Let's celebrate a little tonight; it's a good week for us." He set his keys, phone and files down on the kitchen counter. "Hey, kiddo, you want to go play for a little bit in the backyard before dinner?"

"Yeah!" Sasha screamed.

"Let me go change and I'll meet you out there." I stayed by Kallistos and Natalie.

While Milo was upstairs changing, his phone vibrated; a text. Natalie picked up the phone and read it.

-Need another pic?

Natalie held the phone for moments while the water in the sink ran. She searched the history of texts and pictures on his phone and found nothing that alerted her.

She texted back,

-He is spending time with his family tonight

There was no return text.

Milo came down from the bedroom.

"Hey Milo, who's Lilly Maneyu?"

"Huh, Lilly, oh she's just a closing agent at work."

"She texted you asking if you needed another picture. Care to explain?"

"No biggie, babe. We had a problem with a file today. She was just making sure I had everything I needed."

"A picture, though?"

"Yeah, it's an insurance thing. Pictures of the house, you know. Don't worry about it."

He went out and played with Sasha and they had a nice evening, though Natalie was subdued and contemplative all night.

Before Milo turned out the light at bedtime, he took a sheet of paper from his night stand and wrote, 'how do I solve the Ludlow file problem?' He dropped it on the floor and turned out the light.

"Savlo, he lied so effortlessly tonight, and this paper on the floor method is an invitation to demonic influence," I said.

Savlo did not respond because it was not a direct question.

Kallistos was interceding Natalie's silent prayers as she lay in bed, unable to sleep.

"Milo's daily ritual resembles a pact with a demon. He calls it his subconscious, but it's a deception. How long has he done this?" I asked my one question.

"Seven years ago," Savlo said, "he was a ninety days away from declaring bankruptcy and foreclosing on his house, but kept it secret from her. He went to a coffee shop every day and sat alone, depressed, riddled with despair, when an advertisement posted on a bulletin board caught his eye. It was for a seminar that promised to change his life through sharing the 'Secrets of Financial Success: How to attract wealth through unbreakable universal laws.' There was a small money back guaranteed entry fee. He went to a pawn shop and sold his baptismal cross and watch. That night he went and learned these secrets. Ever since he has called upon these 'laws,' and gradually ceased to pray," Savlo said.

I paused and said, "I knew the watcher angel who taught the image bearers these enchantments long ago. We were close friends. His name is Armeros and he remains in the prison, begging for mercy, even now. Being a watcher, I constantly hear their dirge and his regrets. I spoke against their evil plans and chose not to join their pact against the Almighty One. My heart long suffers for them even more now that I see their teachings continue to this day, albeit in a different form."

"Zazriel, I know now why you were sent to me. Long ago, just before the Archangel Michael expelled the now-fallen from heaven, I was sent with the message to convince some of them not to go along with Lucifer's rebellion."

"Savlo, I must confess, I've heard the aerial demons slander you throughout the heavens."

"My heart long suffers as yours does every time I hear their mocking rumors about me, for I remind them of the Almighty One's plea for their repentance."

I still had more questions about Savlo's history, but dared not inquire further. Savlo silenced himself, enclosed in his wings. I stood by the window for a time and watched as the demons danced outside on Milo's well-manicured lawn. I now carried Savlo's burden for Milo.

ENTRY 4

The Last Thursday of Milo's Life

It had been four turns of the planet, and with sadness I had watched Milo's soul sickness unravel his life and hurl him towards death, blind and disillusioned. He woke up early on this morning and stepped out of bed onto another piece of paper. He proceeded with his usual ritual in front of the mirror:

"I am an amazing real estate agent—

I give others positive energy—

I am powerful—

I am resourceful beyond measure—

I find solutions to every obstacle."

He stopped his incantations and opened his eyes. "I got it." He smiled in the mirror again. "Thank you, subconscious."

He took his shower.

Natalie was still asleep when he bent down and kissed her on the head and whispered, "You're an amazing woman." She stirred and smiled. He proceeded to his den and logged into his online bank account. On the bookshelf next to his computer were several books about neuro-linguistic programming, secret knowledge, laws of attracting wealth, and how to trick the mind with thinking patterns.

"These books teach a version of Armeros's sorcery of the mind," I said.

Savlo nodded.

Milo snapped up his keys and hurried out the door.

— • —

We remained close to Milo as he walked into the bank. He was greeted and sat with a personal banker in a small over-furnished office. Everything was tidy and clean, and reflected the fluorescent light. Milo slid his driver's license over to the young man, who was named Brad. As they exchanged pleasantries, Milo started to mimic Brad's speed, tone and body gestures. It was the way he learned to build rapport from his books on mind trickery.

"Well, what can we do for you, Mr. Christopoulos?"

"Well, for starters, call me Milo."

"Okay, Milo." Brad smiled.

"Okay Brad, I have a question for you. Do you believe there are good deeds done in the world today with no other ulterior motive?"

Brad laughed. "Interesting question. Um—yeah, I think people still do good deeds just for the good of it."

"I have a good deed I'm trying to do, just for the good of it. I want to put someone on my savings account so that I can help her out, but I want it to be a surprise." Milo noticed a Habitat for Humanity award next to Brad's computer and continued, "Like a cross between Extreme Makeover and Habitat for Humanity."

"You're going to buy someone a house?"

Milo laughed. "No, that *would* be a really good deed, though. What I have in mind will change her life for the better. You know, make a small difference in the world—a good deed."

"Sounds good. Let's look at what type of accounts you have with us." He pulled up Milo's accounts and looked surprised at the balances. "You probably could buy someone a house if you wanted to."

"I know I have several accounts, checking and savings. I do a lot of business with you guys. So, do I have a smaller savings account with at least ten thousand in it?"

"Yeah, actually you have a simple saver account with just over ten thousand, labeled Sasha."

"Okay, so can you help me do this good deed?"

"Well, it's pretty easy, actually. I just add the person's name, and then they can have access to the account. They'll have to sign a form, but they'll be on the account with you and Natalie."

"Okay, let's do it," Milo said.

"Sure, but let me tell you this. Once I add a name and they sign a form, they'll have access to the account just like you, and they'll get statements."

"If I add her name today, can I get a printout of the last couple of months' statements?"

"Um, yes, I guess, but why?"

"I just want to make it look official. I don't want any questions about the good deed being a sure thing. It's important not to let her down."

Brad paused and just looked at his computer screen. His guardian appeared, acknowledged us, and whispered cautionary promptings to his mind.

"So, you're a hockey fan, huh?" Milo asked.

"Yeah, big Wings fan as you can tell from my pictures. I'm a little obsessed, actually." He smiled.

"Yeah, hey, sometimes I get tickets to Red Wings games. I don't always get to go. Should I keep you in mind?"

"Yeah, that would be awesome."

"I'll do that, another good deed." He smiled. "Plus, it's a sin to let Wings tickets go unused."

Brad smiled too. "Okay, what's the lady's name?"

"Karen Ludlow."

— • —

Milo walked into the office and emailed the account statements to Doug, Karen's lender, who instantly replied;

-*I'll make this work —You're the man Milo, see ya Friday @ 4*

He walked down to Lilly's office. "Hey, we're all set on the Ludlow file. I had to play in the gray a little, but it'll close."

"Milo, that's great. Oh, and I'm so sorry for last night," Lilly said, turning her desk chair to face him.

"Sorry for what?"

"The text during family time—your wife texted me back."

"She did?" He smiled. "Wow, bold of her. What'd she say? Ah, doesn't matter, I took care of it."

Lilly stood up. "Milo, can you shut the door? I want to tell you something."

He held the door close to him, straddling the threshold.

"We've been flirting pretty hard lately and I really don't want to ruin things for you. We can cool it for a while, if you want."

"Well, it's all harmless fun, right?" Milo said.

"Yeah, but honestly, you're the first guy I've been revved up about in a long time."

"Really? I find that hard to believe. You seem pretty comfortable with flirting."

"Well, I've been on kind of a woman thing for the past couple of years," Lilly said, taking a step closer to him. "My friend Sheila would really dig you. We probably could hook up some night, the three of us."

Pharzuph appeared behind Lilly with a thin grin on his face.

Milo's mouth was agape.

"But if you want to cool it, I understand," she said and sat back down in her chair.

"Lilly, I want—oh, God." He dropped his head and rubbed his face. "You're so, man o' man, not like other women, but I won't leave my wife and family for you."

She laughed the words, "Do I look like a girl who wants to be locked into a marriage? I just want to have some fun, no strings attached. If nobody knows, nobody gets hurt."

Milo started shaking his head but his heart was racing. "Wow, you're an amazing woman but I got to get back to work. You're too much."

"Hey, I have to work late tonight."

Pharzuph laughed and said, "He's no match for her."

Milo meandered out of the office; conflicted with thoughts but energized by temptation.

The rest of the day carried on as normal until five o'clock. An abnormal silence of inactivity descended upon the office. Everyone had left except Lilly and Milo. The infestations of demons quieted and remained hidden in shadows. We hovered above Milo, looking across the maze of cubicles at Lilly sitting in her office. Next to her office, in the darkened doorway of the conference room, Pharzuph appeared, smiling and as grotesque as ever.

Milo gave out a deep sigh and straightened his posture, popped a mint in his mouth and headed for the bathroom.

Savlo reverberated telepathically, "Kallistos!" and then positioned himself right behind Milo, whispering to his mind.

His cell phone rang as he entered the bathroom.

"Hey Nat, what's up? ...Oh, in about an hour or so... No, spaghetti is fine. I'll try and hurry home? ...Alright, gotta go, love ya too."

Milo bit his lower lip as he stood looking at the mirror for almost two minutes. He said nothing.

"Just go home, you're needed, you're loved, you're wanted at home." Savlo pleaded his suggestions to his mind. Milo did not move, just stared at his reflection.

He walked out of the bathroom and headed for Lilly's office. The light was out. He looked in. "Lilly?"

She answered from the adjacent conference room. "Milo, in here."

He stepped into the darkened conference room. She walked right up to Milo, and whispered, inches away from his lips, "So you want to have some fun?"

"Um—"

"Milo, no strings, just fun."

She moved in closer so her breasts were touching his chest and her lips were close to his ear. "I know you want me. Milo, you can have me, right now, right here. Come on, take me. I want it."

Milo stood there, frozen, and said nothing.

One of her hands slid up his thigh. "Oh my, you are interested in having some fun." She kissed his cheek, then his lips.

"C'mon, take her. Grab her breasts, she's hot, she wants it!" Pharzuph now appeared in all his lusty disgust on one side of Milo. "Take her already."

Standing on the other side of Milo, facing Pharzuph, Savlo said, "Don't do it. Milo, go home. Push her away. Run."

"What will she think? You flirt and talk big, but when it comes time to put out you pussy out. Be a man. Take her. She wants to have some fun, no strings attached." Pharzuph said in one ear.

Milo grabbed both her arms, kissed her and moved her so she was leaning on the end of the conference room table. "Walk away!" Savlo screamed.

Milo looked into her deep green eyes and time stood still. Dimensions collapsed. "You're right. I deserve to have some fun." He put his hand up her blouse, placed it on her breast, and kissed her.

"Yes!" Pharzuph cheered and continued to feed words of passion and pride into Milo's mind. Savlo withdrew, enclosed in his wings, with his head bowed and glowed in intercessory prayer. Milo and Lilly clawed each other. They aggressively shed their clothes. She bit him and he grabbed at her. It was controlled violence. He lifted her on the table and grunted. She spread her legs and he pressed against her. They acted like animals in heat.

"Take me," she whispered. He did.

"Wait, this doesn't feel right. Something's wrong," he said.

"Stop talking and take me," she said as she sunk her nails into his back, pulling him close.

As soon as he put his seed in her, she pushed him back, hopped of the table and pulled up her undergarment. He stepped back, pants at his ankles, shamefully naked and visibly sickened.

"You naughty boy," she said as she playfully slapped his face and adjusted her skirt down. "That was fun, wasn't it?" He said nothing. "Bye-bye, sweetie pie." She kissed him lightly, bit his bottom lip, and then walked out of the room, leaving Milo standing there.

As she passed me I thought I saw reptilian scales appear on her neck. I motioned to Savlo but he was attending to Milo who stood disorientated and muttered, "What just happened? I don't feel right." He pulled up his pants but could not connect his belt.

Pharzuph stood on the table in congratulatory reverie for his conquest. Milo lowered his head. Pharzuph laughed and said, "You know what the best part is, Savlo? He has to pass the Porsche dealer on his way home, and he'll think of this ride every day from now on."

Milo went to the bathroom to wash his hands and face.

He drove home in silence, startling himself as he crossed over and back on the highway rumble strip. I could tell he was in deep despair. He walked into the house with a hero's welcome from his little girl, warm food on the table and a clean house. Natalie, with Kallistos behind her, stepped out from the kitchen. He looked at his wife, beautifully domestic, the miracle of life in her womb, a loving smile on her face. He lowered his head, shamed by her virtue.

"Oh honey, you're home. Perfect timing. Dinner is ready. Come on, sit down."

Milo sat down. He looked over the dinner table. He looked at Sasha and then his wife. He reached up to wipe his mouth but paused and smelled his hand. He lowered his head in silence.

"Okay, daddy's going to pray. Let's bow our heads and close your eyes," Natalie said.

I looked at Kallistos and he knew what had happened. Milo started to pray, holding back tears, "O Heavenly King, O Comforter, the Spirit of Truth, who art in all places and fillest all things. Treasury of good things and giver of life, come dwell in me, cleanse me from every stain and save my soul, O gracious Lord." Then he stopped.

"Okay, then, thank you Milo for that prayer. Sasha, go ahead and eat," she said as they ate in silence.

When Sasha had finished, Natalie cleared the table and put Sasha up in her room. Milo did not get up from the table. He had barely eaten. He just sat there looking at the plate of food. Natalie came back down and sat next to Milo at the dinner table.

She reached out and grabbed his hand and looked at him, head lowered.

"The last time I heard that prayer was at our wedding reception. Do you remember?"

He looked at her, tears welling in his eyes. "Natalie——" he said.

She interrupted him. "Was it Lilly?"

"What? No, why would you say that?"

"Milo, your cheeks are flushed and you smell like sex."

He dropped his head again and mumbled, "It's not what you think. I'm not having an affair, I just crossed a line, but something is wrong. I don't feel right."

She got up from the table and grabbed her keys. "I knew something was wrong, and you lied to me the other day about the texting," she said as she slammed the door and left.

He was defeated. After some time he walked out the back slider into their slightly wooded back yard and wept bitterly. He fell to all fours, like a beast of the field, wailing and moaning. It reminded me of God's curse on Nebuchadnezzar.

Pharzuph appeared and hovered over his back, riding him like some sort of horse. His hissing laugh at first was constrained in his belly, then it burst out full throated with spittle everywhere. Milo could barely get any words out. He said he wanted to die for his sins. Savlo encouraged him to transform his remorse into repentance. Pharzuph just laughed at us all. "Well, my work is done here. See you at the seventeenth toll house, Savlo. Oh, I almost forgot, we've been ordered to ask you to join us every time we see you. And that comes from the big man himself. He holds us accountable to work extra hard to keep every soul that is committed to your guardianship in our toll houses. There's a contest actually, and I may be the winner with this piece of work," he said pointing to Milo, groping around in the dark. "So what do you say?" Pharzuph descended into the earth. "Because you can give up on this poor monkey—I mean, just look at him. What a rube." He laughed.

"Be gone, you foul creature," Savlo replied as he placed his hand on Milo's shoulder.

Several minutes later, Milo came back into the house and waited for Natalie to come home. He had retrieved a suitcase from the basement and was thinking of where he could spend the night. His tears were gone and his eyes were darkened with fatigue. The door opened and Natalie came in the front room where Milo sat with his suitcase.

"Where are you going?" she asked.

"I, I was gonna go away. You probably need time, I need time, I don't know."

She just stared at him, lip quivering. "Milo, I'm hurt, I'm pissed and I'm so disappointed in you right now. How could you?"

Her eyes, red from crying, welled up with tears again. "You've hurt me so deeply, but we're married and…"

Milo interrupted, "Natalie, I'm so sorry. If you want to divorce me, I understand. I…"

"Milo, just shut up. Your actions have spoken louder than your words can tonight." She sat down in the front living room and stared at him for some time as he sat across from her, dejected and humiliated.

We all stood around also, wondering what would happen next.

Finally, she broke the silence. "I think I need some time to sort through my feelings. We have a lot to work through, and I have lots of questions, but not tonight. Milo, we're married and that means we don't give up on each other, no matter what. But I'm so sad right now." The tears flowed down her cheeks. She sniffed and wiped her nose with a wad of tissue she held. "But tonight, let's just go to bed."

So they did. He lay on his back staring at the ceiling fan, listening to the gentle sobbing of his wife.

I had no questions for Savlo. The demons were festive that night. Self-congratulatory cheers were audible outside the hedge of our protection.

ENTRY 5

The Last Friday of Milo's Life

Milo woke up and followed his routine of affirmations with less positive verve, and more aggravation in his tone. Natalie woke up and immediately made a phone call. We all located in the corner trying to discern their emotions.

After she hung up she walked into the bathroom. "Milo, I don't want you to freak out but I had some spotting this morning. So I called Dr. Bowne and he can see me today at 4:45. Can you make it?"

"Really? Oh, man. Is that serious? Should I take you to the emergency room?" He turned off the shower.

"No, it's dried blood. Dr. Bowne said just take it easy and come in, it's probably just stress. Can you make it to the appointment today, though?"

"Um, depends. I have a couple closings, but I'll try—no, I'll make it work and Nat, I'm so sorry, this is all my fault too."

"Milo, you have to stop apologizing. I know you're sorry, and I've already started forgiving you but..."

He stepped out of the shower and robed himself, "But what?"

They stood looking at each other in the mirror. "I don't know who I'm married too anymore. I need you to be completely honest with me when I ask you questions."

"Okay, I will be, I promise, from here on out, full disclosure."

"No promises, no sweet talking, Milo, I'm serious. If I'm ever going to trust you again it will begin with honest answers. I'm not going leave you, but I need to know who I am married to. You've changed."

"I wouldn't blame you if you wanted to leave me."

"I am not going to leave you, you idiot, 'no exit plan.' That's what we said when we got married, remember?" Her tone was stern and she was showing great emotional restraint.

"So we'll work this out somehow. I mean, we'll get back to the way it was, right?"

"We may never have sex again, but yes, we'll work it out."

He tried to smile, but held an expression of confusion. He did not understand her emotions.

"Milo, there's a lot going on right now. I hope you can tell that," she said.

Natalie left the bathroom while he stood looking at himself in the mirror.

"You got away with it," a voice whispered. We could see his hindering angel in the mirror, still in the form of a vagabond, this time exposing his black feathered wings singed by fire. I knew from this that he had been a guardian before. Savlo went into high alert, growing in stature and emanating light.

The hinderer wrapped his burnt wings around himself and disappeared, leaving awful incense in the air. Milo sniffed his hands and vigorously washed them again.

Savlo turned around and communed with Kallistos. I could not hear their words, but stood watching Milo and pondered the enigma of his life liturgy. I wondered what he truly thought as he said with more conviction this time, 'I am the captain of my own soul,' over and over.

— • —

In the closing room Lilly was dressed in a green blouse and a knee-length skirt. She glowed this morning, giving off an aura of a fun loving professional to the clients with a slightly inappropriate air of promiscuous femininity. Milo was less captivated by her seductive ways, obviously still confused about his peculiar carnal knowledge of her.

"Milo, would you please sign the FHA Amendatory Clause?" She slid the paper over to Milo while half standing up. Her blouse gaped open. Milo saw her lime green bra. When she knew he was looking she placed her hand on her chest, closing the blouse in obvious fashion, embarrassing him in front of his clients.

"Mr. and Mrs. Kline, these last forms waive any rights you have to the property, including your rights to live there during the six month redemption period of the foreclosure." Lilly moved papers around just as easily as her explanations filled the room.

While the clients were signing, Lilly sat in the same place where she and Milo had conjugated. She nonchalantly rubbed the table edge. She smiled soullessly at him. The Klines signed everything without a question. She left to make copies for them. Milo asked, "Would anyone like a cup of coffee or a water while we wait?"

"Sure, bottled water if you have it," Mr. Kline said.

Milo walked out of the room and found Lilly.

"Good job, Lil." Milo stood next to her, putting his arm around her as the copies lapped out one over another. She pulled sharply away.

"What's wrong?" he said.

"Nothing. So how was dinner at home with the family?"

His head dropped. "We should probably talk about that. Natalie knows."

"Is she going to leave you?"

"No."

"Good, then you got away with it."

"Can we talk about this later?"

"No need. I don't care, I got what I wanted."

"Damn, you're cold."

"Your next client is here. Why don't you go greet her and show her to the other closing room?" She walked away as he did.

"Hey, Karen. So are ya excited?" He extended his hand.

"I'm a little nervous, Milo, I have a bad feeling about this. Doug said my payment went up a little because he was floating the rate, or something like that, and rates went up." She brushed back her dark curly hair and searched for something in her large shoulder bag. She nervously adjusted her blouse as it slid up, exposing her tattooed torso, sat down in the chair and exhaled.

"Nonsense, you'll be fine. The monthly payment is spread out over thirty years; the difference in payment is like going without a pizza once a month. No biggie. Everyone gets cold feet but hey, we'll just sell it if it gets too much for you. Come on, let's do this; right this way."

As they walked past the counter, a demon, appeared as a small bald man; dressed in a three piece suit. He addressed us, "Mr. Christopoulos is really very good at what he does for a descendant of Crete. Like Saul wrote to Titus, *'Cretans are always liars, evil beasts, lazy gluttons...*' I'll have to remember this when he gets to my toll house. It's hive two, in case you were wondering, watcher. Say, what's your name? I don't think we've met yet. I'm Mr. Nisroc." He extended his hand.

Savlo and I ignored him and passed by. I looked back. His eyes had turned black and his face deep red. "Dismiss me at your own peril. Somebody must pay, the House never loses, just ask Savlo. We hold many of his monkeys."

Lilly pulled out a form. "Ms. Ludlow, this is a form that states there are no side deals between you and any other party involved in the sale, and that the price stated on the purchase agreement is the price today, with no other money exchanging between the buyer and seller or real estate agent."

"What do you mean?" Karen asked, smiling nervously. Her guardian remained silent in prayer, standing behind her.

"I mean that you are getting your money from the bank to buy the house. Even though Milo is technically the owner of the house, 'on paper', he is not helping you buy it." Lilly exhaled condescendingly.

Karen signed everything Lilly put before her and did not ask another question. Milo sent Karen on her way with the normal parting words then walked back to Lilly's office.

"What the hell was that?"

"What was what?" Lilly asked.

"The attitude—why are you being such a bitch today?"

"Well, excuse me, I'm still dealing with how you forced yourself on me last night. Now you're calling me a bitch. I might have to talk with HR about how threatened I feel because of the hostile work environment you're creating."

"What the hell are you talking about? I didn't force myself on you."

"I'm not sure HR will see it that way."

"Lilly, what's going on here?"

"How much did you make this week in your little gambit?"

"What? What does that have to do with anything?"

"By the way, I was ovulating last night and felt a little sick this morning."

"Oh, I see what's going on here. A little early for morning sickness, isn't it?"

"I don't know what you're talking about. I'm just not comfortable talking about this or working with you right now. I need some time to figure out what I'm going to do," Lilly said as she sat down at her desk and fanned herself.

"Whatever. I can't deal with this right now."

He stormed out and she smiled while attending to some files on her desk.

"Savlo, I fear she is not an image bearer. I saw her appearance flicker to that of a reptile last night, she has neither guardian nor seal, and her conscience is obviously seared."

"Confront her, then."

Savlo followed Milo as he headed to meet Natalie for her ultrasound, and I went back to Lilly's office. I watched her, while she remained busy, stopping in complete silence and staring off into space for conspicuous amounts of time. During one of these staring spells, I positioned myself in her line of vision, extended my wings and with booming reverberation throughout our dimension proclaimed, "Demon, I command you to reveal yourself. By His Holy Name, reveal yourself."

She broke her focus, shook her head, and continued to organize files on her desk. I drew close to her face and tried to look into her soul. "Who are you? You are very clever but you cannot fool me, I have watched all kinds."

She stood up, walked out of the office, down the hall and engaged another image bearer about a transaction.

I caught up with Savlo. "Nothing," I said.

"This is the work of Pharzuph. He must have her under an oppressive delusion. If so, her soul is in great darkness. Go ahead to Kallistos now. You will hear the heartbeat of your image bearer. I'll make sure Milo makes it before she leaves."

— • —

With haste I found Natalie with my mind's eye. She was still driving.

"Greetings in His Holy Name, Kallistos," I said, flying at his side.

"Greetings and glad tidings are indeed in order."

We positioned ourselves in the back of Natalie's beige Volvo sedan. Despite all that she had been through her demeanor was peaceful.

"She is uncommon," I said.

"Yes, her inner stillness is a harbor for her, and since her youth she has always prayed with clarity of mind, absent of distraction."

There was a pause. Kallistos asked, "You're aware that special women bear special children?"

I nodded.

Natalie pulled into the parking lot, and parked in the nearest space reserved for expectant mothers. She almost floated into the brown brick one story building, through its tinted front doors. We followed her in. She was filling out some paperwork while the doctor was with others.

"Is Milo going to make it?" Kallistos asked.

"On his way," I said. "Forgive me for asking, blessed Kallistos, but shouldn't I be your apprentice and observing Natalie, since I'm going to be the child's guardian?"

"Young one, be cautious with your questions. Only one thing is needful. I see now Savlo's wisdom for the rule of one question per day. He sensed in you something, a weakness that the aerial demons could exploit. You were sent to Savlo primarily and me secondarily. God's will be done in heaven as it is on earth."

Natalie was called into the room, instructed to undress and put on a gown. I had never let myself see a naked pregnant image bearer this close before. So delicate and mysterious is an incarnation, I thought.

"Hello, Natalie. How are you? How you feeling, today? Go ahead and lean back. Put your feet in the stirrups," Dr. Bowne said as he washed his hands, joined by a nurse.

"Oh, I'm fine, doctor. Just a couple spots got me nervous," Natalie said.

He smiled. "Everything alright at home?"

"Milo and I are going through a rough patch, but we'll be okay."

The doctor put on protective gloves and hunched in between Natalie's legs. "Now, you're going to feel a little pressure from the wand, but I want to check out the cervix first. Then we'll check in on the little one with an ultrasound."

The nurse stopped watching the doctor and seemed to be either looking at me or out the window.

"Okay, everything looks really good." Dr. Bowne rolled his chair back and disposed of his gloves. He glared at the nurse, who snapped back to the present moment and readied the machine.

"This will feel a little cold." The nurse squirted some gel onto Natalie's exposed stomach. She rubbed it around. Natalie cocked her head and looked at the nurse, then to the doctor who was looking at some charts, trying to draw his attention. The nurse kept rubbing her belly as if it were a magic orb.

"Okay, that's good," Natalie said, interrupting the nurse, who seemed entranced.

"Yes, that is good. Thank you, Julie." Dr. Bowne stepped in front of her and reached for the ultrasound wand.

Everyone looked at the screen as the doctor swirled around her life-filled womb. He stopped every so often and clicked as he measured and took pictures. I was filled with such joy.

"Everything looks really good, Natalie. Good work." He smiled and grabbed her hand to encourage her. "So, would you like to know the sex?"

"Yes," the nurse blurted. Then she appeared to blush. "Oh, I'm sorry, this is the first time I've temped in an OBGYN office. Seriously, I am so sorry."

Natalie smiled. "That's okay; it's very exciting for us too. We thought we wouldn't be able to have any more children and then wham-o, surprise. Dr. Bowne, I've had enough surprises lately so please tell me," she said, her eyes beaming with joy.

"It's a boy," he said.

I smiled. Kallistos smiled. The nurse smiled and looked at me again. This time, Kallistos noticed and his wings flared alert. She abruptly walked out of the room. Natalie and the doctor were taken aback. The doctor's guardian appeared and told us he didn't know about her.

Dr. Bowne gave his attention back to her and said, "Natalie, everything is just great. You are twenty-five weeks, so right on schedule. Stay active but don't overdo it. Find a stress reliever and we'll see you in a couple of weeks. Any questions?"

"That nurse?"

"We were short staffed today. I don't think we'll be asking her back. I apologize."

Natalie nodded. "That's alright." The doctor left the room and she got dressed.

I looked to Kallistos and we looked out the window at the nurse walking to the parking lot. She stopped at the end of the sidewalk, turned and looked back at our room. Her eyes were black. Her lips were moving rapidly.

"Kallistos?" I called.

"You have just met the image bearer's hindering angel," he said.

"What? She touched the womb, as if she was holding him."

"Yes, seems we have a special child here. Assigning a hindering angel and a watcher to an unbaptized image bearer is rare."

"What should I do? The demon was so close to my image bearer. I failed already."

"You did not fail. You won't see her again until the child dies and must travel to the toll houses, but you'll battle with this foe throughout his life. You'll feel her presence sometimes and see her work. Hindering angels like to work undetected, I'm surprised she showed up at all. Take great care, for just as the doctor measured the infant, the demon measured you."

Natalie was dressed and headed to the office front desk.

"It's because I'm a watcher. Raphael warned me the aerial demons would be curious."

"Welcome to the front lines of the battle, my young friend. The great war rages in the hearts and wills of the image bearers until the Ancient of Days calls all things into account."

Natalie was walking to her car when Milo pulled into the parking lot. He hugged her but she looked upset at his tardiness. She told him it was a boy and he fondly engaged her roundness.

They got into separate cars and headed for home. Savlo was inside Milo's SUV; I stationed myself with Kallistos above Natalie's car. Kallistos was watching the oncoming traffic.

"Watch with me. If the little one's hinderer was around, then Natalie's is too. There's great attention from the aerial demons for this family. Let us attend."

"Kallistos, I must know. Has Savlo ever successfully translated an image bearer to paradise, past the toll houses?"

"I don't know all of his history. What I do know is that the free will of image bearers who are sick with sin is a terrible burden for those who truly love them. In the end, all things will be reconciled and I believe you'll play an important role in Milo's trial, but for now, learn all you can from Savlo. There is much to learn from the last angel who attempted to counsel the Seraph of Treason before he and his army were cast out of heaven," Kallistos said.

I nodded. "Savlo told me he was sent to plead with the angels that they might not rebel against the Almighty, but I didn't know he was the last to talk with Lucifer."

"Curiosity into divine mystery should not distract you. Let's count that as your one question for the day," Kallistos said.

The family spent the evening as they did every Friday, watching animated movies with Sasha. Milo sat in the chaise lounge while Natalie and Sasha were cuddled in an embrace on the sofa. I could discern, Milo's mind remained distracted as he waited for Natalie to ask him questions so he could be honest with her. They did not speak, but shared the comfort of household duties and rituals. Savlo tried all evening to counsel him, but Milo could no longer discern his promptings from the cacophony of lies the demons reinforced daily. Later, while they slept, we all spent the night huddled together within vibrating wings, in a collective meditative communion, sharing light.

ENTRY 6

The Last Sabbath of Milo's Life

Natalie was up early with Sasha while Milo slept in for the first time in seven years. There was no sheet of paper to step on as Milo woke up and stumbled to the bathroom. He looked in the mirror waiting for the shower water to heat up.

"Some captain I am."

He showered until the hot water turned tepid and headed downstairs in a much more apathetic mood, but with irritation percolating. Savlo descended through the floor while I remained and entered the steamed mirrored bathroom.

"Hello, watcher, you're a long way from Laodicea." A clear mist from the water twisted and formed into a demon I recognized.

"Remember me?" she said.

"You also are a long way from our old region, Chliavos. Why are you here?"

"I'm here because you're here. By the way, you beautiful bird-man, why are you here?" she asked.

"I will call his guardian and we will banish you to the abyss if you remain even one more moment."

"Relax, I'm leaving. The toll house generals asked me about you. After I told them everything I begged them to let me give Milo a reminder that no captain with any self-respect goes down with his ship without a fight."

She evaporated. I joined my mentors.

Natalie was preparing breakfast. "Do you want some coffee?" she asked.

"Whatever, if you have extra," Milo mumbled.

"What'd you say?"

"Hell yeah, I want some coffee."

Natalie perked up without looking at him. "Hey, will you drop off the videos? Oh, and drop this package off at the post office and then go to the store, really quick, and get these things before we go to brunch with your parents?" She handed him a list and a travel mug of hot black coffee.

"Brunch?"

"Uh, yes, dear."

"Fine, but if she pisses me off again, I may just smack her."

"That's your mother, Milo."

"Hey, you wanted honest. I'm just saying, if she wants to fight, I'll give her a fight."

Natalie raised her eyebrows and whispered to Sasha, who was sitting on the counter, "He's just in a bad mood. He's not going to smack yiayia."

I told Savlo about Chliavos, her interrogation by the toll house generals and her influence on Milo in the shower.

Kallistos said, "I know her well. The demons are watching you now."

Milo left for the store, angered and energized by the vices he had nurtured for so many years.

He texted Lilly several times while stuck in the parking lot of the video store:

-lets talk monday. Have idea how we can all benefit

-hello Lil u there

-u there

-wtf

Several moments passed; she replied,

- k

After completing the other errands, Milo entered the grocery store and quickly gathered the things on Natalie's list.

"Ah, come on lady, really, a coupon dispute for fifty cents?" Milo said, standing next in line at the grocery store. "Can you believe this dumbass?" he said to the image bearer behind him.

"Excuse me," the woman in front of him responded. "Who you calling a dumbass?"

"You, that's who."

"Well, screw you mister high and mighty, I've got a bunch a coupons to dispute so you might as well change lanes." Her guardian appeared, prompting her to calm down, as did all the other guardians of the surrounding image bearers.

"You know you're only going to save, like what, five bucks. Here, just take my five bucks and go away."

"I ain't taking your money; I clipped all these super savers out and I'm down right gonna use every one of them."

He lowered his head, visibly angry. "I'm so tired of you people."

"What do you mean by 'you' people?"

Milo did not respond.

"Hey, I'm talking to you."

He looked up and was enraged. "Poor, fat, lazy people with a fucking entitlement attitude. That's what kind of people—rats."

Everyone in the line was looking at Milo with wide eyes, as he continued to voice his rage, "I've been hit up for money by a lazy bum this week; got stuck in the video store parking lot; mailed a package with no help from the inbreeds at the post office; and now I have to wait for some big assed woman to try and save fifty cents on a supersized tub of butter. For God's sake, do you really need all that butter?"

"Sir, I think you should calm down or I'm going to call security," the cashier said as she put her hand on the phone.

"Crazy man thinks he's better than everyone," the woman with the coupons said.

"You know what? I am. I am better than all you people, and I don't need to shop here anymore." He dropped his basket and walked out. The cashier called security, but Milo was out the door before they responded.

We could hear demons mocking us. "Butter get ready for us, birdies!"

Milo drove home festering and muttering. He walked into the house, was greeted by Sasha hugging his thighs, and brushed her aside as he made his way back to the kitchen. Natalie was wiping a counter. We stood to the side. I looked at Kallistos and shook my head.

She turned when he came in. "Hi, did you get everything?"

"Hell no, I didn't."

"What's the matter with you?"

"Lines. Lines are what's the fucking matter with me."

"What are you talking about?"

"Do you know how many lines I have to wait in throughout my week? There are lines everywhere—the video store, grocery store, DMV, Starbucks, on and on, lines everywhere, wasting my life. This is time I will never get back. Do you realize this?"

"Milo, other people have to wait in lines. It's just part of life."

"Well, they piss me off. I fucking hate them."

"Okay, that's enough of the cursing, Milo. Really, get a handle on yourself. So you didn't get the eggs?"

"Well, I was in line to pay for them and some fat-assed woman was insistent on saving fifty cents on a bucket of butter. We got into it a little."

"Milo Christopoulos."

"I know, I just couldn't take it. She was fat and buying butter and I—I just snapped."

Natalie shook her head, disappointed.

He looked at her and waited for a response, then stormed off to his den.

"Savlo, is it the state of his heart or the aerial demons stirring this anger?" I asked.

"Both. To stand in lines and not sin requires image bearers to maintain several virtues in concert, and lines are a favorite tool of the hinderers."

"Waiting in line? What other simple things do hinderers use?" I asked, still thinking about the nurse the day before.

"One question per day, that's the rule. You'll have to wait until the planet turns to ask another." He paused for a moment and then looked at me with a smile. "Think of waiting to ask your question as standing in a line."

Forty-five minutes later Milo, Natalie and Sasha were sitting at The Nautilus restaurant in a large corner booth covered in mauve vinyl. Kallistos informed me that every visit here captivated Sasha, with the restaurant's nautical decorations, pictures of ships on the open sea, fish tanks, and the endless omelet buffet. They were waiting for Milo's mother and father to arrive. Milo looked at his watch as Sasha walked over to the fish tank.

"They'll be here. There're just running late. Why are you so agitated today?" Natalie asked.

"I'm not." He forced a smile. "It's Sasha. She shouldn't have to wait for food. It's America, for Christ's sake."

All three of us blessed His Holy Name in unison.

"Milo!"

"Just a little shock humor—c'mon, Nat."

"Don't you 'c'mon Nat' me. Your language has been horrible lately, especially around Sasha. Are you this foul-mouthed at work?'

"Foul-mouthed?" Milo laughed. He leaned over to give her a kiss and break the tension.

Natalie pulled away.

Helen and Nico walked up to the booth.

"Sorry we're late. I dropped off some cheese bread to sell before Lent starts. It's Cheese Fare Sunday tomorrow, you know?" Helen said.

"Hey Papa, how are you feeling?" Milo stood up to greet his dad and ignored his mother's comment.

Nico smiled, winked and whispered, "Thank God." He was small in stature, smiled profusely and walked with a slight hunch, continually ailing in pain and bearing it humbly.

Sasha greeted her grandparents affectionately. Helen handed her a package marked 'cheese bread.' "Sasha, Cheese Fare Sunday marks the last week we can eat cheese before the Great Fast called Lent," Helen said.

"Yiayia, you don't eat cheese?" Sasha asked.

Helen pulled Sasha in closer to her bosom and explained the fasting rule for Great Lent.

"Well, come on Sash, we better make an extra cheesy omelet before yiayia tells us more about food we can't eat," Milo said. They slid out of the booth and headed for the buffet line. He told her that today they would eat until their bellies almost burst, but they would leave a little room for ice cream to fill in the gaps.

"Savlo, I have observed that vices and a love for food are deeply woven together in his life."

"You've observed a great mystery concerning the incarnation of image bearers."

A creature appeared to be following Milo and Sasha as they returned from the omelet station. Kallistos and the other guardians, all over the restaurant were in silent meditation. Savlo and I stood in their way as they walked through us.

"Hey, hey, Savlo baby, who's your new pet?" The creature said as she stopped following them. She looked me over and laughed. The rolls of fat under her pig shaped face jiggled like sacks of liquid behind what appeared to be a wedding veil. She was unpleasant to look at, purple and deep blue in color, bruised like tenderized meat, with another mouth in her belly chewing.

"I'll know soon enough. Rumor has it the she-monkey is carrying this watcher's offspring," she said as she drew close to me. "What's your name, little birdy? Wings and feet of purple, just my favorite color, mmm." She reached for my leg. I took my staff and struck downward to slice her away from me but missed, even though she was fat, she was quick.

"Easy does it, we've just met," she said.

Savlo's stern look amplified the situation, so I said nothing and held my staff at ease.

"Be gone. I rebuke you, Moria. Go back to the bowels whence you came," Savlo said maneuvering between her and me.

"Milo is one of my favorite toys, so hungry and never satisfied. He eats out of spite against his mother's beliefs." She started to walk away, then turned and said to me, "Like father like son, lil' birdie. I'll be seeing you around for sure." With a wink and a snort she vanished.

I was quiet as I followed Savlo back to the table. The family ate for some time and laughed. Natalie seemed to gain much encouragement from Helen's presence. As his parents sipped their black coffee, Milo had been up to the buffet twice more and was picking at Sasha's plate while leaning back and fiddling with his belt buckle.

"Oh come on, honey. Keep your pants buckled at least until we get home," Natalie said.

"That was awesome. That last mini omelet was delish, but the extra cheese did me in. I'll be napping in twenty minutes."

He jolted up in his seat as he held in a belch. Helen looked disgusted. Nico smiled. Natalie snickered and Sasha said, "Daddy, we got to fill in the gaps with ice cream."

"By God you're right, lil' birdie," Milo said as they headed off to the sundae bar.

"Lil' birdie'? She must still be here," I said to Savlo.

"She is like a mistress, always lingering in the background," Savlo said.

They left for home. Helen and Nico had taken Sasha for the day and evening.

After a short nap, Milo spent the rest of the daylight cleaning the garage. Natalie rested, cycling through many different emotions. She would check on Milo in the garage and then wander into his office and search through his personal items, curious as to what was really going on in his life.

That night, after Sasha had gone to sleep, Natalie asked him three questions as they lay in bed. The first was did he love her? He replied; yes. The second, how many times and with how many women had he 'crossed the line' with? He replied; just this one time and one woman. And thirdly, could she meet with Lilly? He answered; hell no, it was a done deal and they should move on. She cried herself to sleep again.

I had asked my question for the day, so I meditated all night concerning the next day. It would be the first time I would visit an earthly place of worship in many centuries.

ENTRY 7

The Last Sunday of Milo's Life

The clock flicked 6:01. The blaring buzzer shocked them both awake.

"Damn it, you know why I'm so negative? It's because every fucking morning that buzzer puts me in a bad mood. I mean really, can't we invent a better way to wake up?" Milo asked.

"Honey, the f-word is the first word out of your mouth—really? On Sunday?"

They went back to sleep for a couple hours, then Milo flung the covers off. "I'm getting in the shower," he said, startling Natalie.

Milo took an extra-long hot shower. I located in the bathroom in case Chliavos returned. The steam filled the bathroom, making the vent fan useless, and the mirror dripped, leaving runs like bars in a cage. Milo leaned forward with his forearms against the shower wall and rested his head on his arms. His legs were red, numb from the scalding temperature. The tub was filling because Natalie's hair had clogged the drain.

Natalie abruptly opened the door. The waft of cold air made the shower curtain stick to his leg, "Err, I hate that," he said.

"Hate what?"

"The shower curtain sticking to me. It makes me mad."

"Hey, do you know what time it is?" Nat asked him, arms folded and lips tight, as steam billowed out the door.

"Uh, no Nat, I don't. I'm not wearing my watch in here."

"Well, you've been in the shower for thirty two minutes and you're going to make us late for church if you don't wrap it up," Natalie said.

"You're timing me now? Sheesh," he exhaled. "Hey, are we going anywhere this afternoon?"

"My brother's house. It's Joshy's birthday party. It's on the calendar. My Baba's going to be there."

Milo sighed as he dropped his head onto his forearms again and muttered to himself, "Man, I need a new life."

Natalie, still standing there, quipped back. "What'd you say? You need a new wife?"

"No. I said I need a new life." His voice lost its conviction.

"Nice, Milo. Either way, nice," Natalie said as she shut the door with force. The shower curtain billowed and stuck to his leg again.

"Damn it," he said.

They finished getting ready in silence and headed to their place of worship visibly distracted in thought.

As they walked into the plain, square-shaped building, we heard the wind whispering, "Soon, soon."

The family sat in the second-to-the-back row of the large gathering room. They were greeted by their friends, the Armstrongs, who sat in front of them.

"Hi, guys," Katy Armstrong whispered. Savlo had told me she was responsible for inviting Milo and Natalie to Dogwood Bible Church and helping them make friends. He also said that Katy grew up with Milo at Holy Resurrection Greek Orthodox church, but married Kevin Armstrong, the son of a Baptist preacher, and never considered going back.

I didn't recognize the liturgy of worship, and there was only one icon in the building: the podium, shaped like a cross. The congregation sang songs of the Crucifixion, but they were not the songs given to the monks by the choirs of angels.

The leader stood up and spoke with authority and persuasion; "Dear brothers and sisters in Christ, I would like you to open your Bibles today to the Gospel of Luke, Chapter 16, verses 19 to 31, the parable of the rich man and Lazarus. While you're finding the passage, I want to perk your imagination and ask you to think about what Lazarus would say to the rich man now, who is in hell this very moment. The title of my sermon is Listen to Lazarus."

Milo was not mentally present most of the homily. It was as if someone had kicked a beehive in his head and now he was distracted with buzzing thoughts. His eyes glazed over and he was deaf to the preacher, just as he had grown deaf to Savlo. The preacher spoke passionately, as if he was upset. I was confused by his words. The other guardians in the room were scattered and silently hovering over the heads of those committed to their care. We looked at each other but no words were shared in our minds. We were all in the same space, but we were separated, individualized, lacking a sacramental act of unity.

"Hey Nat, did you see this in the bulletin here?" Milo whispered and pointed.

"What?"

"It says right here that member number one forty three should see the church treasurer."

"And?"

"What the hell, I should've at least been called on the phone, not just a number in a bulletin or a journal entry. What the—" Milo's whispering grew louder.

Katy turned around and hushed him.

"What are you talking about? Named? Called? How do you know if we're number one forty three?" Natalie asked.

"It's right here on our offering envelopes. Right at the bottom, we're number one forty three. I'm telling you I'm pissed off about this. How can they put this in the bulletin?"

"It's no big deal, just calm down," Natalie said.

"Sweetheart, we are real people, we have names. If they can't keep our names connected with our numbers, how can I trust them with my money? This is just incompetence. Here the preacher is talking about some rich man who goes to hell and they can't even keep track of my number or keep my name connected to the damn number," Milo said, disturbing those around them.

Katy turned around and shushed him. Milo gave her the evil eye.

"Honey, just calm down."

Milo got up during the homily.

"Where are you going?" Natalie grabbed at his shirt.

"I'm going to find the treasurer. This is bullshit."

Katy turned around again.

"And if you hush me again, I'll, I'll..." Milo snapped his fingers and pointed at her.

Natalie and Katy just shook their heads. Milo walked around the back of the pews, scoping out where the treasurer was sitting.

He tapped him on the shoulder. "Hey Bob, can I talk to you a second?" Milo whispered in his ear.

"Now?" Bob asked.

"Yes, now." Milo walked back through the double doors and waited for Bob to join him.

"Milo, what's going on? Pastor Dan is still preaching."

"Why don't you tell me what's going on. I'm member one forty three. But my name is Milo Chris and my phone number is in the directory, in case you forgot. What the hell, Bob? Am I only a number to you?"

"Whoa, Milo, there's no need to swear." Bob looked around for others within ear-shot.

"Swear? You're worried about my language? I'm worried about my money, and just being considered a 'giving unit' and not a person. It's insulting. You're insulting." Milo was red in the face.

"Brother Milo, there's an easy explanation." Bob remained calm. "The church's computer—"

"Don't give me that bullshit, Bob. Computer problems don't put my number in the bulletin, do they? Now everyone is going to think that something odd is going on with me and the money I give to the church—like a check bounced or something. This is unforgivable. I may just leave the church over this, and it's going to be your fault." Milo shook his finger at Bob.

"Milo, just calm down. No one knows your number. We should talk to the pastor about this."

"You're damn right we're going to talk to the pastor, right after this service. And Bob, everyone knows everyone's number. This place is so inbred with gossip it's pathetic."

Milo walked away and went to the bathroom. Bob walked back in and sat down.

Milo washed his face and looked into the mirror. "What the hell is going on with me? I'm going insane." He tried to calm himself by repeating his affirmations from his morning routine, but they had lost their charm for him.

"I can do this, the power of positive thinking." He walked back and sat down.

"...dear brothers and sisters in Christ, in conclusion, I would like to remind you that a simple reading of the text, which is the only way to read the Holy Scriptures, clearly states that upon entering death, you go to heaven with the poor man or to hell with the rich man. So it's heaven or hell, folks. Now is the time of decision. Today you must be sure, beyond a shadow of a doubt, where you will be one second after death. Jesus died for your sins on the cross. He took your place on the cross, hanging between heaven and hell as your substitute, He paid the debt that made it possible for you to be in heaven with Him and Lazarus. Maybe you have your eternal destiny settled, but a loved one needs to listen to Lazarus. You can go to the media center in the rear of the church and pick up this sermon for a ten dollar donation and give it to that someone, today. If the Holy Spirit has laid someone on your heart then, quench not the Spirit, brothers and sisters, and make sure you buy this sermon and give it to them today. Nancy's going to play *Just As I Am,* and we're going to have an altar call for anyone who doesn't have this matter settled today."

I looked around for the altar, but did not see one.

Milo leaned over and whispered to Natalie, "Now, that guy can sell."

She just shook her bowed head and quietly sang the words to the funeral dirge of a song.

After the service meeting, Milo, Bob and Pastor Daniel talked passionately for a brief moment, then Milo walked away.

As they got into their vehicle, Natalie buckled her seat belt, Milo did not.

"Milo, what was that all about with Bob and Pastor Dan after church?"

"Oh, nothing. I have a meeting tomorrow morning with Pastor Dan."

"Honest answers," Natalie said.

"I'm going to resolve the number issue in the bulletin with Pastor Dan tomorrow, that's all."

They drove home with the windows down and the warm spring wind whipping loudly through the SUV.

"Hey, what did you mean Pastor Dan could 'sell'?"

"Huh? Oh, it was his sermon."

"You were around enough to hear it?" Natalie asked.

"Shut up." He smiled at her.

"No really, honestly, what did you mean?" She closed her window.

"Well, Jesus died for your sins on the cross and if you accept this, you're saved from hell. He took our place. He steps in and makes things right and we get to live a blessed life, waiting to go to heaven or for the good Lord to come back. That's the basic message, anyway, right?" Milo said as he turned down the radio. "And get your CD for only ten bucks in the back." He laughed.

"Okay, but what's that got to do with sales?"

"Well, it's essentially what I do. These poor sinners are going through financial hell, I step in, pay their debt and then give new life to another couple in homeownership heaven." He laughed. "The only difference, my dear, is I get rich and God does it for free."

"Dang, Milo, nothing like having a messiah complex."

"Hey, just spreading the good news. When you think about it, Christianity is just like sales and marketing, same tactics, different product."

"Sounds crass. Your mother would light extra candles and pray all night if she heard you talk like this."

"Well, it's all pretty clear to me. I mean, who wants to go to hell when it's so easy to go to heaven?"

"I remember my parents and especially my Baba always praying for God and Mary to save them. It seemed like they were…" She paused then asked, "Do you ever miss it?"

"Bad marketing babe—not user friendly—ancient and unsellable."

"Milo, you're going to get struck by lightning." She shook her head.

"Nah, I got my fire insurance. Just like the preacher said, I listened to Lazarus, my debts are paid, just as I am, baby, no worries." He laughed.

I looked at Savlo and Kallistos. Both were ministering to Sasha, distracting her from retaining the conversation by showing refracted light on her lap as she giggled and tried to catch the little rainbows.

"All right, that's enough, you're going to get us both sent to hell now," Natalie said and opened her window again.

He turned up the radio and drove to Natalie's brother's house for the birthday party.

— • —

We arrived at the home of Mikhail Myshkin, Natalie's brother. Kallistos told me that her parents, who had died when she was in college, were very holy people. He cautioned me to be careful around their Babushka, who was so holy she often could see angels. When she was around, we were to remain unseen even to each other.

Milo slammed his fist on the steering wheel as he parked the SUV and said, "Damn it, Natalie, I forgot my Zoloft."

"Milo, please. It's not that bad."

"You're right," he exhaled. "It's just that your Baba creeps me out. It's like she's a fortuneteller or something. She stares all crazy at me, with her lazy eye and all."

"Stop it. My Baba's a holy woman, full of love. It's just, she's from a different place and time. She's old school Russian. Cut her some slack, and don't start anything with my brother, either."

Sasha dashed out of the SUV to find her cousin Joshua and the other children gathered for the party. Milo slothfully shuffled in as he carried the dessert Natalie had baked the day before.

From around the tree a swarm of bees started to coalesce into a funnel and float towards Milo. They rested right above his head. As they formed into a face they sang, "Fun, fun! His sin scrolls are almost done! Just a curse or two before the hearse is due!" Then the face dissipated, but the bees kept swarming all around Milo's head. They buzzed and crawled into his ears, nose and all over his face. He looked agitated.

Milo walked up to the front door and was greeted by Natalie's brother, Mikhail. "Hey Mike, how the hell are ya?" He set the dessert down on the side entry table and greeted Mikhail by shaking his hand and drawing him close, kissing first one side of his cheek and then the other. He actually kissed his second cheek firmly and said, "Mikey, how long has it been since you were last kissed by a man?" Milo seemed to find amusement with this distasteful humor.

Mikhail pushed Milo back a little and looked at him sternly. Milo laughed and said, "Damn, just kidding with you. Lighten up, man." Mikhail stepped aside and let him pass. Milo grabbed the dessert and walked down the hall into the family room to join the others.

"Uncle Milo!" young Joshua shouted.

"Hey buddy and hello to everyone. Glad to be here," Milo said. He scanned the room. Natalie's Babushka was sitting in the corner, dressed in black. She adjusted her embroidered head covering as her eyes met Milo's. The look on her face was one of horror. She did not stop looking at Milo as he moved towards the kitchen countertops to set the dessert down, looking over his shoulder a couple of times at her. He found Natalie talking with her sister-in-law, Jessica. He bent over, interrupted her conversation and whispered into her ear.

"See, this is the shit I'm talking about. Your Baba is staring at me. She's burning a hole in my head. I mean, *damn*! Nat, look at her stare at me."

She intensely focused on him only and would not break her gaze. We remained invisible but the old woman could see the Beelzebub which still buzzed around Milo.

Natalie stood up, looked at her and said, "Baba? How are you, Baba? Do you want something to drink?" She mimicked a drinking motion.

"Until you have smoked out the bees, you can't eat the honey," the elderly saint replied in Russian with a proverb.

"Bees, Baba?" Natalie could only make out one of the Russian words.

"What the hell did she call me?" Milo asked so only Natalie could hear. Natalie just put her hand on Milo's shoulder and gently forced him to sit down, never breaking eye contact with her Baba.

"Baba, what did you say? I don't know all the words. Bees? What about the bees, Baba?" Natalie asked from across the room. Everyone else was talking and laughing about other things.

Her Baba started to roll a string of black prayer beads through her fingers, and then leaned back to get another look at Milo. Milo saw this and hid behind Natalie to block her Baba's gaze.

"What the fuck is she saying, Natalie? Is she cursing me?" Milo whispered.

"Milo, please, the language lately is so gross and beneath you," Natalie said.

"I really needed my Zoloft today to deal with her," Milo said.

Beelzebub formed a face of an old man and said to us, "We know you're here. That was too easy, guardians." Then they disappeared. Baba continued to roll her beads and pray the 'Jesus prayer'. She watched Milo throughout the evening.

— • —

On the way home from Natalie's family party, the shadows made the drive even darker. Sasha was asleep in the back seat. We were behind her. Natalie's interactions with her brother and Baba had showed me the vestiges of her parents' strength of faith and love they had instilled in her. It was the core of her personality. Natalie's Babushka did not speak any English, and though we could see her holiness, she appeared crazy to most, but not to Natalie. She was comfortable with spiritual expressions that were sometimes out of the ordinary.

"Nat, your Baba was really creeping me out tonight," Milo said.

"I could tell you were really bothered by her."

"Yeah, but tonight she was a little out there, like mentally ill."

"What do you want me to say? She's not mentally ill, Milo,' she said sternly and appeared frustrated. She took a deep breath then said, "She's a classic Russian Babushka. She still lives in Russia, in her mind, but she's certainly not mentally ill. She cares for you, Milo. When I was growing up she would always pray for people, and when something was up she would take out those prayer beads and really pray."

There was a pause in the conversation for several minutes. Natalie nestled up against the door, removed her seat belt strap from across her chest and flipped it behind her.

"Honey, can you turn up the heat? I'm cold."

"Sure," Milo said, and then opened his window a crack.

"Milo, I don't want to sound like your mother, but maybe we should go to Holy Resurrection more often, like on Easter or some other feast day."

"Absolutely not. Listen Nat, you sat through the same services I did. Yours were half in Russian and mine in Greek. They did no good for us. We made the decision to go to DBC for Sasha and to hear sermons that nourished us. It's just that 'off the boat,' old fashioned mentality of our parents and especially your Baba, that are not in step with how church is done here. Trust me. I've given this a lot of thought."

"You're probably right, but there's something off about us and you especially. I'm worried about you." Natalie sat up and looked at Milo. Kallistos was prompting her and holding her head close to him.

Milo let out a big sigh. "Sweetheart, you worry too much. We're going through a rough patch right now, that's all. You're my wife, not my priest, pastor, or even my therapist. I'm trying to be honest with you, but it does no good to let you share in all my unhappiness. That's for me to enjoy." He smiled at her.

"You're unhappy, then?" she asked.

"Sheesh. See, this is what I mean. Don't psychoanalyze me. I made a mistake and we're working through it. Most of the world is unhappy to some degree. They work through it. They make do. It's life."

"Do you still pray?"

"Holy shit, Natalie, what kind of question is that?"

"Just a question, Milo. You can answer it honestly."

"Alright, Natalie. You want a glimpse into my head?"

Not being privy to the inner thoughts of image bearers, we all kept guard, emanating great light, to keep the demons from hearing his words and recording them on a sin scroll.

"Who do you pray to?" he asked.

"God, of course. Sometimes Mary," Natalie said.

"So do you really think that the all-powerful God is concerned with the details of your life? I mean, think about that for a second. How many billions of people are in the world, suffering, dying, and most are unhappy? How can God be concerned with all that?"

"I don't know. Maybe because He is all powerful and has saints and angels to help Him," she said.

"If He is all powerful, then why does He need saints and angels? It doesn't make sense. Praying is for your own psychological benefit, and that's it. So no, I don't pray. I see little benefit in confessing sins to a priest when my pillow will do. I see little benefit in participating in boring irrelevant rituals of crazy backward thinking Greeks or Russians. Okay? So is this the kind of honesty you want?"

"So, you don't pray for me or Sasha?"

"I'm done talking about this."

They drove for a while. Natalie closed her eyes tightly. Milo's jaw was clenched. He had turned the radio up a little and was driving faster than the speed limit. He started to drift to the side of the road and straddled the rumble strip. The initial rumble caused all to stir but not wake. He increased his speed. The reflector mile markers were flickering by as he reached eighty eight miles an hour.

Kallistos prompted Natalie awake.

She screamed, "Milo!"

"Aahh!" Milo yelped and jerked the SUV back into the lane.

"Milo, what the hell are you doing? You could have killed us."

"Calm down. I wasn't sleeping. I was just driving on the side of the road."

"What?" Natalie said. Her heart was racing. She awkwardly leaned back between the seats to check on Sasha, who was still asleep.

"Milo, I don't even know what to say."

"Then don't say anything. It was no big deal."

Natalie turned off the radio and they drove in silence. The rhythmic thumping of the road joints seemed to tamp their tempers down. Milo pulled in the driveway and didn't open the garage door. They both just sat there, staring straight ahead. The automatic light in the cab shut off after ninety seconds. Neither of them moved. Natalie popped the door open, got out, retrieved Sasha, held her close, bumped the door shut with her hip, and headed inside the house. Milo's hands were still on the steering wheel. He dropped his head. The demons nested in the trees roused themselves as he got out and walked into the house.

They soon found themselves getting undressed and ready for bed. Natalie rolled away from Milo's side of the bed as he got in. One could only hear them breathing, one after the other. They both stared at the walls. When they were breathing in unison, Natalie would change her breathing rhythm.

"Milo, I'm not sure what's going on with you, but you better fix it. I don't feel safe around you."

Milo said nothing. They went to sleep. We prayed and watched the demons dance on the lawn as the underground sprinkler system shushed its water in the air.

ENTRY 8

The Beginning of Milo's Personal Eighth Day

At 6:01 the buzzer blared and Milo did his routine again. He stopped in the office before anyone else was there and sorted through some files. He stopped by Lilly's office and left her a note telling her to text him when she was in. Then he left for his meeting at Dogwood Bible Church. Milo drove intentionally slow, deep in thought the whole way. He pulled into the parking lot, let out a big sigh, and walked in.

A murder of crows with red glowing eyes, were flying in unison from the telephone wire to the ground and back again. Milo didn't see them, but Savlo and I did. After flirting mildly with the Pastor Daniel's secretary, Milo walked in to meet with him.

"Have a seat, Milo. How's your day going?" Pastor Daniel asked. I could see he had a sincere heart. He was almost six feet tall, a bit portly with broad shoulders. He wore a blue suit and tie and had a black gold-leafed Bible on the mahogany desk in front of him. His guardian angel was visible but remained silent in meditation.

"Thanks, Pastor. I think I will." Milo sat down in a chair opposite the desk, which was loaded with papers, Bible commentaries, and a Tony Romo bobble head. A sign tacked to the bulletin board behind the desk read, "I'm a Christian first, a Texan second and a Republican third."

"How about them Cowboys, Pastor?" Milo asked.

"Good night! They need to do something this off season, for sure."

I could tell Milo was apprehensive about being confronted. He usually led every conversation, but this time he waited for Pastor Daniel to start.

"Milo, after you stormed off yesterday, Bob briefly told me about the conversation y'all had during my sermon."

"What'd he say, specifically?" Milo asked.

"Now, Bob Sterling is a good man. I've known him for a long time. He said you were angry and threatened him over some accounting error. Sound 'bout right?"

"Well, it sounds like that's what he heard, but that's not how I meant it." Milo looked to the floor.

"By all means, tell me what you meant then."

"Pastor, have you ever been misunderstood?" Milo looked Pastor Daniel straight in the eye now.

"Of course."

Milo went on to describe how passionately Greeks communicate and how he meant no harm to Bob, but was offended that he didn't get a call from him or try to settle it face to face. He skillfully turned the issue around as an attack on Bob, insinuating he had an effeminate way of dealing with confrontation.

"Milo you're right about face-to-face talking and I wouldn't be a good Texan if I disagreed. However, brother, I would not be a good Christian if I didn't tell you that settling things like Christian men should involve a little truth and love."

"Pastor, I didn't grow up knowing the Bible like you, but I seem to remember stories of Jesus turning over tables of money collectors, calling all those religious folk "vipers" and "tombstones" and pretty much insulting and threatening them to get it right when it comes to money and God. Now am I right about that or not?"

Pastor Daniel leaned back in his high-backed leather swivel seat, put both his hands behind his head, and just smiled at Milo for a couple of moments.

"Milo, you're a smart son-of-gun. Maybe too smart—so I'm going to do this gently like it says in Galatians chapter 6 verse 1. Do you know this passage of scripture?"

"No, not right off hand."

"Well, I always have my Bible on hand. Let me turn to it right here real quick."

He did, then read, "Brethren, if a man is overtaken in any trespass, you who are spiritual restore such a one in a spirit of gentleness, considering yourself lest you also be tempted."

"So what trespass has overtaken me?" Milo asked. His jaw was tight.

"It's a hard sin to recognize unless you have it. So that's my confession to you. You're overtaken by the sin of justifying yourself by way of spinning the events a little, which means pride. You don't want to be in the wrong. You use your verbal skills, your tongue to manipulate others and get them to believe your side of the story. This is a dangerous sin, and you, my friend, are good at it."

"So what are you going to do about it?" Milo asked. "Preach about it next Sunday?"

"Now, now, boy, there's no need to get combative with me. It's your sin. My job is to protect the flock. Before I had the 'calling' to join the ministry, I wanted to be a sheriff. I even had thoughts of being a Texas Ranger. Now the good Lord's seen fit to put me here in Michigan and be the pastor of this here church. But you can see that my calling is still to be a protector and root out sin, even though I ain't in law enforcement. I don't got a gun here, but I got a King James Bible and boy, do not let your tongue loose on one of my sheep again. You hear me?

"Aren't I one of your sheep too?"

"Not when you act like that," Pastor Daniel said.

There was a long pause while Milo just looked across the desk. I had seen this expression before, on many of the aerial demons, filled with all the vices of hell.

"Loud and clear, Pastor. Sheep number one forty three reporting for duty," Milo said, then stood up and extended his hand. Pastor Daniel stood and shook it out of habitual gesture before Milo left the office.

The murder of crows was flying about as he got into his car. "This is all a fucking scam—screw that self-righteous, Jesus selling cowboy."

Milo turned on the radio and headed out on the highway, music blaring, fueling his emotions. We located in the backseat.

We were on the highway and Milo started to speed up, eighty eight miles an hour and climbing. I noticed the reflector mile markers whizzing by. Then he caught my eye, the mumbling vagabond, Milo's hinderer. He was dressed as he was in the coffee shop, in the same overcoat, camouflage and scarf. He stood smiling at each mile marker as we passed them. Savlo opened his wings to full protective extension and now floated above the SUV. Milo drifted to the right and straddled the rumble strip. Savlo screamed in his mind, "Center the car, now. Do not do this. Straighten the car! Now!"

I drifted outside the car and around front. I hovered in front of Milo's face, separated by the windshield. "Stop doing this! Milo!" I yelled. I turned and saw the hinderer at another mile marker, laughing. We both were prompting to get Milo's attention. I looked up.

Savlo, who could see farther down the road said, "There's a parked truck ahead."

It was a green and white truck. I could see it now. I looked back to Milo. Another mile marker flashed by and I heard the hinderer laughing even harder. I saw him holding his belly.

"Milo!" I yelled, and decided to break my apprenticeship rules, show myself to Milo, and scare him into straightening his vehicle. But at just that moment he looked down at his phone.

A text from Lilly:

-*Goodbye Milo. See you in hell*

He was texting back when his SUV reached ninety nine miles an hour and slammed into the abandoned truck. He was leaning sideways on his elbow towards the center of the vehicle so the air bag did not stop him from flying through the front windshield. Milo's forehead caught the top edge of the windshield, just like stubbing a toe, it snapped down on the top of the hood. His momentum sent him into a series of somersaults. The last tumble ended as the back of his head thumped on the rumble strip with a blood-soaked splat. The hinderer and I watched the whole spectacle of carnage happen. He laughed. I bowed my head. He vanished and Savlo hovered over Milo.

Milo's soul tried to rise, but could only sit up. He expressed the usual disorientation the dead feel. He did not realize fully what had happened as he looked at his own mutilated, crumpled body while the mangled steel, smoke and fire from the crash flickered in the distance.

He looked up at Savlo and said, "I know you. You seem familiar."

"Yes, Milo, I am your guardian angel. Be not afraid," Savlo spoke to his mind.

"Yeah, you're the voice in my head, aren't you?"

"You used to be able to discern my voice, but yes, that is how you know me."

"Guardian angel, hey?"

Savlo nodded.

"Hey, nice job here," he said.

He was barely alive and with every fleeting pump of his heart, his soul was jerked back down and into his bloodied fleshy body. It would be seventeen minutes until the ambulance reached us. I stood over Milo, now unconscious, comatose. We waited. Savlo was in a meditative trance.

The ambulance arrived, establishing a parameter from the onlookers who had stopped. The hindering angel stood in the crowd, watching his work. The medical workers shoveled Milo onto a board, then a wheeled bed and were about to load him into the ambulance.

"Do you see his hand?" one image bearer said to the other.

"It's over here," someone yelled. The young image bearer with a belt full of medical gear hurried over to it, grabbed it and placed it in a red plastic bag. He set the bag on Milo's stomach.

"I don't think we should take him. Let's stabilize him and call for Areo-med," the female image bearer told her partner.

It would be another seven minutes until the medical helicopter would arrive.

The police arrived, trying to make sense of what had happened. The medical team did all they could to stabilize life in Milo as he gasped for breath, choking on blood bubbling out of his mouth every couple of breaths.

The helicopter arrived, but it would be another seventeen minutes until we reached the helio-pad and the doctors at the hospital could properly evaluate him.

As we lifted off in the helicopter, we could see demons dancing in the fields below. Milo's hindering angel was the only being in the crowd of people still looking up. Dark storm clouds billowed overhead. Milo was not ready for the valley of the shadow of death that was yet to come.

"Go to Kallistos," Savlo said to me.

— • —

I arrived next to Kallistos, who was meditating in the corner of the kitchen.

"Greetings, Milo's been in an accident, and his hinderer was there."

He didn't break his meditation. He must have known.

Natalie, dressed in a black sweater with an apron tied at her neck, stood at the granite center island in the kitchen. As she rolled and cut the dough for a pie she remained silent, not distracted by other horrible events being reported on the television or by Sasha's rather rambunctious play.

"She reminds me of a priest at the altar," I said.

He opened his eyes. "More than you know."

I started to watch her with increased attention. She was an industrious woman, even in pregnancy, and held an inner joy that warded off the darker powers surrounding her. She compartmentalized the stress of Milo's infidelity; processing the emotions a little at a time. Image bearers make a liturgy of their lives and that is what I beheld in her. Even with all that had happened, with bright sadness, Natalie embraced the sacredness of every moment. Soon, this was all to be tested.

"Look Mommy, it's Daddy's car on TV," Sasha said.

Natalie stepped away from the kitchen island and took notice.

"...Details of the rollover accident on highway 131 are still coming in, but all traffic is stopped and we're told that it was just one man driving. Police have not released the name. We talked to witnesses, driving several hundred yards behind the vehicle, who told us he was driving on the shoulder of the highway, straddling the rumble strip until he hit an abandoned vehicle. Suzi, we will stay with the story as it develops."

"Thanks John, in other news..."

Natalie called Milo's phone with haste, hands shaking. There was no answer and she left no message. Sasha continued to play. Natalie assumed her position at the altar of her kitchen and started to mentally pray. I could hear her prayers, now. Kallistos stood right behind, both hands on her shoulders, and prayed with her. She knew in her heart the driver had been Milo, and was going into shock as thoughts of his possible death moved from intuition to reality.

The doorbell rang. Natalie set down her knife. Her hands shook, the neighbor's dog was barking, and life as she knew it would be different in a matter of seconds. She could see through the glass in the front door that a police officer and an older man with a white shirt and black v-neck sweater were standing on the other side.

"Good afternoon, ma'am. I'm Officer Don Krowkoski and this is our Chaplin, Reverend Steven Snyder. Are you Natalie Christopoulos?"

"Yes, I am. It's my husband, isn't it—on the highway?"

He frowned and dropped his head momentarily. "I'm afraid so, ma'am. Miletus was in a serious accident. He was flown to St. Jude's Hospital, downtown."

Natalie held her womb and leaned against the door. The reverend dropped his Bible and pounced to catch her from falling.

"Please, Mrs. Christopoulos, you should sit."

He led her to the sofa in the adjacent living room.

"Is he dead?" She was welling up with tears and her fair skin started to blotch around her neck.

"We were told that he is unconscious and the injuries are severe. It's a miracle he's alive."

"Did Savlo intervene?" Kallistos asked me.

"No, he did not. I tried but—"

"Transitions are treacherous. This must have been an action of Milo's free will."

"If the hindering angel was present and visible, he's dead and we have the toll houses to go through. Those evil dark hives along the passageway to the next life will terrify him. He died with no peace in his soul," he said.

"We?" I said.

"Yes—'we.' Surely the divine movements have not escaped you. Three guardians shined together in communion over the past week; three image bearers, one losing his faith, one full of faith and one not yet living the life of faith. This journey is never sojourned alone. As they are bound together by mystery and sacrament, so are we."

Natalie had taken the news with calmness but was clearly in shock. She instructed the reverend to call Pastor Daniel and have him meet her at the hospital. She called Helen and sent Sasha to the neighbors' house while she prepared for the trip to the hospital. Officer Krowkoski insisted with gentleness that they leave, and that he drive her to the hospital. We followed.

— • —

Natalie took the elevator to the second floor labeled, Intensive Care Unit. She walked past the nurses' station and asked where Milo was. Great sadness filled the three nurses' eyes as they saw she was pregnant.

"He's in room eight, the one on the end. I'll let the doctor know you're here," one of the nurses said following behind her.

Natalie walked down to the room and opened the door. A nurse with her guardian followed her but did not enter the room.

The only lights on were dimmed over Milo's head. The curtains were drawn. She gasped at the blinking cacophony of machines and the ventilator, held her womb and put her other hand over her mouth. He was wrapped in shrouds from head to foot, his eyes closed. She began to cry as she walked over to the bed and searched for some part of him to hold.

"Oh, my sweetheart. What's happened to you?" Her hands trembled over his. She stood there weeping, looking for some way to connect with him or touch his skin, for a movement behind his closed eyelids.

I stood next to Savlo at the foot of the bed as he watched Milo and Natalie. Occasionally he glanced off to the right. A black swirling inter-dimensional portal opened in the room. This is how the passage to the toll houses appears to the soul of an image bearer. This vision was for Milo. Kallistos was in deep meditation, ministering to Natalie close behind her.

The doctor and a nurse entered the room. He was of Indian descent, speaking with a slight accent and a kind tone, dark skinned, dark haired, small in stature with rimmed glasses.

"Mrs. Christopoulos, I am Dr. Dayaal. I am overseeing your husband's care. The ER doctors did most of the work and have sustained him to this point. You can see his injuries are severe and he needs the assistance of the machine to breathe. He is in a coma and in no pain due to the medications he is on right now. Have you been briefed as to what has happened?"

She said nothing and did nothing.

"Mrs. Christopoulos, I understand this is a terrible shock."

"Just Natalie Chris, but please call me Natalie." She looked into the doctor's eyes.

"Okay, Natalie, when you are ready, I would like to talk with you in one of our hospitality suites—only when you are ready of course. Just notify the nurses and I will meet you there and we can talk some more."

"Okay."

Dr. Dayaal and the nurse left the room, closing the door behind him.

Natalie wept.

Helen soon rushed into the room and burst into tears and wails. She wanted to embrace her son and Natalie at the same time. When Nico arrived, the three of them huddled next to each other looking at Milo, mourning and weeping with hearts torn asunder.

— • —

The amount of time it would take for a monk to say fifty psalms had passed, when the room filled with a noticeable coldness and the calm silence of the spiritual dimension enveloped us. We could hear jeering. "He is ours," some demon whispered from deep in the black portal. We could see no one just a light starting to illumine. The whispers began to grow louder. "He is ours, and we've come to harvest that which we've grown."

The voices we had heard earlier began to manifest themselves as little lights. They started to collapse on each other and formed a bodily figure. Their whispers now chanted in rhythm, "Come with us, follow the light. Come with us."

"Why do you always try to confuse the children of the Resurrection with your deceitful snares and lies?" Savlo demanded of the figure.

"We know our bounds, and we know about you, mighty Savlo, who gives us souls to keep until the appointed time," one of them hissed.

Milo's soul began to float up from his broken body, but was disoriented as he became aware of his trans-dimensional state of being. He looked around, down at his body, at his wife and parents, still in shock and weeping, then to the creature posing as an angel of light.

"Come with us, follow the light. Do not be afraid, Milo. What you truly desire is waiting beyond," the fiery being said.

Milo looked with confusion at the scene outside his body, again. He looked at Savlo, then to the creature calling him.

"Come with us, follow the light. Hurry," the manifestation said with more urgency. It was waving its hand, bidding Milo to come toward the portal. "Follow me, for our way is easy."

"Enough. He has at least three turns of the planet before we sojourn," Savlo said.

"Three turns of the planet. Really Savlo, is that your best attempt to stall us? You're such a failure at guarding souls. We laugh at you. Come with us, Milo. He cannot save you."

"Silence, I command you," Savlo said.

"We will leave for a time to go tell the hive generals you bring another soul to the toll houses. Dumah, the Shepherd of Hell, will be pleased to see you again."

They dissolved, and Milo grasped in the air, trying to find the light again.

Only Savlo appeared to Milo, for he was not used to this mode of existence and my presence would confuse him more.

"Now I am really dead, aren't I?" Milo said.

"Yes," Savlo said to his mind.

"I can hear you in my head, but how do I know if this is real or a dream? Talk to me directly."

"Telepathy is preferred for we have no bodies. Milo, you stand at a crossroad. Look at your corpse." Savlo pointed to it and the family standing around it. "Now look to the desert of infinity." Savlo then pointed to the black portal. This is where you must eventually sojourn. You know it as the afterlife."

"I don't understand this. I don't know what to do," Milo said, his soul growing downcast.

"You have a long hard journey before you. I will guide you, but you must decide to leave of your own free will."

"If I don't, will I just be a ghost forever?"

"If you don't decide, then the demons will trick you into coming with them."

"I am not going with any demons. No way," Milo said.

"You did not resist them for the last years of your earthly life, so now you are easy prey for them. Do not trust what is comfortable or familiar, for you did not die in a state of grace or repentance."

Milo looked at Savlo and said, "Speak plainly to me. Are you for me or against me or just a guide?"

Savlo's angelic reaction could not be described with human emotions. He spoke the words of love that echo in silence.

Milo drifted back down next to his body and stood beside Natalie.

"She can't hear me, can she?"

Savlo shook his head to say 'no.'

"Natalie, my dear, I love you so much. I'm so sorry. I was an idiot. I was driving over the rumble strip and not paying attention. I didn't mean to kill myself." He tried to stroke her head but his hand went through her.

"I have some other things to tell you. Bad things…"

Savlo interjected. "Do not. The time for repentance has past. You cannot change one thing you have done."

"But I've done terrible things."

"Yes, you have, and they have kept a scroll of every sin. They are preparing them now, to accuse you. They're spreading their sin scrolls all over the seven hives clustered with the terrible toll houses in the city of doom, beyond the river of fire, Styx."

"Who?" Milo asked.

"Aerial demons," Savlo said.

"So I'm going to hell?"

"Not as you understand it."

"Purgatory?"

"No, not as you understand it."

"Well, tell me something I do understand. You're not being very helpful. You're freaking me out," Milo said with frustration in his voice.

"I will tell you more when you decide to make passage with us."

"Us?"

"Yes." Savlo permitted me to reveal myself. "In time, all things will be revealed to you."

Milo scrambled away from us, startled by my appearance. "Whoa, where'd that thing come from?" He studied us. "Angels, demons and now a purple feathered giant— I don't understand all this. I don't know what's going on." He turned away from us to his family and pleaded, "Ma, Dad, Natalie, help me!"

"My name is Savlo. I have been yoked to you since your baptism. I have watched over you, and tried to guide you your whole life. I will continue my job, for He who sent me has so willed it."

"This is too much. Natalie, Nat, what's going on, here? I don't want to die. I'm scared, baby. Help me." Milo knelt down at Natalie's feet as she continued to hold his body's hand. He wept without tears, confused and downcast.

Natalie blew her nose and dabbed her tears, took a deep breath and walked out of the room. His parents stayed.

"Where are you going? Hey! Nat?" He elevated. "Savlo, where is she going? Make her come back."

"Life moves on. She has holy work to do. We have time before our journey starts. Do you wish to visit anyone or go anywhere?"

Milo ignored the invitation and looked in silence at his parents mourning the death of their only son.

ENTRY 9

"you dwell in the midst of a rebellious house,
which has eyes to see but does not see..."

- The Prophet Ezekiel

The next day, Milo's body still lay comatose and attached to a breathing machine as a heart monitor beeped. Tubes snaked into his nose and his hand was wired to monitor vital biological functions. He gasped for air every few seconds. The room was warm but stale. Natalie sat in the dull teal vinyl reclining chair and stared at the blinking lights, flashing numbers and graphs.

She had been there all day. Her cell phone rang.

"Hello...Hi, Helen...Yeah, he's still the same. I met with the lawyer today and all that's left to do is to sign some papers and then let him go. How's Sasha?" She started to cry, but no tears were left.

"The doctor said the same thing, as soon as we take him off the machines he will die. They say it is a—um— a biological certainty... My brother wants to take Sasha for a couple of days. So, I'll come get her tonight. Oh Helen, a priest is here, I've got to go, but I'll call you later, okay? ...I love you too."

She sniffed, wiped her nose, and walked around the bed to greet the unexpected guest.

"Hi, Father, I don't think we've met before?"

He extended his hand as if to have her receive it, kiss it and be blessed, in old Russian Orthodox fashion.

"Oh, Father, we're not Orthodox anymore," she said, and extended her hand to shake his. He withdrew his hand, made the sign of the cross over her, and blessed her anyway. When they were standing closer she seemed mesmerized by his deeply tender yet uneven eyes.

"My child, I am Father John from the Russian Orthodox Church," he said with a thick accent.

"I'm Natalie Chris and I know that church very well, St. Mary's." She smiled. "Father, how did you get in? It's after visiting hours—Father Luke from Holy Resurrection, the Greek Church, has already been here several times."

"You were baptized at that parish by Orthodox priest, were you not?" Father John said.

"Um, yes, after my parents died my Babushka took me to church until I was older. How did you know you that?" She could not stop looking into his uneven eyes. They seemed to glow above his thick black and white beard.

"I know," was his only response. He smiled at her, and then walked closer to the bedside. Natalie went over to the other side of the bed; she and the priest faced each other. Father John looked at Milo, and then he looked at her, then back to Milo again.

Natalie broke the silence. "Father, they say as soon as I take him off the machines, he will die."

"He is dead already," Father John said.

"What?"

"Yes, he is dead. His soul is waiting to go down the path."

"What path?"

— • —

Milo sat next to his body, watching it gasp for air. The ventilator was hypnotically consistent. He could not make out what Natalie and the holy priest were saying.

"Isn't technology amazing? They think I'm alive but here I sit, outside of my body, looking at them. I spent my whole life looking out for others, and now it's reversed, I guess. Isn't that ironic, Savlo?"

"You didn't spend your life like that," Savlo said.

Milo laughed, then wept. "You're right. What am I going to do?" Savlo was silent.

"Hello. I'm dead, you crazy old priest." Milo tried to get Father John's attention, but with no effect.

Another angel of light appeared to Milo, coming closer through the darkened portal, growing bigger and brighter. Its light filled the room. It was a different kind of light than we possess, manufactured, not emanating from the Holy One.

Milo spun around, lowered to one knee and bowed his head. I wanted to interrupt these demons of deception, but Savlo stayed me with a wave of his hand. For the first time I realized Savlo's patience and how his great respect for the image bearers' free will governed his actions.

"Miletus, son of Nicholas, we have come to reason with you and offer you a choice."

"What choice do I have?" Milo said.

"During your life you were a man of respect, of means and of action. You were a self-made man. Is this a true testimony of you?"

"Yes, yes and yes. You speak plainly to me."

"We understand you, because we have lived with you too, watching and waiting for you to come with us," the angel of light said.

"I want my life back. Can you grant me this?"

"This is beyond the established way of things. However, we can give you the fruit of your labor on earth. We have things to eat, drink and be merry with. Many things you worked for we can give you for all of time to enjoy. We speak well of you in our house."

"Now, this sounds good, better than what Savlo has offered so far."

"You have lived this way for many years, but it was only a means to an end. The end is what we offer. Your life was just a shadow of your truest desires."

"But I was sinful." Milo lowered his head.

"Have no thought of that, or of this guardian. Embrace our hospitality."

Milo rose to his feet and drifted in their direction. Savlo motioned for me to follow him, and we stayed close to Milo.

"This is an old trick. Make careful note of this, for your true education is at hand," Savlo said to my mind.

A great light far off in the vastness, of the portal, caught Milo's eye as his perception was adjusting to the spiritual dimension." Look, there must be heaven? Follow the light, that's what they all say." He arose, looking around, as though he did not know how he was moving towards the light. There before him appeared another angel, clothed in white with a human face and beautiful wings, who bid Milo, "Come, follow me."

Milo followed, though squinting; he thought he recognized people from his past that had died. "Hey, I think I know them!" he yelled. Many were bidding him to come. The angel of light lured him farther into the vision, up a mounding grassy hill to a great gate encrusted with jewels. Milo with building animation looked around. He floated up to the gate and peered through. There, a distance off, was a magnificent garden enclosed with a fieldstone fence.

"Welcome home, Milo," said the angel. "Go and see."

Milo went towards the stone fence, seeing all the people waving at him. As he grew closer he slowed down and saw that the people were not waving him closer, but waving him away.

He looked back. The angel of light was now a flaming fire, his human face now hollowed to a skeletal figure. Milo tried to turn back to where he had come from, but he was being drawn towards the fence. Horrible demons yanked by the neck those who he thought were people he remembered, and threw them down behind the fieldstone wall.

The fiery demon split apart, shedding his angelic appearance, and closed in on Milo. Milo tried to get away, but he did not know how to move his soul. The multiplying demons reached for him. Their energy formed darkened features, horrible looking faces of dogs, owls, ravens, rats and disfigured humans, cackling and laughing, trying to pull him toward a river of dark water beyond the fence, which was licking with bursts of flame. Demons appearing as naked women with tails and reptilian skin jumped up and stood on the wall. They carried goblets of blood-thick wine and loaves of bread so stale they appeared to break their teeth as they gnawed through them.

"Come dine with us, Milo. We want you," they said.

Milo shrieked in fear but no sound came out. Then he noticed a large she-devil that resembled Lilly from his office. Her mouth was full of sores. He looked down. The she-devil came close to him, leaned into his ear and whispered. He wagged and flailed to get distance from her and the dark ones who pressed in on him.

"We want to eat you, digest you and stick our claws into you," one demon said as he cleared away the she-devils. His appearance was fierce; his reptilian eyes squinted with intense anger. He was muscular, hairless, pale white and had four arms. He started to pummel Milo with all four fists. Milo somehow felt the blows. He was in torment, real torment. He fell down and cried for help. The demons pressed in closer, a squalling crowd, the sounds of their voices a whirlwind of slander and sarcastic mocking. All were phrases he had uttered in his life.

"Savlo!" he screamed.

Savlo secured Milo's soul and yanked him back. The demons pawed at him and tried to seize him. We travelled with great speed backward towards the portal opening. Savlo hurled Milo into the space of the hospital room where his body lay.

Milo sprawled to his body, trying to reunite with it.

— • —

Suddenly, the heart monitor sped up, as did all the graphs and lights. Natalie looked at all the monitors and then down at Milo. He turned a jaundiced yellow and the bones in his face protruded as if his skin was being pulled tight. Instant beads of sweat appeared on his brow. His legs and arms straightened too rigidly for a human body as broken as his was, and his fingers clawed at the air. He opened his eyes and looked at no one. His eyes were dark and sullied. He opened his mouth wide and looked like he was screaming. The veins in his neck were strained like a hundred different cords being pulled against their will. His body rose from the bed as if to sit up, but he only got half-way. He turned his head to Natalie and looked at her, still mouthing a silent scream.

Natalie took a step back and covered her mouth with both hands. Milo somehow vocalized the words, "I didn't know. Help me!" Then he was gone again, lifeless, all the monitors returned to their hypnotic pulsing and blinking.

"Oh my God!" was all Natalie could say. She grabbed the call button for the nurse and kept pushing it as she stared at Milo. She then looked up at Father John, who was staring at her, unnerved.

"So he's dead, Father? Did you see that? What the hell was that, Father?" she said hysterically, still mashing the call button, holding it up in front of her.

"My child, go, learn what he did not know. Learn about the toll houses of the aerial demons. You have forty days," Father John said, as he headed towards the door. He bowed his head to us and said, "Greetings in the name of our Lord." Then he left.

Two nurses came rushing through the door.

"What's wrong, sweetie?"

"I, I— he came alive, and sat up and spoke," Natalie blurted.

"Oh, sweetheart, you're tired, very tired. You've been here all day," one nurse said.

"No, you're wrong. He sat up and said 'I didn't know.' He was in so much pain and so scared. I've never seen anyone look this way." She started to cry, and sat back down in the recliner. "Ask the priest, he saw the whole thing."

"Natalie, there's no priest here," the other nurse said.

"Oh yes, he's got to be here still. He was old, big beard, black cassock with a hat and staff. You can't miss him. He's right out there, he's slow. He couldn't have gotten far."

"No honey, he isn't. No one is out there. I've been at the desk watching the monitors all evening, and no one has come in."

"But—" Natalie held her face in her hands. "Where's the doctor? I want to see the doctor, now. I've got to help my husband. He asked me to help him!"

"Okay, you just stay here. I'll get you some tea, and we'll get Dr. Dayaal. He's on call tonight," the nurse said.

Natalie sat back in the recliner and kept staring at Milo.

The doctor soon came into the room and extended his hand, just like the priest had done. She stood up and just looked at it.

"Mrs. Chris," the doctor said, "I understand you've been here a long time today and are very tired."

"Do not patronize me, Doctor. There was a priest who was here. He and I saw my husband sit up. Milo looked as though he was paralyzed with fear. He said he didn't know about something, and then flopped down on the bed again. I saw it. I'm not crazy or tired. I saw it, Doctor," Natalie said.

"Okay, Mrs. Chris, calm down. Take a seat and let's talk about this. Your husband is doing fine now," the doctor said as he sat down first in the extra chair.

"I am calm—of course he's *fine*, he's in a coma, on drugs and breathing machines, waiting for me to pull the plug and end his life but now asking me for help! He's doing real great," Natalie said.

"I mean no disrespect, Mrs. Chris."

"Natalie, please."

"Okay, Natalie, please tell me exactly what you saw."

She took a deep breath and exhaled. "Well, I was on the phone with Milo's mother, and an old Russian Orthodox priest, Father John, came into the room. My husband and I both grew up Orthodox, and many priests have come by this week. We talked a little and then Milo sat up in bed. His body was stiff. He looked like he was screaming, but no sound came out. He looked like a ghost or something. Then he looked at me, said, 'I didn't know. Help me.'

then flopped back down on the bed. The lights were going crazy on the machines. It was the scariest thing I've ever seen." She started to cry again. "Then the priest told me to go find out what my husband didn't know. But the nurses say no one has been here."

"Natalie, listen to me. I do not doubt that you saw a physical reaction. I do not think you are crazy. Can I explain what I think happened?"

"Yes, of course."

"Your husband has been in a severe accident and has been medicated heavily for the last couple of days. I know you have a very difficult decision ahead of you and are under much stress. Now it doesn't happen often, but it is possible your husband could have had a chemical reaction, perhaps an adrenaline rush if the IV's were pinched or there was a break in the medication. Where were you standing when this happened?"

"I was standing by the side of the bed," she said.

"Where all the IV lines are?" he asked.

"Yes."

"Well, it is possible that you were standing on the IV and created a break in the sedation."

She just looked at the doctor with no real expression.

"Natalie, are you a religious person?"

"Yes, I go to church every Sunday. Why, why are you asking me this?"

"Maybe you can admit that you are under some stress and are very tired, and somehow this biological reaction awakened these religious elements in your mind."

"I won't admit that. I saw a ghostly version of my husband, in pain and scared as hell and he talked to me."

"A djinn," the doctor mumbled.

"What?"

"Nothing—I apologize."

"Dammit, doctor, what'd you say?"

"When I was a child in India, my grandmother told us stories about the djinn that would torture the soul at the gravesite before they went on to the next life. They were like your demons in Christianity. Your story reminded me of that."

"Demons? Are you saying my husband is what, demon possessed?" she asked.

"No, no, no, I am not saying that at all, Mrs. Chris—Natalie—angels and demons are a very old superstitious belief system. In our day of medical advancement we know what happened here. It can all be explained medically. If you want, I can go and do some research and pull some articles about this biological reaction. There is ample proof of this type of seizure and scientific explanations for all of this. This we know by reason and it is sound," he said.

She stared at him for a while and said, "Thank you doctor." Then bowed her head; he left her.

She remained at the hospital in silent contemplation until ten thirty that night. She called Helen to let her know she would not pick up Sasha until the next day, and then went home, exhausted. Savlo told me I should remain with Kallistos, for Milo would not leave the hospital.

ENTRY 10

"But blessed are your eyes for they see, and
your ears for they hear."

- Matthew 13:16

Natalie tossed and turned that night after Milo's awakening. She lay on his side of the bed where she could smell him, clutching his pillow. The words of the old priest perplexed her, and she pondered them in her heart. It was 2:23 when she finally threw the covers back and walked downstairs into Milo's office. She turned the computer on. Google was the homepage. She hesitated, resting her fingers on the keyboard and looking at her wedding ring as the cursor blinked.

toll houses

She hit the enter key.

9,120,000 results. The first web site was;

Aerial _Toll-Houses_ - OrthodoxWiki

Posted Jul 10, 2007 ... The teaching of Aerial _Toll-Houses_ regards the soul's journey after its departure from the body, and is related to the particular judgment.

Patristic evidence - Liturgical Evidence - The Number of the Toll Houses _orthodoxwiki.org / Aerial_ **_Toll_**-**Houses** - Cached - Similar

She read for hours.

She typed in aerial toll house on YouTube.

76 videos were listed.

She watched several hours of videos theologically critiquing the hidden teaching until 6:01 a.m. when the alarm clock buzzed upstairs. She was emotionally and physically exhausted. She walked upstairs, turned on the shower, turned around and looked at herself in the mirror. She wore one of Milo's t-shirts under an untied white cloth robe. His shirts were big enough to cover her hard, round womb. Her navel had popped out, which caused her to smile slightly as steam billowed over the shower curtain. She had no more tears to shed.

"Angels, demons, toll houses and Orthodoxy, hey?" she said and dropped her head and leaned on the counter.

Kallistos and I just stood in the bathroom with her, looking at her in the mirror.

"Show yourself to her, Kallistos. She needs to see she's not alone," I said.

"The righteous shall walk by faith," he said.

I wanted to explain my suggestion; how I didn't do enough for my brother watchers, but he silenced me with his hand.

Natalie stepped into the shower. Kallistos turned to face me. His beauty was powerful and his wings shimmered many shades of white. "Milo is exactly where he needs to be—purifying himself.

Savlo is experienced with the aerial demons of the toll houses. Natalie believes we are near. She is coming to terms with a cosmic spiritual reality and you should remember your role. You are zealous, but zealots lack patience. Creatures who lack patience become distracted and miss the miracles of faith around them."

I was silent, for he was right.

While she was rinsing her hair, Natalie said aloud, "Lord, I need a sign. If there are angels out there to help me, please tell them to help me now. I don't know what to do. I don't know how to help Milo. Lord, please, hear me and help me."

She dried off, robed herself, walked into the closet and sighed as she looked at all of Milo's clothes. Something on Milo's tie rack caught her eye. It was the cross necklace Helen had given Milo for the infant's baptism.

Natalie walked over to it and picked it up. She kissed it and put it on, holding her hand over it tight against her heart. She was remembering something. She began singing Orthodox hymns, half remembered. Kallistos sang too and finished the words for her. It was amazing to witness such love between a guardian and an image bearer.

She finished her routine, made the bed, picked up clothes and soon would go downstairs to make something to eat. We drifted down through the floor and noticed a demon sitting with its back to us at the dinette table next to the kitchen. Its head was cocked slightly as it looked out the window at the empty bird feeder. The demon took the form of a young woman's body clothed in a dark ruby red cloak. It had small black slender wings and an owl's head, but when it turned we saw a human face.

"What are you planning, O beautiful one? And who is your friend? What's your name? Are you a special one? In training, perhaps?" It didn't look directly at us.

"He is of no concern to you, demon of doubt. I know who are you, and I can assure you her faith is stronger than your doubting questions," Kallistos said, positioning himself between the demon and the place where Natalie would fix her breakfast.

It turned its head almost all the way around.

"Are you sure her faith is strong? Is yours strong, after all these ages? What about your friend? I missed his name in my briefing, what was it again?"

"Let me ask you a question for a change. Why are you here?" Kallistos said.

"You think you can ask me questions? Or that I'll give you any answer at all? How would that benefit me? Are you willing to trade information for information, oh beautiful one?"

"No, I will give you nothing. We have nothing to fear, for she walks under His care and she hears His voice. Do you remember what that is like, to hear His voice, Onoskelis?

It spun around and hovered above the table. Its raven black wings extended and vibrated with anger. Its eyes were blackened and bleeding. "You dare torture me with memory?" It angrily said and glared at Kallistos. Its wings retracted, and then it lowered its gaze to me.

"You have a zealous heart, don't you?" It said and smiled. "Will you say anything at all?"

"This is not your soul to hinder. She has already decided to learn of the toll houses and the passage therein. You are too late, Ono," Kallistos said.

"Don't you know my work just begins when someone makes a decision?"

"I know you cause the faithful to doubt, but you will not cause this one to stumble."

"Are you challenging me? Oh my, why are you so good to me? Tell me, when was the last time she partook of the Holy Mysteries? Huh?" Onoskelis laughed and started to descend through the table into the floor.

"You know I would love to stay and chat, right? I never tire of you, you're my favorite, Kallistos, but you know that already, don't you? How many have we battled over? I will leave you little birds alone for now but I must say, she is just something else, isn't she?"

Natalie had made her way to the kitchen and the demon could see her now.

"Oh, is she carrying your Nephil, you dirty bird you? Do you remember those times? Are you starting another race of giants for the great Ego to destroy? What did you do when the other watcher angels slept with the women? Where were you? Did you want a daughter of man for yourself?"

I was silent as flashbacks of the giant Nephilim, those monstrosities sprouted from mixed seed, feasted on flesh, drank blood, raped the woman image bearers, and laughed as the births of their giant babies split the women open, killing them. They used all angelic knowledge to create new ways to maim, deform and destroy the male image bearers for sport. I watched and did nothing. I looked at the demon and she smiled for she knew I was remembering.

"I command you, be gone, Onoskelis," Kallistos said.

It disappeared.

"Who was that?" I asked.

"Onoskelis is one of the aerial demons of hive seven holding the nineteenth toll house, where they judge doubt, denials of faith, and heresy. She puts doubting questions concerning faith into the minds of the image bearers; she always speaks in questions, which annoys me. She has taken pleasure in battling me especially through the ages, though I do not know why. We all have special foes, who work hard on tempting those committed to our care."

As Natalie was rinsing some dishes left in the sink, Kallistos went over to the library in the family room and removed a book. It was an old red Orthodox service book with a folded bulletin inside it. He placed it on top of some of Sasha's toys that were strewn on the floor next to the basket where her books and puzzles were kept. He came back beside me.

"The righteous shall live by faith?" I questioned him.

"She asked for help, with pure intention."

"So finding this book on the floor is going to help her?"

"No doubt about it," he said and smiled ever so slightly.

Natalie fixed her usual breakfast, bagel and cream cheese, yogurt, and coffee with a flavored cream mixture. She carefully balanced them all as she walked past the dinette to the family room with the fireplace. She set everything down on the oversized chaise lounge where Milo had sat last Friday night. She was looking about the room, at the mess Sasha had left, puzzles and books and figurines lined up in patterns on the raised base of the fireplace. She smiled and then her eyes welled with tears.

She noticed the red service book lying amid the mess. She walked over to it, hand on her womb, and picked up the book. As she flipped through it, a bulletin fell to the floor. She picked it up, paged through it and smelled it. It was still imbued with incense. She went and sat down.

The bulletin was quite old. It was from her Babushka's church, St. Mary's. She recognized some of the names of families listed as being sick or that had died that month. She was paging through when something caught her eye. Kallistos smiled at me, and I went to look at what she was reading;

To remain in communion with the Holy Orthodox Church one must not be absent without good cause from a Divine Liturgy, have participated in the sacrament of confession monthly and observed the practice of fasting from meat and animal products during the major fasts throughout the year, including Wednesdays and Fridays.

"Yes, yes, I know Mom, our family just does not eat meat on Friday," she said obviously remembering her childhood.

She scooted to the edge of the chair and brought her bagel, yogurt and coffee back to the kitchen. She scraped off the cream cheese into the sink, put the yogurt back into the fridge and snapped off a banana from the fruit rack on the counter. She was about to pour out her coffee and then grabbed the flavored creamer mix from the fridge and read the label.

"Go figure, a creamer with no cream," she said out loud.

She returned to the chair and enjoyed her breakfast. As she held the bulletin and paged through the service book, she looked around the room as though she knew she wasn't alone.

She glanced back at the book, smiled and said, "Thank you Lord—okay, after I call Father Luke, I'm going to take a step of faith and go hear what the old priest downtown has to say."

She would continue to talk out loud, in complete faith that we could hear her.

— • —

St. Mary's Russian Orthodox Church was located on 8th Avenue in an impoverished, ill kept neighborhood of Grand Rapids. The temple was a converted home with white vinyl siding and a gold onion-style dome. Old stained glass windows lined the sides of the temple. The backyard held a prayer garden with an icon I recognized as the Sweet Kissing Theotokos and Child, at its center. Birds and bees were always trying to nest under the Virgin's care. Kallistos told me, Natalie's Babushka attends here from time to time, especially on Russian Christmas.

Inside was quite beautiful. The white and gold iconostasis stretched from floor to ceiling; red carpet, stained glass icons in the windows and oversized candle holders blazing with beeswax candles sufficed for the parish's needs. I learned it was a humble parish whose greatest quality was liturgical zeal. They held a service almost every day of the week. The priest was a celibate. He was not particularly striking in appearance, lanky in stature. His hair was a mess with a fair attempt to hold a blotchy beard. He held a warm and inviting expression, ready to listen. I liked him and thought he would be a good priest for my image bearer.

Natalie stood in the vestibule for a moment as the priest was tidying up. She took a deep breath. The incense lingered in the air like prayers.

"Smells like church, doesn't it?" The priest walked over to greet Natalie. He extended his hand for her to reverently kiss.

"Oh, yes, smells like church, that's a good way to put it." She awkwardly grabbed his hand with both her hands and shook it.

"May I bless your baby, then?"

"Um, of course."

He was wearing a pectoral cross hanging from a long gold-plated chain, a sign of honor among priests. He held the cross out over her womb and spoke a blessing in Slavonic for the child. I started to shine and a flame burned in me. I looked at Kallistos, who just smiled at me.

"Thank you, Father."

"Thank God. I'm Father Job and I'm new here. We haven't met yet. Do you go here?"

"Oh, I was expecting the older priest, Father John. But yes, well, I used to go here with my parents but—my Babushka goes here—but I, I haven't been in fifteen years."

"Did you move away?"

"No, not physically, but I guess you could say I did move away, in a way, if that makes sense."

He smiled. "Well, you're here now. What's your name?"

"Sorry, Father. Natalie Chris."

"Natalie, welcome back. What brings you here today?"

"Can we sit down? This may take a while."

"Of course, yes, beg your pardon. We could sit here." He pointed to a side pew. "Or in the fellowship hall. We have a kitchen and tables. Can I also offer you some tea?"

"That would be nice, Father."

They convened in the fellowship hall.

"Do you take cream in your tea?"

"Cream, Father? It's Wednesday," Natalie said.

"Of course, you're right." Father Job was holding non-dairy powdered creamer but did not want to embarrass Natalie or presume anything about her. From this I discerned he had a humble soul. He sat down opposite her.

"So what brings you here today?"

She started to bite her lip in hesitation.

"It's okay. I have large ears and a small mouth. Who am I going to tell, sworn to secrecy, you know?"

She laughed. He did have large ears.

"Well, several days ago my husband was in a terrible accident. He's on life support right now at the hospital."

Father Job looked very sympathetic. He crossed himself and his eyes softened. It was sincere, and Natalie recognized this and decided to tell him the rest of the story. He listened with silent, undivided attention until she told him about the visit from Father John.

"Wait. Are you telling me you saw a Father John in your hospital room? Big hat, all in black, with a staff?"

"Yes, exactly. He said he was a Russian Orthodox priest and I assumed he was the priest here."

Father Job laughed in amazement, beside himself. He pulled out his phone and conjured a picture of John Maximovitch, Bishop of San Francisco.

"Is this the priest you saw?"

"Yes, that's him. He even knew I was baptized here."

Father Job laughed again.

"What's so funny?" Natalie asked with a tone of offense.

"Forgive me, Natalie, I'm not making light of your situation. It's just that Father John Maximovitch is known to do such things, but he goes by another name now. Saint John Maximovitch. He died in 1966 and was canonized as a saint. His body is actually in San Francisco right now, in a shrine uncorrupt."

"Uncorrupt? What do you mean?"

"When some saints die, they are so holy they emit a flowery fragrance and are very slow to decay."

"Wait. So he is a saint and his body is in San Francisco right now; so he's dead?"

"Yes, very much dead. You could go there and see his relics, his body, right now. Look it up online. It's real."

"So I saw a spirit? A ghost?"

"No, you saw a saint, my dear—a real miracle."

Natalie sipped her tea and held a glazed look at the floor.

"I don't understand, Father. Why would a saint come to see me?"

"I don't know. What'd he say?"

"Well, after Milo woke up and yelled 'I didn't know. Help me.', this Saint John, I guess, told me to go and find out what Milo did not know, and something about the toll houses. I called Father Luke from Holy Resurrection, because that's where Milo's family goes, and he wanted to talk more in person about it. I will visit him but he did not object to me coming to talk to you, something about the Russians being more versed in the discussion or something like that."

Father Job leaned back in the tan metal folding chair, took his hands and ran them through his thick hair. He took off his glasses and set them down on the table.

"I think I am involved in something supernatural," she said.

"Oh yes, dear, you are—very much so."

"So what do I do?"

Father Job looked at Natalie for several moments, making her feel uncomfortable.

"Natalie, beloved of God," he leaned forward with arms on his knees, "I have three pieces of advice for you. First, read up on the toll houses. Be aware there is some controversy regarding this teaching because of the imagery and it delves into the mystery of the afterlife— always a controversial topic for people."

"I did. I've been up since two-thirty in the morning reading about them online," she said.

"Okay, the second piece of advice is for you to reconcile your-self to the Holy Orthodox Church, either here or Holy Resurrec-tion, as long as it's a canonical Orthodox parish."

"Is that necessary? We go to Dogwood Bible Church; Pastor Dan is a good man."

"I'm sure he is but my advice remains unchanged. You are wel-come to go and share what has happened with the pastor over there, but this mystery is not part of their tradition."

"But they are very biblically centered."

"I don't doubt that. Protestant clergy certainly do know the Bible, but it's only in the Orthodox tradition you will find a biblical interpretation that spans church history; but more importantly you need protection."

"Father, I don't have time to debate which church reads the Bible correctly. My husband is in some kind of hell or toll house place and needs my help."

"I know your needs are urgent, Natalie, that's precisely why my advice still stands. Come back to the Orthodox Church. You have left it but it has not left you. You're involved in something supernatural, as you say, and reconciliation with us is the best way for you to figure out what an actual saint has instructed you to do."

"And your third piece of advice?" she asked as her tone grew cold towards the priest. Kallistos leaned in and prompted her to be more open and humble.

"You need to go and speak with Father Lazarus."

"Why?'

"Oh, Father Lazarus has a specialized understanding that I don't have. Let's just say he has had firsthand experiences with the afterlife and the dead."

"Okay, so where's his church?"

"Well, that is the peculiar thing about Father Lazarus. He lives at the Grand Rapids Rehabilitation Center."

"Isn't that where addicts and alcoholics live?" she asked with a most skeptical look on her face.

"Yes, it is. Natalie, we are all wounded healers, even priests need spiritual medicine, but that doesn't render us of no use to God."

— • —

Natalie left Father Job at the church. She could still smell the incense on her clothes. The baby had been active during their talk, but now was calm. She drove, crisscrossing through the streets which were laden with trash, furnished front porches, sprinklers watering patches of weeds and small children scurrying everywhere. A little boy, wearing only ripped shorts, ran out into the street. She abruptly stopped. He had dirty knees and was holding an orange popsicle dripping down his arm. Their eyes met. He smiled at her and waved. She opened the window and yelled, "What's your name, little boy?"

He looked at her with eyes wide open, bursting with joy. "Emmanuel!" he shouted.

"Don't you know you're not supposed to play in the streets, lil' boy?" she asked. "No ma'am, I didn't know," he said and ran off. She paused for a moment and held a pleasant expression. Something had changed in the way she understood the world. She now could see the Kingdom of God at work.

She drove on, past the street to the hospital where Milo lay. Kallistos was in high alert, watching oncoming traffic and the demons of oppression nestled in the poor city neighborhoods hissing as we passed. She drove down Eastern Avenue, and then I realized we were going to see Father Lazarus right away.

"Kallistos, what do you know of this Father Lazarus?"

"He lost his parish many years ago due to a demon of drunkenness, a true nemesis for him. He spent his times of sobriety, which were few, walking in local cemeteries weeping over his sins and praying for the dead. One day the regional bishop was contemplating how to discipline him, for the complaints and rumors had reached a height of sensationalism. A dead man named Augustus Woodward, barged into the bishop's office demanding that Father Lazarus not be transferred, for he was doing good works in Grand Rapids. The bishop asked the apparition what good works the priest had done, because his desk was full of letters alleging the opposite. Augustus slapped his fist down on the bishop's desk, leaned over to meet the bishop eye-to-eye and said, 'Saving us wayward souls.' He then disappeared. The bishop was troubled from this meeting and prayed many days. Finally the bishop removed Father Lazarus from his parish and made him the unofficial chaplain of the rehab-center and the Kent County Jail. Now, Father Lazarus's life consists of praying for the dead, drinking and repenting. He attends Divine Liturgy once a year, on the feast of the Holy Resurrection."

I refrained from asking any more questions and watched with great interest.

Natalie pulled into the parking lot. She walked into the stale smelling room with white walls, stained fabric chairs, fake plants, and a patterned tile floor. She stopped at the reception counter which was separated by a glass wall with a voice intercom system.

"Can I help you?" a short round woman of Ethiopian descent pleasantly asked through the intercom.

"Yes, I am looking for a Father Lazarus."

"Why?"

"Why? Well, I want to talk to him, that's why."

"Who are you, and is your visit personal or business in nature?"

"I am Natalie Chris and this is a personal visit."

"One moment, please," she said and picked up the phone. After a moment, the woman shook her head and said, "He says he doesn't know you."

Natalie dropped her gaze and held her womb. "Um, wait. Tell him Father Job from the Russian church sent me."

The receptionist passed on the message, waited a moment, and said, "He said he still doesn't know you and you should go back to Father Job."

She was about to hang up the phone when Natalie yelped, "Wait. Tell him I have a problem with a toll house."

The nurse put the phone back to her ear and told him just that. Then she nodded. "He said he will see you, but not here. He said go to the cemetery down Eastern Avenue, and find the pyramid tomb. There should be some benches close by in a clearing. Wait for him there."

Natalie hastily drove to Oakhill Cemetery. The cemetery was a walled off city block with old oak trees and wispy grass that was hardly cared for. Hundreds of worn slabs and some large tombs bore symbols of the fallen watchers, protractors, triangles, as well as angelic letter characters. Small blue cloaked statues of the Blessed Virgin Mary stood all across the burial grounds. The clearing near the pyramid shaped tomb was where the poor families, long forgotten, had buried their dead. This was now the parish of Father Lazarus.

Natalie drove the winding roads with caution, pausing at a site of a fresh interment, with no grass or flowers to beautify it. Finally, she saw the pyramid and parked her car. She got out, sat on one of the benches, and looked around. The warm spring breeze quieted the busy traffic noise outside the walls. But she was not really alone, for we could see the spirits of the dead rise up as Father Lazarus walked past the gravesites to the pyramid.

He was a long ways off. His walk was more like a stagger, as though he was forcing his legs to take him to his destination. He wore an old black cassock, frayed and mud-stained at the hem. He wore no collar, but his unkempt black and gray beard and long curly hair savagely thinned in the center gave him the appearance of a disheveled monk or a fool for Christ. He had kind eyes, a scar on his forehead, and a moist, jowled mouth. He approached Natalie with hesitance, leaning from side to side, looking at her womb and then her face. He licked his lips, and then stroked his beard.

"You're pregnant. Mrs. Natalie Chris. Is that short for Christopoulos?"

"Yes, Father, my pah-pa was a Russkie, named Myshkin. My mother was a Greek, Stephanopoulos, and I married into a Greek family—but I go by Natalie Chris."

"All are good surnames. Choose one and go by it, don't Americanize it. Names are too important."

Natalie straightened her back and adjusted the lapels on her jacket. "Won't you please sit down, Father?"

He twitched his mouth and looked to the side. "Not now, please," he snapped.

"I'm sorry?" Natalie looked to see who he was talking to.

"Nothing—yes, I will join you, and I would like to hear more about your problem with a toll house."

"So you know about them?" she said as she studied him, squinting. She lightly turned her face into the wind and caught a waft of him. He may have smelled bad, but I could discern he had not been drinking.

"Yes, I know about them, as much as anyone can know about them this side of the grave."

He locked eyes with her now and did not break focus.

She stopped squinting and said, "Well, I think I may be involved in something supernatural."

"How do you know if something is supernatural or if something is just natural?"

Her expression revealed puzzlement. "I don't know, I guess."

"You don't know, so you guess? I am confused, Mrs. Christopoulos. Which is it?"

"So am I." She laughed nervously.

He quickly smiled then asked, "Where's your husband?"

"That is what I don't know. He was in a terrible accident several days ago. His body is at the hospital and he's on life support. The doctors told me he is clinically dead, but the other night he woke up and screamed 'I didn't know. Help me.' then fell back as though he was dead. He looked like he was in great pain. Then Father John, who I guess is a saint, visited me, and he told me—"

"Stop." His look grew intense. He leaned forward with one elbow on his knee and held his tightened jaw. "Saint John Maximovitch visited you?"

"Yes, the saint of San Francisco. He told me to find out what Milo, my husband, didn't know. He said it had to do with toll houses. I researched toll houses on the internet, and now I have even more questions and no answers. This saint has led me to you. So you tell me where my husband is."

He continued to stoke his beard and stare at her. His eyes were not threatening, but showed concern.

"I am sorry for your loss, Mrs. Christopoulos. I may have some knowledge which may help you and your husband, or it could scandalize your faith and leave him, well, leave him where he is. I do not know what to say to you exactly at this time. Some things are best left to the angels."

"With all due respect—"

"I do not deserve or desire respect from you, young lady. I should not counsel another priest's parishioner. I'm sure Father Job's a good priest. Go to him and pray for your husband."

"I'm not Father Job's parishioner. I was raised Orthodox, but my husband and I left that church after we met in college."

"You're not in communion with the Orthodox Church, and yet you claim to have seen a saint? Are you Catholic?" he asked, even more perplexed.

"No, we go to Dogwood Bible Church and we really care for the people there."

"I'm sure they care for you too, but God placed you in a tradition. You have been sacramentally sealed to Holy Orthodoxy, baptized and I assume married in the Greek Orthodox Church, right?"

She nodded.

He stood up and looked out over the cemetery, his shoulders tensed up as if carrying a heavy burden.

There was a long pause as the breeze picked up again and seemed to soften the tension between them. Natalie's eyes started to well up with tears.

"I just want to help my husband. You don't know...you didn't see him."

"Young handmaiden, listen to me. If you want to help your husband, then do what he can't do for himself. It's not safe for you to continue down this path without the sacraments. Reconcile, be in communion with the One, Holy, Catholic, and Apostolic Church. After that, I'll tell you more."

"That's coercion."

He smiled at her. "Not coercion, no, not coercion at all. More like a protective requirement necessary if you're going to wage battle for a soul that goes from the natural world to the supernatural, as you say."

"Protection? Battle? From what?"

"You need protection from the aerial demons who want to tear you apart, girl. There is a battle for your husband's soul going on right now. You must fight so he is not stranded like the hundreds standing around us right now."

She looked around but saw no one.

"Father Lazarus, I'm a pregnant woman with a dying husband. I need to have a moment of clarity and honesty with you."

She stood up and stepped toward him until they were face to face. He stepped back as if intimidated. "Are you crazy?"

He gave a deep belly laugh and said, "We both see the dead. You saw St. John Maximovitch, and I the dwellers of this place. So I'm as crazy as you are."

She smirked. "True. So will you help me?"

"Possibly, if you speak to Father Job and reconcile this issue of who you are in communion with. You're grossly underestimating this matter, by the way, and—"

"Why Father Job? Why not you?"

"Shush, my dear, I'm not worthy of such activities. I'll teach you to fight, but you, like your husband, do not know what you are in for. If you're not in good standing with the Church then it's best to leave it to angels, my dear. That's all I have to say for now."

He walked away, chastising unseen souls surrounding him. She saw it as ranting into the air. She watched him descend the rolling hill of the pathway until he was out of sight. She then left for the hospital as the breeze played with her hair and her soul found new hope.

— • —

At the hospital Natalie was greeted with smiles of sympathy and whispers as she passed the nurses' station. The normal errands of the staff and their portable machines filled the hallway, along with the smell of sterilization as another room in the ICU was vacated.

Kallistos and I watched her as she walked into Milo's room. He lay there as he had the night before, mechanically gasping for air every few seconds. The sunlight shone on his face but did not give him light. She grabbed his one hand, placed it on her womb, and waited until the baby kicked. She then leaned down, kissed his cheek and stroked a tuft of his hair as the nurse came by to check some vitals.

Milo's soul remained in the corner, unable to hear his wife's muffled words as his bodily senses faded and grew more accustomed to the spiritual dimension.

"How are you today, Mrs. Chris?" the nurse asked.

"I'm doing okay." She continued to hold Milo's hand. "By the way, please call me Natalie and tell the others too. The formality of all this makes me feel uncomfortable."

"My name is Sandy." The nurse rolled her lips in and nodded cordially. "I'll tell them Natalie." She recorded some data, checked the connections on an apparatus, then left.

Natalie whispered to Milo, "Well, sweetheart, I'm not sure what's going on with you. Remember how you always told me, I worry too much? Well, I am worried and—" She dropped her head, overcome with emotion. "I met with two Orthodox priests today. Can you believe that? They were both characters. They weren't at all like Pastor Dan. They tell me the best way to help you is to go back to the Orthodox Church." She wiped her eyes. "I'm going to trust this is the best way to help you. Your mother will be pleased. I suppose my Baba will be too." She smiled.

She sat down in the recliner next to him and said, "I read some pretty scary stuff online, and so I'm going to talk with Pastor Dan about it. I know you always liked him."

She leaned back in the recliner, laid her head back, and closed her eyes.

"You're a good man Milo, even with our recent problems. You've provided for our family. We've always had the very best of things. You were respected by everyone you knew."

She paused for a couple moments.

"It doesn't seem fair. I mean, what kind of God does this? God is love, right? So why are you not loveable by God? Is it loving to leave me and your children fatherless? You won't even get to meet your only son. God knows what it's like to have a son but you won't. I just don't know, honey. I just don't know any more what to believe."

"Young one, do you recognize this line of questioning?" Kallistos said as he looked at me.

"Yes, it reminds me of Onoskelis."

Kallistos positioned himself by Natalie's ear. His wings rose and fell in rhythm with her breathing and he whispered to her mind. She was very still and relaxed. It was an act of subtle intimacy. If there had been any distraction or other noise, she would have missed his delicate prompting. This went on for quite a while.

Finally, she opened her eyes. She sat up from the reclining chair and walked over to Milo, holding his hand again. She spoke confidently, "But one thing you must remember, my love, if you can hear me at all, I am strong enough to stand by you. You may have gotten lost, but I believe I have enough faith for both of us. I don't know how, but with God's help I'll see this through. We're married and through our son, I carry a little bit of you in me. That connects us way beyond death." She patted his hand and squeezed it. "I'm going to speak with Pastor Dan to see what he has to say, then I'll come back with Sasha later on. I love you, Milo." She kissed him on the forehead and gathered her things to leave.

"That looked quite easy," I said.

"Yes, it is when they are quiet. The war is waged in the heart, the very core of their souls. If they are still and quiet in their being, they can hear us and we can guide them. But if not, well, then it becomes very difficult."

A large black raven landed on the window ledge and cawed violently. Kallistos had won another battle with Onoskelis.

Natalie left to go meet with Pastor Daniel. Savlo retained me for some instruction; Milo observed our activities with great interest. I then joined Kallistos and Natalie at Dogwood Bible Church.

— • —

"Hmm, well, I don't know much about the Orthodox, but they are a lot like the Catholics and they have many traditions, just less organized. What it all boils down to is this one question; do you believe Milo was saved?" Pastor Daniel asked Natalie.

"Well, of course. He believed in God and he was raised in a very religious home. His mother and father are very good Christian people. He prayed, I think, maybe not so much recently but he did," she explained as if trying to defend him.

"Natalie, God doesn't have any grandchildren. Do you follow me on that?"

"Yes, I think so."

"Well, each one of us individually must make a decision to accept Jesus Christ as our personal savior. Your parents can't do it for you. A pastor or priest can't do it for you, even the Pope can't manage that. It's just between you and God. The Bible says, 'For there is one God, and one mediator between God and men, the man Christ Jesus.' There is no way around that. Do you think Milo ever did that?"

"I don't know anymore. I don't know what to believe. It sure looked like he was in hell when he awakened. He was in real torment, Pastor, the kind of pain I can't describe." She dropped her face into her hands. "Are you saying Milo is in hell?" She started to cry.

The preacher was quiet for a while, thinking with his hand on his Bible.

"Natalie, there's a lot about life after death we just don't know about. The Bible is silent about many things. When the Apostle Paul tells us in his letter to the Corinthians that 'to be absent from the body is to be present with the Lord,' that's about all we know. So if you believe Milo was saved, then you have to have faith God has him in His presence. Maybe the pain you saw was just a bodily spasm and looked like physical pain. You know, a medical anomaly is a reasonable possibility. He is relying on life support and on a lot of drugs, right?"

She continued to cry with her head in her hands. He sat across the desk from her, watching, tears welling up in his own eyes. She blew her nose and wiped her eyes.

"Pastor, I've talked with a couple of priests, and they both think something very different is going on here," she said.

"Young lady, you be careful when you talk to priests. I strongly disagree with the Orthodox and the Catholics, theologically and biblically. Truth be told, if you read your Bible on your own and walk in the Spirit, you'll get through this and be a lot better off than if you get mixed up with those priests. Nat, they believe you have to work for your salvation and a bunch of other non-biblical teachings, like purgatory."

"Pastor Dan, I'm not a theologian, and I don't know my Bible as well as you, but this is heaven and hell we're talking about, and my husband's soul is at stake." She wiped her eyes. "To be honest, I'm a little confused about what's going on— it's like something super-natural, and I feel like I need to know more than only what the Bible says. I'm sorry, Pastor, but I feel like talking with the priests, especially Father Lazarus, is the right thing to do. They seem to know how to help me. I feel I'm being led to him."

"Natalie, please, I care for you, and I cared for your husband very much. There is a lot we don't know, but the Bible is not the enemy, it tells us it is all sufficient for our faith and—"

"What did you say, Pastor?" Her demeanor changed.

"I said that the Bible is not the enemy and it is sufficient—"

"No, before that. You said you 'cared' for my husband—past tense."

He was silent.

"Pastor, the Bible may say it's sufficient, but what happens when every person tells me something different about the Bible? What happens when the Bible doesn't seem to have the answers? I need to know how best to show love for my husband right now. What's your advice for me, now? Because I'm getting ready to take Milo off life support and I could be sealing his fate forever. Dan, what can I do for him, today?"

"Natalie, all I can tell you is what I read in the Bible and how best I reason it out. Beyond that—" He broke eye contact with her.

She sniffed and wiped the tears from her face again. Then she smiled at him. "Please come to the hospital when it's time, and to the funeral. Milo's mother has made arrangements to have Father Luke do the funeral at Holy Resurrection."

"I can do that, Natalie," he said.

Natalie left Pastor Daniel to go pick up Sasha and visit Milo again. His guardian angel appeared and positioned himself close to him as he sat with his hands folded and head bowed in prayer.

Kallistos sent me to Savlo with a message and then bid me to come back. The message was cryptic: The whiskey priest will teach her the ways of Theodora.

ENTRY 11

How shall I understand what I read if no one guides me?

- The Ethiopian Eunuch of Acts

I stayed with Kallistos the whole night. Natalie and Sasha visited Milo, cried, held each other, went home and made cookies, then slept together. Milo did not leave the hospital room where his body was. He seemed sad and full of regret as he watched his wife and daughter and other family members come at different times throughout the day.

The next morning Natalie dropped Sasha off at Helen's again and went to St. Mary's temple at eight-thirty in the morning for a daily liturgy. It was a cold spring morning, the kind that might have called for a winter coat. She walked through the front doors of the temple and her face changed as if she had stepped into a different time and space. Orthodox temples have that effect on image bearers.

Father Job was vested in gold. One other image bearer stood at the chanter's stand off to the right. Her name was Catherine and she sang the Znamenny style chant in the clearest tone an image bearer's alto voice could. Her head was covered with a thick black shawl. A scrawny, ragged she-devil standing in the choir loft looked down on me and said, "She covers her head so you won't lust after her, watcher."

Kallistos floated up and cleansed the choir loft.

The litanies of 'Lord have mercy' raptured Natalie into a spiritual reverie. Kallistos was now bringing back all the memories of her youth, warming her heart with tender moments; how she took communion with her mother, how she watched her father weep after confession and the crowning of her and Milo at their wedding. These moments held cosmic consequences for all of us, especially Milo.

The service concluded with its usual seasonal blessing and the calling of many saints to intercede for them, names she had forgotten and which were only truly remembered by God and some of us.

She went up to venerate the hand-held cross and receive a more personal blessing.

"May the Holy Trinity bless and keep you this day," Father Job said.

"And blessings to you, Father. Do you have some time to chat?"

"Of course. Let me put some of this gear away," he said, smiling at her.

Natalie looked at all the icons of saints and feast days and remembered the prominent place the Blessed Mother held in their veneration. She held her own womb and let the incense absorb into her being.

"So, what brings you here today? Do you want to sit?" He motioned to a side pew in the nave.

"No, I'm fine. I met Father Lazarus and he gave me some advice."

"Advice is good. What'd he say?"

"Well, he looked a little ragged and he's quite a character."

"Yes he is, and may God bless him for it."

"Say, Father, do you know where I could get him a new cassock? His is in pretty bad shape."

"You know, we have a similar build. I just might have something. But, how did it go, otherwise?"

"Well, among other odd things, he insisted, for my protection, I should be reconciled to the Orthodox Church before he would discuss anything supernatural with me."

"Really?" Father Job said.

"Yep, and the saint I saw in the hospital, Father John…"

"St. John Maximovitch, yes, I remember."

"He knew I was baptized here, so I thought it fitting to go back to the beginning. But Father, everything seems so strange right now," Natalie said as she looked over at Catherine, who was quietly reading some post communion prayers.

"How so?"

"I mean, am I crazy? I see my husband wake up from a coma. I see a saint, and now I'm taking advice from an alcoholic, homeless priest who talks to dead people. I don't know, Father. Pastor Dan says to stick close to the Bible and not discuss this situation with priests. Crazy people never think they're crazy, so who's to say I'm not going crazy with all the grief?"

Six white-skinned, red-robed demons with solid black eyes appeared in each of the stained glass windows, looking in with great concern. Kallistos ordered me to keep guard and stand by the demons to the south, while he stood against the others.

Father Job again, offered her a seat on the side pew right under the three demons I was watching.

"Natalie, have you ever considered that God is trying to get your attention?"

"What do you mean?" She offered him the seat next to her.

"It seems to me that God, for whatever reason, has given you a great gift. A special type of vision or awareness, and He is bidding you to believe beyond what you have believed before."

"Hmm." She stared off into the distance.

"I can tell you this. You're not hallucinating. There are stories upon stories of similar visions where God lets people see into the life beyond."

"Really?"

"Yes. Isaiah was before the very throne of God, Saint Paul was caught up in the third heaven as was another man he knew, Saint Peter saw a vision of clean and unclean animals and Saint John the Evangelist wrote the last book of the Bible, which is a vision of heaven so far beyond our understanding very few church fathers felt worthy to interpret it. Just off the top of my head, there's four saints describing their visions in the Bible, so you can see we are biblically based, too." He winked at her and handed her some papers.

"What's this?"

"It's an account about the toll houses by Blessed Theodora. I thought you might find it interesting."

"Thanks, Father," she smiled and put it in her bag. "Father, I don't have good logical reasons for what I'm about to ask you. Deep inside I know it's right and true." She paused for a moment. "How do I reconcile with the Orthodox Church?"

"Natalie, understand that you're not just switching teams. We don't view it like that. You are actually connecting to God by putting yourself in communion with the mystical Body of Christ, here on earth, the Holy Orthodox Church. This is a big deal, are you sure this is what you want to do?"

She nodded with full consent.

"Well, you were baptized here. I checked the records—not that I doubted Saint John." He smiled at her. "So you simply join in the proclamation of the Nicene Creed, go to confession, and start partaking of the Holy Eucharist on a regular basis."

"What prevents me from doing so now?"

"Nothing."

"Will you hear my confession, Father?"

He paused for a moment, smiled and said, "Of course."

He went back behind the iconostasis, through a door adorned with the Archangel Michael into the sacristy, and put on the appropriate vestments. Then he came out the other door bearing, the Archangel Gabriel's icon and asked her to step up close to the holy doors of the altar and bow her head in front of the icon of Christ. He opened a prayer book and instructed her to read the fitting sacred prayer as the first step on her sacramental journey.

The demons in the windows bared their jagged yellow teeth and seethed with anger. The power shut down in the temple.

Father Job and Natalie looked around. "Catherine," he said as she was still reading the post communion prayers, "Will you please go check the circuit breaker box?" He turned his attention back to Natalie. "Good thing we have candles. Now, my child, have you any sins to confess?"

I positioned myself nearer to them when Kallistos halted me and bid me to switch places with him. I watched Kallistos emanate a great light that filled the nave, and I could hear rejoicing from unseen angels nearby. The demons covered their black eyes, for it was too great a light to bear. I was energized as the physical means of grace were executed with all holiness.

Father Job drew close, heard Natalie's confession, and began to cry, himself. He put his vestment over her head and pronounced God's absolution. Her face glowed looking relieved as if a heavy burden had been lifted.

"Natalie, come to Divine Liturgy and commune with the One Holy Catholic and Apostolic Church."

"Any church?"

"Any Orthodox Church in the world. I also would like to say that if you want me to come pray over Milo, I will."

"Father Luke is already helping us, at my mother-in-law's request, but please come to the hospital, I have to, um—" she paused to wipe her own tears from the confession, then continued, "The hospital and insurance company have suggested a decision timeline for me."

"Absolutely—I'll be there. Father Luke is a good priest. I'm sure everything is as it should be."

— • —

Natalie left and went immediately to find Father Lazarus. As we drove across town, hovering over her care, I asked Kallistos, "Why was I not allowed to hear the confession?"

"The sacrament of confession should be witnessed only by the priest and the angel committed to their care," Kallistos said. "All you need to know is she confessed the sins of Eve and will now do the work of Mary."

"Who were the red-cloaked demons? Did they hear?"

He did not answer, but held up his finger indicating one question, "hell is full of many courts, and now we know they are paying great attention to us."

We arrived at the rehab-center and Natalie walked into the reception room. She engaged the receptionist to summon Father Lazarus again.

"I'm sorry, ma'am, he says he's in no mood to talk with anyone today."

"Can you open the door and hand me that phone?" Natalie said.

The look of determination in Natalie's eye convinced the receptionist to allow this obvious breech in protocol.

"In my opinion, he needs a swift kick in the ass every now and then," the woman said as she opened the door and handed Natalie the phone.

"Hello, Father Lazarus, this is Mrs. Christopoulos."

"Mrs. Christopoulos, what do you want?" We could hear his loud voice.

"Well first of all, Father, how are you?"

"My state of being is inconsequential."

"I respectfully disagree. Father, your state of being is paramount."

"I told you to get reconciled, and then we would talk."

"I have been reconciled this morning, and now I need a priest. There is no rest for the wicked, so get up and let's talk."

His gruff laugh was so loud Natalie pulled the phone away from her ear.

"Ut—um, yes, yes, there is something nice about being insulted by a Russian woman. So what do you want of me, again?"

"I want you to tell me about the toll houses and what I should do."

"Pray for your husband, live a good life, and follow the piety of the Orthodox Church. That is the best thing you can do."

"Father?"

There was a long silence. "What?"

"Every now and then crazy people need someone to share their craziness with. Can't we have some tea—no, on second thought,

I'll buy you whatever you want but we need to talk and I need your help."

He laughed again. "That's either temptation or coercion."

There was a long pause. Natalie smiled at the receptionist who had been silently cheering her on until she heard what sounded like an offer to buy him alcohol.

"Very well, Mrs. Christopoulos. After lunch meet me at the pyramid again in the cemetery."

"Fine, I'll be there."

"Oh, and Mrs. Christopoulos."

"Yes?"

"If you happen upon some Russian Imperial Standard, I would be much obliged."

She laughed. "We'll see, Father."

While she drove around searching for the requested brand of vodka, Kallistos sent me to check in with Savlo.

— • —

When I arrived, Milo's soul had positioned itself on the floor next to his body. Savlo stood against the opposite wall in a meditative state. Milo looked at me, then dropped his head, despondent and in misery. I was briefing Savlo when Milo interrupted us.

"Thank you. Thank you both for saving me from them."

"You're welcome, but we must go back," Savlo said.

"I'm not going back. I am guilty. There is no way around it. I'll burn in hell forever."

"Guilty of what?" Savlo asked.

"Guilty of my sins—you should know. You've witnessed my whole life, the good and the bad. You know I'm guilty. I'm ashamed to even be in your presence. I will burn in hell, I just know it. I feel hot even now, even though I don't have a body and can't figure out how I feel anything," Milo said.

"Even though your mind perceives a hell, despair not. You're still acclimating to the unnatural state of life without a body. You're now outside of time and space as you understand it. All that is left is the record of your life; both they and I have records of your deeds. It will soon be time for the fire of the All Holy One to test your deeds. That is what you are feeling."

"I feel nothing but regret and remorse. I was so blind. Is there nothing I can do? I'll repent now. I'm a sinner. I accepted Christ into my heart again and again. Didn't He pay for my sins?" Milo said with desperation.

"Of course he would repent now. They all repent after they die," a voice coarsely whispered through the darkened portal. "Savlo, it's time to close this deal. Let us take him to our toll house and you can move on to your next soul assignment."

Milo looked scared and moved away from the portal, closer to Savlo.

"Milo, come on, it was just a joke, but you know, eventually you'll have to renegotiate those double standards," the voice said with a whisper, then laughed.

"He still has time," Savlo said.

"Maybe they're right. You said it yourself. I can't stay here," Milo said.

"Be patient, Milo," I let it slip out. Savlo looked sternly at me.

Suddenly a pack of three, muscular bodied looking demons, gray skinned with glowing red eyes, and black wings, advanced through the portal and swirled just above our heads. One of them swooped from their cyclonic circle. "So it does speak. Why are you here, watcher, who sent you? Rafe? Perhaps Mike? Or are you here on another quest altogether, maybe to free your kind? Do tell, we are all crazy to know." He leaned into my face. It was putrid to see him so close.

Savlo grew to double his size and hovered, spreading his wing and gathering Milo and I underneath him. The demons mocked, swirled and hurled insults at us, vicious slanders and lies of Milo's sins, Savlo's past failures and my role in the perverting creation with the Nephilim.

Savlo instructed me to leave, for my presence was stirring too much negative energy and unsettling Milo even more.

— • —

When I rejoined Kallistos, Natalie sat on the same bench in the cemetery. She seemed to be enjoying the breeze, as the morning warmed up and crocuses opened their petals to the heavens. She looked over the wilted bouquets, shiny plastic arrangements and empty metal holders across the studded landscape of green grass and gray lime stones.

She got up and started to walk the lines, standing in front of each stone, offering a simple prayer for the named dead. Kallistos stationed me on top of the pyramid to watch for Father Lazarus while he walked in the lingering cool of the morning with her. She stood longer in front of the simpler marker stones and the graves worn down and weathered, crossing herself. She walked past a statue of Mary, arms raised, forever interceding for those under her shadow.

On her way back to the benches, Natalie stopped and looked at a grave where a husband and wife were named. It was ornately engraved. It listed their names and their birthdates but only his death date. The inscription read, 'Even in death let us not part.'

She walked over to the benches and waited for Father Lazarus. Kallistos stopped prompting her and located below me.

It was twelve fifteen when the old priest managed to make his way to the cemetery. Natalie pulled out a small bottle wrapped in a brown paper bag and he smiled.

"I have questions for you. You must answer to my satisfaction before I tell you more. I will not give pearls to swine. Deal?" Father Lazarus asked.

"Father, are you calling a pregnant woman a pig?" She smiled, acknowledging her affection for his gruff nature.

He smiled back, blushed, then looked around with an old man's grimace.

"Are there many of them around?" she asked.

"Yes," he said, lowering his head.

"What do they want?" she asked.

"I'm the one asking the questions here. They call me a whiskey priest. What do you say to this?"

"Who am I to judge what kind of priest you are?"

"Hmm." He sat down across from her. "Next question—you have seen something frightful in your husband. Are you not afraid?"

"No. I mean it was scary, but now it's like I'm standing at a balcony watching the world busily go by. I'm probably in shock, but that can't be. I feel many things, sadness, I cry all through the day; but I also have a certain amount of distance from it. It's strange, but no, I don't feel fear," she said.

"Detachment—it's called detachment. You still feel and have emotions but you are not governed to them."

"Yes, exactly. Do you have this, too?"

"No. Only the pure in heart have this. Next question—why did you leave the Orthodox Church?"

"I just followed my husband's lead. I missed it all, but it didn't seem wrong to be with people who were excited about their relationship with Jesus, studied the Bible and enjoyed life."

"That's what's best about the Protestants. What do they tell you to do?"

"Well, Pastor Dan sticks pretty close to the Bible and its advice."

"He keeps close to the red letters, doesn't he?" he asked.

She laughed.

"Yes, he says the red letters are the best parts, as well as some passages that should be underlined in every good Christian's Bible."

"Well, Natalie Christopoulos, you're about to learn about the parts of the Bible that are never underlined, and you may not have their support once they hear you've talked to the insane whiskey priest."

She dropped her head. "I think you may be right, but I hope you're wrong."

"Next question—have you seen any angels or demons?"

"What?"

"You told me you've seen a saint and your husband is in torment—have you seen any other creatures?"

"No, I haven't seen anyone else. Should I?" she asked.

"Not necessarily."

"I will tell you this, Father. When I am most quiet, I feel like I'm in the presence of a heavenly energy."

"Energy?" he laughed out loud and slapped his knee.

"Well, I don't know what to call it. It's not words in my head and not really feelings or emotions, just a part of me warmed, like energy."

He straightened up his back, cocked his head, and looked wildly at her.

"Does this energy prompt you to action?"

"Yeah, you could say that."

He laughed out loud again, stood up, and turned his back to her. "I'll be with you in due time, good sir!" he yelled to the open air.

He spun back around. "Listen to me very carefully, young lady. You keep your inner heart quiet, listen to that energy, and doubt it not. That is the best advice anyone can give you."

He sat down, looked at the bagged bottle, then back to Natalie.

"Father, are the aerial toll houses real, the ones I read about online?" she asked.

He twitched his lips back and forth. "Yes and no. Yes, a real attack, a taxing of sorts, by the demons of the air but—no, not a physical toll house. It's a terrible truth that is difficult to describe this side of the grave. It's not a teaching most can live with. Saint Matthew tells us, 'the kingdom of God is taken by violence,' and that, my dear, is a dreadful mystery that is not underlined in the Bible. Most refuse to believe in spiritual warfare beyond death."

"What about love, Father? God is love, right? So how can there be terrible places like hell or toll houses?"

"Don't ask so many questions," he said.

I smiled, empathizing with her inquisitiveness.

He stood up again. "The universe is full of terrible and irreconcilable mysteries that can only be dealt with by the strong in faith, energized by great devotion to God, who is love."

"So if I have enough faith and devotion, can I help Milo out of the toll houses or whatever he is in?"

"You need love, my dear, and I don't know for sure if you can help him."

"Well, do you help the dead you see in whatever hell they're in?" she said as he became distracted by other things around them.

"I believe they are helped, but only through great battles."

"How?"

"Love wins because love fights. But it's not how you think, not like Hollywood movies. Sacrifice. Read the Gospels with a prayerful heart."

"I don't understand, Father."

The bottle wobbled a bit as a breeze picked up. We could see the Father's demon of the noon day fingering the bottle to draw his attention away from Natalie. I wanted to act on the demon but Father Lazarus's guardian appeared for the first time, placed his hand on the priest's shoulder, whispered in his ear, and then disappeared from us.

"I'll tell you this. The weapons for your fight are not what you think. If you try to help him, the demons will fight you. You will not be alone and you must remember who you are, Natalie Myshkin Christopoulos; baptized, sealed with the Holy Spirit, and in Eucharistic fellowship with the Holy Orthodox Church. Yes, remember who you are and listen to your heavenly energy, and it all will work out for you. I must go now."

He stepped toward her and reached for the bagged bottle.

"Father?" She stood up and put her hand over the bottle. "Will you come to the hospital? If Milo is there, can you talk with him? I beg you, from the bottom of my soul, please, Father."

He looked into her eyes and his face softened.

"Don't beg. I like you better when you are insulting me."

She smiled at him and their kindred spirits ignited.

"Yes, but leave me alone after this." He winked at her.

"Good. Be at the hospital before six o'clock tomorrow."

He picked up the bagged bottle but did not look inside. He paused for a moment, then set it back down on the bench next to her and left it. He walked away reciting in the air, "Have mercy on me O God, according to thy tender mercies…Yes, yes, I know the person you are talking about…"

Natalie sat back down for a few moments and watched the tormented old priest make his way out of the cemetery, blessing the dead with the sign of the cross and flailing his arms at others unseen.

— • —

The rest of the day was busy for Natalie. She met with lawyers and insurance representatives about the end of life instructions for Milo, made funeral plot arrangements, and visited Milo until well after the Vespers service was prayed on Mount Athos. Then she went to pick up Sasha.

Distracted with thoughts, she pulled into the driveway of Milo's childhood home. I looked out into the darkness and noticed a glowing red eye peering from behind the maple tree in the back corner of the yard. I alerted Kallistos. Natalie walked in the house, announcing her presence.

I ventured around the side of the house's attached garage. Kallistos went around the other way to complete the ambush.

"Ah, there you are demon. Are you alone?" Kallistos asked.

"Pft, we never run alone, mighty Kallistos, as I see you don't either," it said as we had cornered it.

The small blackened figure stepped out from behind the maple tree. As I approached it, the hair on its back arched to razor sharpness. Its eyes glowed red with hate and its rat face frothed and grinned as if it were keeping a secret from me.

"What do you want with me, watcher?" It hissed.

"Why are you here? You know this house is holy ground, blessed every year by the priest," Kallistos said, seizing its attention.

"For the child, of course." It laughed. "We want that little monkey. Milo left her with no guardian."

Just then four smaller rat-faced demons scurried from out of the house in pain from the sacramental hedge of protection in the house and huddled together. They whispered to each other and started to wail and moan. "I hate Helen" were the only words I could make out.

Then one of them turned to us. "Hey fowl, leave us alone. We're not interested in your she-monkey." They all chimed in, cursing at us. Kallistos ordered me to stand at the back door while he searched for other rat demons.

One of them came from inside the garage. "Hey, beat it, you damn doormat. You have no power here, watcher."

"I'd rather be a doorkeeper in the house of my God than to dwell in the tents of wickedness, the psalmist writes," I said.

Several joined in behind him and faced me, razor-haired, teeth showing, growling to a dull roar.

"Don't you quote a psalm to us, defiler of daughters," one said.

"By the power of His Holy Name, be gone, you rodents of hell, before I send you to the abyss for good!" I yelled. They scattered, leaving behind a foul mist.

I proceeded to enter the house and found Natalie foraging in the refrigerator.

"They left?" Kallistos asked as he walked through the fireplace from the side of the house.

"I banished them."

He looked at me, for he knew I was not to engage in battle.

"Kallistos, you sent me to guard a post. So I did what was necessary to protect her," I said in defense.

He smiled. "Your protective instincts will serve you well, but exercise wisdom. They were leaving anyway, but now they will remember you forever. Each confrontation breeds more enemies, personal ones who will work extra hard on your image bearer."

We drifted upstairs to check on Sasha.

"Greetings in the name of the Holy One, who bid the little children to come unto Him," Kallistos said to Helen's guardian, Cassiel, who bowed to me, then went back to watching from the foot of the bed.

"What happened?" Kallistos asked, "The rodents sped out and were very angry."

"Helen taught Sasha some ancient prayers tonight, the prayers for the dead and to the Holy Theotokos—more honorable than the Cherubim and beyond compare than the Seraphim. They prayed for Milo tonight."

"Powerful intercessions from an innocent child," Kallistos said.

"Helen told her that whenever she thought of her dad or missed him, but especially right now, Sasha should pray these prayers, and that sent them away." Cassiel said.

"Yiayia, I miss Daddy right now," Sasha said.

We all stopped and listened.

"Me too, sweetie."

"Is he going to sleep at the hospital forever?" Sasha asked.

"I don't know."

"Is he going to die?" She started to cry. "I don't want Daddy to die."

"Me neither, sweetheart, but remember every time we get sad, we can pray to Mary, Pangaea, for him, for her love is more spacious than the heavens," Helen said.

"Do you think Daddy misses me?" Sasha asked.

"Yes, of course he does."

Natalie walked into the room and sat on the bed next to Helen.

"Mama, I miss Daddy so much."

"Yeah, me too."

"Can you read the prayer yiayia was reading? Again and again until I fall asleep?"

"Yes, I can do that. I think Daddy likes it when we pray for him," Natalie said.

"Me too," Sasha said as she pulled her blanket close to her face.

We all prayed with them. Natalie slept with Sasha that night at Helen's house.

ENTRY 12

"I will utter dark sayings which have been from the beginning."

- Psalm 77 Septuagint

Due to the annual blessings by Father Luke after the Feast of Theophany, the house was rendered a sacred place, hard for demons to work. We watched Natalie's first peaceful night's rest since the accident. She awoke early and readied herself to go pray the daily Matins at St. Mary's.

After dropping Sasha off at her brother's house, she stopped by the rehab-center in hopes of another audience with Father Lazarus. She was told he was not in. She then drove to the cemetery on Eastern, where they had met before. Entering the driveway, she looked carefully for the staggering figure in the tattered black cassock. She was about to leave when she noticed someone sitting slumped over on the ground by the pyramid shaped tomb. She backed up, parked, and approached the person. It was Father Lazarus, either weeping or coughing.

"Father Lazarus!" she called.

His head bobbed up and he managed to get to his feet, dizzy but cogent and sat back down.

"Father Lazarus, it's me, Natalie Christopoulos."

"I know who you are, child. What do you want?"

"Are you okay?"

"Yes, yes, I'm fine. What is it Mrs. Christopoulos?"

"I wanted to talk with you again about the toll houses, and I have a gift for you."

"More Russian Standard?"

Natalie smiled. "No, something better." She held a paper bag by its handles. "But first, Father, I have some questions for you this time. Are you sure you're okay?"

He coughed and cleared his throat. "Uh, child, you don't need my twisted testimony, you have the saints' testimony. Read Blessed Theodora, she saw all the toll houses in one night."

"I have read her account." From her bag she pulled out the sheets Father Job had printed and held them up to his face. "It was very helpful. But I have more application type questions."

"Application questions and angel energies—speak clearly, girl." He stood up and leaned against the pyramid.

"I want to know how to get my husband through the toll houses. Theodora had Father Basil giving angels magic dust, prayers and good works. That doesn't make sense, how does that translate into the real world?"

He gaffed and started coughing with a sickness deep within his lungs. Blood splattered down his long scraggily beard and he bent over in pain.

"Father," Natalie reached for him and helped him sit down, back against the pyramid tomb.

"You're really sick, Father, and I don't think drinking is going to help you."

"Sometimes drinking is the only thing that helps."

Natalie slowly slid and sat next to him, as only a fit pregnant woman could. She sat in silence for several moments, looking over the cemetery tombstones.

"What do you know of the real world, girl?"

"Well, I know what I see."

"And what of that which you don't see? Is that part of the real world, too?"

"What do you mean? Like air?" She dared to look at him in his discomfort. He waved her eyes away.

"No. Like angels, demons, toll houses and even dead spirits. Are they part of the real world?"

She thought for a moment.

"Yes, I believe they are. God created all things visible and invisible."

"Ha, Father Job has done his job. You remember the Creed. Well, there you have it."

"Speak clearly, old man."

Father Lazarus closed his eyes and smiled. I could tell he liked her feistiness.

"What do you know of God's plan for saving the world?"

"Well, that Jesus died on the cross for our sins, and anyone who accepts Him as their personal Savior goes to heaven."

"No—that's not a plan, that's a transaction." He crossed himself and continued, "God's plan is about the Incarnation and the process of theosis."

"Father, I don't really know that much about theology."

"You don't have to be a theologian to understand this. Do you want to know it?"

"Maybe, a little, I mean—yes, Milo talked about being saved and how it was like sales, the day before he died."

He rubbed his whole face with both hands and paused for a moment.

"God, who is spirit, unseen, unknowable, and all those words that make Him seem so far away, became bodily, seen by all and knowable. Christ, who is God, united us and really all sinful humanity to Himself by becoming one of us. With me so far?" he asked.

"Uh-huh, I get that, I believe that and all, but what does that really mean?"

"What that really means is now the visible—" he grabbed his sleeve and tugged it— "and the invisible—" he pointed to the dead souls lingering in the distance which Natalie couldn't see but looked to anyway—"are united in one 'real' world, as you call it—physical and spiritual together. It's the only way to make it right because we can't just decide to be saved. That's the Incarnation in a nutshell. God unites man to himself by becoming man so we can be with God."

"Okay," she said.

"At baptism you were given a white garment, both physically and spiritually, because they are united right? Body and soul—visible and invisible—are you with me? I'm talking about sacraments here." He looked at her.

She nodded.

"It's now our job to keep that garment pure, by cultivating virtues until we die or He comes back. Our Orthodox faith teaches us how to do this. Virtues and sacraments are real things—bread and wine, physical and spiritual—they join you to God." He paused and thought for a moment. "Salvation involves your mind and the belief that Christ died for your sins, but it's not just in your head—a mental set of beliefs. It's more beautiful than that. It's a journey in communion with others, a process of transformation, body and soul."

She just looked at him as he winced in pain again. Then he said, waving her eyes away again, "And it's hard because we often lose our way and we're prone to vice not virtue. That's theosis, Natalie, and that is how we understand God's plan of salvation." He paused again then said, "And a better way to understand what you must do to help Milo."

"I've never heard it put that way before," she said, pondering his words.

He rested his head on her shoulder in a moment of exhausted vulnerability.

"Father, angels, demons, spiritual warfare, toll houses—I didn't know."

"Now you sound like Milo. This is what your husband didn't know and Saint John Maximovitch instructed you to learn about. The toll houses, as we call them, are the demons last chance to disrupt theosis, the final uniting of our souls to God." He looked at her. She looked back very attentive.

"So what do I do to help Milo? What do you do for the dead who ask you to help them? You must have learned something; you've been at this for a while now."

The cemetery grew quiet. Father Lazarus lifted his head and could see none of the dead now. He looked around with renewed alertness.

"What is it, Father?"

"We're alone," he said.

"Yes, I know."

"No, we are really alone. Come—we must go. It is not safe here for you."

Natalie looked perplexed, "Okay, Father, I'll drive you back to the center."

"Fine—let's be off."

Kallistos and I noticed this too, but saw nothing. As they got into her vehicle and left the cemetery, he appeared, rising from the ground just a few plot sections away, his gaze fixed on us. We could not move. His blackened skin shone a reddish hue. He had long horns, six wings and many eyes looking to and fro.

"Where is the priest Lazarus?" he demanded.

"He left," Kallistos said.

"I have locked away his guardian and now I require his soul."

"His work is not finished." Kallistos dared to speak against the demon.

His stature tripled and a rage-filled growl bellowed out of him. I stamped my staff, revealing its fiery blade.

"I have watched widows and old men conspire and fail a thousand times," the demon said. "This story is irregular—Kallistos, the good guardian and the watcher from Laodicea, a soul-gazer priest with a pregnant widowed woman whose prayers are unusually strong. We have been tricked before by sainted mothers, but not this time. The priest goes with me to the abyss until the end of days."

"You will get no help from us, and Archangel Michael will know that you keep a guardian against his will."

"Come to me, you little snitch!" He advanced towards us quickly. I posed to strike, but Kallistos secured me and we fled into the air.

"We should fight him," I said to Kallistos's mind.

As we sped into the stratosphere away from where Natalie was, Kallistos looked back. He stopped when we could no longer see the demon.

"Young one, that was Satanial, Lucifer's second-in-command of all his dominion. When you see a demon of this rank, you flee and report to the other seraphim."

"I didn't think we could defeat him, Kallistos, just delay him so Natalie could get away."

"Maybe if we had Savlo, for he has special knowledge concerning Seraphim, but even he would flee without at least a Principality or a Dominion."

We surveyed the spatial planes but did not see him. "Come, let us go back."

Natalie had driven Father Lazarus back to the center and they were parting company.

"Father, thank you for your advice. It is hard to believe all this stuff is going on, but I do."

"It's always hard to believe. People have trained themselves to not believe that which is unseen."

Natalie shook her head in response to many of his sayings. "Father, my gift is a new cassock and I want to give it to you, but I have one condition."

"It's not a gift if there's a condition."

She smiled. "I want you to come to Milo's funeral, too. So come to the hospital and the funeral. I would feel much better if you were there, even if it's behind the altar."

He looked at her, seeing the sincerity of her heart.

"I accept your 'so-called' gift."

She smiled and stepped forward to hug him. He raised his hand, stopped her, and offered to bless her instead. She cupped her hands and obliged.

He looked around and acknowledged the presence of the dead.

"They're back, aren't they?" she asked.

"No rest for the wicked, my dear. No rest for the wicked."

"Father, people are starting to say I'm crazy, just like you."

"What do they know of crazy, my child?"

She laughed and seemed greatly endeared to him. Since she had already missed the morning service, she went straight to the hospital.

— • —

Before going up to see Milo, Natalie ventured down to the hospital cafeteria to find something to eat. We followed behind her observing all the other guardians at work. The image bearers are more open to angelic promptings at hospitals. It was a typical Friday menu of roast beef, lasagna and pizza. An older gentleman whose wife was on the same floor as Milo recognized her.

"May I buy your lunch, young lady?"

"Oh, um—no thank you. I'm not sure I'm going to eat here after all," she said.

"The roast beef is actually quite good. I mean for hospital food, it truly is a special."

"I'm sure it is. I may just have some salad. I'm trying to fast from meat on Wednesdays and Fridays."

"Why on earth would you do that?"

She paused. "Why on earth indeed, sir. Thank you for your kind offer, but I'm going to be on my way. Good bye." He shook his head at her.

She went up to spend time with Milo and relieve Helen and Nico to go and get Sasha, who was at her brother's house. Natalie decided that only Milo's parents, Sasha, and some clergy were to attend his release from the machine.

As Natalie walked into the room, Milo tried to plead for his life and alert her to the reality he faced after death. She walked over to the bed and grabbed Milo's bodily hand.

Savlo drew close to Kallistos and asked, "Is she ready?"

"Almost. Is he ready?" Kallistos asked.

"Almost."

"Almost? We should delay it until we have more certainty," I interjected.

They both looked at me and smiled. I didn't know what they were smiling about.

Milo could hear us talking, but looked confused still. He could not make out our words. He just kept looking at his wife, and then to us and back to his body.

Several hours had passed, when I asked, "What are we getting ready to do, exactly?"

They both looked at me this time. Savlo said, "You've been a watcher for many ages, watching moss grow and rocks crumble, now you are about to witness some of the most terrible attacks of the aerial demons since hades was destroyed; but also how an image bearer's true faith transforms the created order."

I wanted to rephrase my one question, but could not due to the number of people gathering outside the room and the clamor of the distant toll house ringing a bell and calling for Milo.

Savlo and Kallistos continued talking. Milo walked into the hall through the door and I appeared to him. I was not allowed to talk with him, but he could talk to me, and so he did.

"He's the priest from Holy Resurrection, Father Luke, the church where I grew up, a good man. This guy in the tie, holding the cowboy hat is Pastor Dan from our church; we just had a bad run-in before I died, but you probably know that already. Of course the doctor who has been helping us. I don't know the lanky priest and I certainly don't know that guy standing down the hall leaning against the wall. He looks like a crazy monk or a patient here."

Then from around the corner came Helen and Sasha walking hand-in-hand, Nico trailing behind at his usual limp speed. Milo ran to them and slid right through his daughter, trying to grab her. He turned to face me and the now small crowd. "What's going on?" he asked.

The crowd of people were whispering and consoling each other. The priests greeted Helen. She grabbed both their hands and kissed them, then held them for Sasha to kiss. They reluctantly obliged. Pastor Daniel gripped his black Bible tighter to his chest, tipped his hat, and nodded to Helen and Nico. Milo appeared concerned as he realized the clash of religious traditions he had brought to their family was about to crash down on Natalie's shoulders. Natalie came out of the room and greeted everyone.

Pastor Daniel was the first to speak. "Now Natalie, I want you to know I have deliberated over the Scriptures, and I want you to know that nothing in this decision goes against what the Bible teaches. All options for life to continue have been exhausted, so rest assured this is God's plan. I believe He's taking him home—done deal."

"Ahem!" Father Lazarus coughed out loud and several looked at him. He did not look back at them.

She blushed and smiled.

"Did he say 'Amen'?" Pastor Daniel asked.

"Never mind him for now, thank you Pastor Dan, and thanks for coming. I know you must feel a little strange with all these priests around, but it's good you're here and that I am sure is part of God's plan today." Natalie embraced him around the neck. He smiled, and with that she anchored him in her harbor of love forever.

Natalie had greeted each person, accepted whatever they said with humility, and spoke gracious words to their hearts. It was an act of spiritual solidarity, across traditions at odds, the likes of which I had not witnessed before.

The night had come and the demons were swirling in the distant portal in the room, watching what was about to happen. The magnetic force that connects soul and body together had taken hold of Milo. He now stood next to his body. Everyone's guardian located above the room, except Father Lazarus's.

The first to enter the room were Dr. Daayal and a nurse. He walked over, extended his hand, and slightly bowed his head to Natalie. He grabbed her thin but warm hand with both of his. She smiled at him.

"I know this has been a difficult decision for you but in my professional opinion, there is nothing more medically that we can do."

"I know," she said. "Thank you, doctor." She smiled nervously at him.

They stood aside, next to the machines to give room for the others to come in.

Helen, Nico and Sasha were the next to enter. Sasha ran to her mother's side and clung to her leg. Helen started to cry and moan. Several moments passed. Nico wept for his son and prayed under his breath for his soul. The aerial demons swore as he prayed.

"Mommy," was all Sasha said as she looked at her unrecognizable father lying in the bed. Natalie leaned down and spoke in her daughter's ear. Her words were a soul salve for the young one seeing death so close up.

Sasha stepped closer to the bed and kissed her dad's hand. "Bye-bye, Daddy. I love you."

Nico snatched up Sasha and walked her from the room. Milo screamed as his conscience came undone with grief and regret.

Pastor Daniel came into the room, black hat and black Bible still in hand. "Nat, how ya holding up?"

"Just fine, Pastor. Thank you."

"Well, you know I like to talk about these things as homecomings. And it's important to remember that God gives you the grace to handle these things and we are here to help you. We can never be sure why the good Lord decided to take him home but we'll miss him, and look forward to the great reunion either at the rapture or when we join Him."

"Thank you again, Pastor," Natalie said.

Milo looked at Savlo. No words were spoken. None were needed.

Father Luke and Father Job came in next. Father Luke was holding a small black bag with brass sacramental tools and a worn out book.

Pastor Daniel looked at them and held an expression of skepticism.

Father Lazarus staggered into the room, muffled a cough in his sleeve. He appeared drunk, but it was due to his limp and suffering from his lung sickness.

"Who's the drunk crazy priest?" Milo blurted out.

No answer was given, but Father Lazarus looked sternly at Milo. "What? That guy can see me? No way."

Again no answer was given to Milo.

Father Luke bowed to Natalie with extreme reverence. "Well, I talked to my bishop today, and after Helen grabbed the phone from my hand and had her say with him, he gave permission to let me pray a Trisagion service on Saturday and offer an Orthodox funeral service on Sunday before Lent, if you think that would have been Milo's desire, Natalie?"

"I think it is his desire now," she said.

Pastor Daniel, the doctor, nurse and even Father Luke made quizzical gestures at her response.

"Alright then." Father Luke opened his book, placed a vial of holy oil on the legs of Milo's body and began to read a prayer for the dead;

Have mercy, O Lord, if it is possible, on the soul of Thy servant Miletus Emmanuel Christopoulos, departed to eternal life in separation from Thy Holy Orthodox Church! Unsearchable are Thy judgments. Account not this my prayer as sin. But may Thy holy will be done!

He sealed the body by wiping crosses of oil with his thumb on the forehead and other visible body parts. Savlo, Kallistos and I started to shine with inner light illuminating the cosmic dimension of the room. The portal demons cackled and wagged their heads as the priest continued. Milo was drawn closer and closer to his body.

"Natalie, per the bishop's instruction that's all I can do for now. So with my blessing, do what you must with great hope in our God as the lover of mankind," Father Luke said.

"Thank you, Father Luke."

The nurse stepped forward. "Natalie, I just need you to sign this final form and then the doctor will tell you how to turn off the machine."

Natalie signed it. "Can I have a couple of minutes alone, please?" she asked.

Soft affirmations filled the room as they all made their way past Father Lazarus, who did not move. He stood looking at Milo. "I will stay," he said.

Everyone else left respectfully, some whispered about the whiskey priest.

Natalie grabbed Milo's hand. Milo's soul was close by. Father Lazarus limped up to the bed, stood across from Natalie, and waited for her to make eye contact with him.

"Natalie Christopoulos," he said when she had looked up at him. "Have you prepared yourself for all that will be required of you?"

"Yes, Father. Can you see him?"

Father Lazarus crossed himself and muttered a prayer, then bent down his head but lifted his eyes. He was face to face with Milo's soul. He addressed Milo directly.

"Son, you've been prayed over with the prayers of the Holy Orthodox Church. The bishop has granted you an Orthodox funeral due to your family's love and devotion to the true faith. I am sure you have guardians near to guide you, so be on your way. Depart in peace and may the mercy of our great God and Savior be with you," he said making the sign of the cross over Milo's soul.

Milo lifted from his body fully, drew close to Savlo, and offered his wretched hand. He was lost in his emanating light.

Milo's bodily lungs closed and refused the air from the machine. Alarms went off and the doctor hurriedly led the others in. They saw Father Lazarus leaning over the body.

"Step away, sir!" the doctor demanded. After assessing the body and making sure the machine was still on and not malfunctioning, he turned to the priest and said, "What did you do?"

"I helped him along," he declared and coughed.

"You should leave, padre, and try to sober up a little," Pastor Daniel said.

"Natalie?" Father Lazarus asked.

"It's okay, Father, you can go."

Father Lazarus was trying to get out the door, pushing himself against the jamb. Helen rushed under his arm into the room just as Natalie said, "Father." He turned back. "Thank you. And pray for him, won't you?"

He snorted and walked out.

There was commotion in the room for several minutes, as everyone except Natalie voiced opinions about how it all had been handled. Natalie went immediately to find Sasha to console her and take her home.

Within thirty minutes, the room held only Milo's body, Milo's soul, Savlo and me.

"So what now?" Milo asked.

"Now, my friend, we go to your funeral, then we travel the way of the dreaded aerial toll houses," Savlo said.

Savlo told him the soul is free to roam for several turns of the planet once sacramentally severed from the body. Milo asked to travel and visit many places that night. He chose places from his youth and reviewed his life, asking many questions of Savlo. Early the next morning we came to the funeral home to watch the preparation for the wake. Savlo sent me to check on Pastor Daniel, and then to find Kallistos and Natalie.

ENTRY 13

"We can do nothing better or greater for the dead than pray for them."

- St. John Maximovitch

With great speed I found Kallistos and Natalie at Dogwood Bible Church. I surveyed the meeting room for any demons and listened to assess the conversations. Pastor Daniel led discussions about finances, attendance numbers, which songs were to be sung, and the Christopoulos family. Natalie sat outside the meeting room in the blue carpeted vestibule. The cartoonish pamphlets of heaven and hell that lined the welcome desk were the only icons displayed.

The building was dark, with only the sounds of the heating system and dull laughs behind closed doors to break the silence. Natalie faced forward, looking blankly out the front windows and watching traffic drive by. Solomon wrote that 'there is nothing new under the sun,' but not everything is common, and Natalie was not. She was gaining inner strength and holding a glow in her face.

I appeared to Kallistos. "Greetings in the Name of the One who illumines us all," I said.

He bowed his head and became attentive.

"Savlo sent me to learn what Pastor Daniel was doing. Strange I should find you here," I said.

"Strange indeed." He smiled, obviously knowing more than I did. We stood next to Natalie, waiting for her audience to be granted, when a shadowy spirit appeared down the hallway. Its true shape was unrecognizable, for it lurked in the darkness, not wanting to be identified.

"Should I confront it?" I asked Kallistos.

"No, it's Natalie's hinderer. He wants to know what we are doing. I suspect Satanial, whom we fled in the cemetery, is taking a greater interest in her and us."

Kallistos took several steps forward and fixed himself between the hinderer and Natalie. He extended his white wings to their full length, twice the size of his body, filling the large hallway as a barricade. He emanated light that dissolved the darkness. A hallway light flicked on and caught Natalie's attention. She leaned forward to see what was there, but nothing was visible to her.

"You have no authority here, hinderer. Her time is not at hand."

The demon dissipated its energy because of the light and could not be seen anymore. Kallistos came back to Natalie's side as she prayed for Milo and for Father Lazarus. Kallistos leaned down and spoke to her mind.

The door of the meeting room swung open. "Nat, come on down," Pastor Daniel said, waving his arm in a welcoming manner. She gathered her things and entered the room.

"Well, Natalie, have a seat next to me. I think you know everyone in the room; Sam, Bob the treasurer, and of course Brooke from the ladies' Bible study group are all here for your support." Brooke squeezed her hand three times as a gesture of affection.

Natalie sat in peaceful silence, and listened to Pastor Daniel. "Natalie, we all know you're going through a tremendous trial of faith right now and you're pregnant, which I know makes its own stress. I asked you to come here this morning so that we could offer our love and support as your church family." Everyone in the room shook their heads and lulled verbal agreements. Someone whispered, "Amen."

Pastor Daniel spoke loud enough for everyone to hear. "Nat, the manner in which your husband passed away impressed upon me the need to reach out to you, strengthen your faith and, well, wrap our arms around ya and love on ya, so to speak."

Natalie smiled at everyone in the room, making eye contact, paused then said, "Pastor, Brooke, and really all of you, my heart is so touched by this." Natalie's eyes welled with tears. "Thank you so much. I welcome any support you guys will offer, of course, Lord knows I need it." She took a breath and then spoke with confidence. "Many things have happened to me pretty quickly, and I ask for your prayers and prayers for Sasha too, she has almost stopped talking."

Brooke's eyes filled with tears and solemnity was expressed by all.

"Pastor, if it's alright, I wanted to bring up something I've been thinking about recently?"

"Of course—whatever's on your heart, dear," Pastor Daniel asked.

"I'm in need of your forgiveness."

"My forgiveness? For what?" he asked.

"Well, I'm ashamed to admit it, but during the past couple of days, Milo told me some very ugly thoughts and interactions he's had recently with you Pastor, and you Bob. I know he was coming from a meeting with you before he was in the accident. I feel just horrible coming to you with this request."

"Did you also have these thoughts?" Pastor Daniel asked, as he and everyone else in the room adjusted uncomfortably in their seats.

"No, Pastor, I didn't then and don't now. I thought Milo would work out whatever was wrong between you guys, but——"

"Well, Natalie, those are not your sins."

"But I listened and said nothing, and therefore participated in his sins." She stood up and took a step toward Pastor Daniel who reciprocated in stance.

"Pastor Dan, please forgive me and my husband for our sinful words." She started to cry again, but tried to hold it in.

"Darling, you're breaking my heart." He opened his arms and they embraced. Natalie was sobbing now and Pastor Daniel shared in her tears. I looked over at Kallistos. He was catching their tears in an angelic vial. They are rare, created by the first Nephilim, and require angelic energy to hold materials from this dimension.

"I forgive you and Milo for any offenses against me," Pastor Daniel said.

Bob, the treasurer, stood up with tears in his eyes as well. "I do too. Milo and I had some hard words over the last couple of times we talked and I—well, just like Pastor, all is forgiven." He wiped his eyes and flung the tears towards the ground. Kallistos caught them too.

"Pastor, what's that verse that talks about confessing sins to others?" Brooke asked wiping her eyes.

"James five verse sixteen says, 'Confess your trespasses to one another, and pray for one another, that you may be healed.' That's what's going on here, people, and God is glorified by it."

After several moments of affirming one another, everyone sat down and calmed themselves.

"Whew, that was something, Natalie. Praise God." Pastor Daniel wiped his face with a pocket cloth and said, "So, I would like to have you and Sasha come forward this Sunday after the service, and we can have the whole congregation pray over you. We'll call the elders and some ladies to lay hands on you and really lift you up to the Lord in prayer," he said.

Natalie sniffed and wet her lips. "Well, Pastor, I normally would be here, but I feel right now, with the situation the way it is, the Orthodox Church is where I need to worship."

Pastor Daniel reclined in his chair at the head of the table, rubbed his chin, and furrowed his forehead. He seemed to be thinking. The rest of the room was silent until Natalie spoke again.

"I just feel like there's something really spiritual going on right now, even on a supernatural level that I can't explain all too well. Milo and I grew up in Orthodoxy, and the people have been helpful and very comforting while I've been trying to figure all this out."

"You mean like the whiskey priest feller?" Pastor Daniel asked.

"Yes. Father Lazarus, Father Job and especially for Milo's family, Father Luke, who will be doing the funeral," she said.

"Nat, you know I care for ya, but what happened at the hospital was, well—let's say it was outside of the Biblical teaching that we hold to here in this church. You know how I feel about the Orthodox and all their rituals, we've talked about this. I mean, First Timothy says, 'all scripture is given by inspiration of God, and is profitable for doctrine, for reproof, for correction, for instruction in righteousness.' So I'm a little concerned about you going back to them, especially that fellow Lazarus, for any kind of spiritual advice."

"Pastor, I hear you, I really do, but like I said in our last discussion, I'm just following my heart and trying to love my husband right now, the best that I can figure it, anyway."

Pastor Daniel dropped his head, as did the others, and the warm affection that was shared before chilled.

She continued, "In all honesty, I've already made amends with the Orthodox Church but please don't think I'm leaving you. I want you to come with me. Pastor, they love the Lord just like you all do. It's really the same thing just done differently. You'd like Father Job. He really knows his Bible."

An unseen demon of dissention whispered, "Divide and conquer, it's worked for centuries." All of the guardians in the room observing, immediately went into high alert but could not detect the demon.

"Natalie, they're doing the funeral, then?"

"Yes."

"Do you think they would let me preach the Gospel at the funeral, since he was a member of our church when he died?"

"Um—I don't know, Pastor. I could ask, but I think it's a pretty set service."

"Natalie, I've done some reading and it's not the same thing. We know no other authority than the Holy Bible inspired by the Holy Spirit," Pastor Daniel said, his face flushed.

"I'm not trying to argue with you, Pastor. But—Please, Pastor Dan, come with me on this journey, learn about how God works in this world."

"Young lady, I'm not ignorant of the ways of God—"

Natalie started to cry and interrupted Pastor Daniel, "You said you wanted to minister to me, 'love on me.' Well, then, support me. Walk with me. I'm begging you, Pastor."

"Natalie, we're always here for you, but as the pastor of this flock I need to take a stand for the truth."

The room fell silent for several moments. I could observe many conflicting emotions.

"Well, I thank you for your forgiveness of Milo and me, but I've got to follow my heart on this one. Please, Pastor, come to Milo's funeral, it's tomorrow after the church service at Holy Resurrection across town. You're all welcome to come. I want you to come. I love you all, I really do."

"We'll bring meals starting next week. If you need to me to watch Sasha, I will of course do that too," Brooke said.

Pastor Daniel said, "I'll stop by after our church service." Natalie stood up again. She bowed her head to them all and excused herself from the meeting. She was on her way to the Holy Resurrection temple, for it was the Saturday of Souls and Milo was being especially commemorated. As she walked to her vehicle, birds swarmed above her head, flying to the ground, then up again to the electrical lines, then off again over her head, hundreds of black birds all in angry unison. Natalie noticed them and hurried into her car.

"One question, Kallistos" I said.

"Yes?"

"Why the tears?"

"Tears of repentance are as powerful as baptismal waters."

— • —

After the liturgy Natalie spent the day helping host relatives at Helen's house. She watched for quiet times when Sasha played with the other children and was gracious to everyone who tried to console her. Evil groans began filling the stratosphere all afternoon as they prepared to go to the funeral home for the wake. The aerial demons hated being shut out from the harbor of love that Natalie had created.

That evening the short memorial service was led by Father Luke and Father Job. Father Lazarus stood to the side. The darkness of night had set in and the throng of people who had paid their last respects for Milo concluded. The funeral directors were cleaning up. Natalie was in the bathroom and a few image bearers remained sitting in the back sharing memories of Milo.

Natalie emerged from the restroom and saw Father Lazarus by the casket.

"Do you think he's watching, Father Lazarus? Do you see him?" Natalie interrupted him as he prayed over Milo's body.

Milo's soul located behind the casket. He had watched in silence and without expression the whole evening as everyone grieved his death. All the guardians gave us encouraging nods for they knew the toll houses awaited us. He could make out only the words and prayers of the holy image bearers who passed by, for they were praying pure prayers.

Father Lazarus looked at Natalie with one eye squinted shut. "Shush. Come pray with me."

The other priests had left after all arrangements had been confirmed for the funeral service the next day. Father Lazarus held a ragged old book. His hand trembled from extended sobriety. One side of the book was in Slavonic and the other in English. He was whispering the prayers of the *Canon of the Departure of the Soul* when Natalie supported one side of the book, slowing his shaking hand a bit. "Where are you?" she asked. He pointed to Canticle Eight. She read in a quiet voice;

"Verses: As the Mother loving mankind of the God who loveth mankind, look thou with calm and merciful eyes when my soul from its body shall part; and I will glorify with thee forever, O holy Mother of God.

"Vouchsafe that I may escape the hordes of bodiless barbarians, and rise through the abysses of the air, and enter into heaven; and I will glorify with thee forever, O holy Mother of God.

"O thou who didst bear the Lord Almighty, banish thou far from me when I come to die, the chieftain of bitter torments who ruleth the universe; and I will glorify with thee forever, O holy Mother of God.

"Glory to the Father, and to the Son, and to the Holy Spirit."

She looked at him. He took the book from her and flipped to another section. "Pray," he said. She did;

"A prayer from the Canon to the Guardian Angel: My holy angel, be my protector and invincible warrior before me as I pass through the toll houses of the terrible ruler of this world."

She finished and they each crossed themselves three times. Natalie looked back to see if anyone remained. Lilly then walked in the room wearing a black dress, which exposed her shoulders. She walked up the center aisle and Natalie met her half-way. Milo dropped his attention, shamed.

"Hello, Natalie, my name is Lilly. I worked with Milo at Open Door. I closed all his deals. We were partners in a way," she said and winked at her. Natalie forced a smile.

"Well, I'm here to pay my respects and offer my most sincere sympathies," she said.

Natalie nodded her head and stood to the side, giving a path to Milo's body. Father Lazarus watched. Lilly stepped forward and put her hand on the swell of Natalie's womb.

"Ouch," Natalie said.

"Oh, sorry, it must be the static in the carpet. I didn't know you were so pregnant. I am so sorry for you." She laid her other hand alongside the first. Natalie winced, but was mesmerized by Lilly's green eyes.

I lifted my staff, but Savlo held out his wing and stopped my advance. Kallistos floated right through Father Lazarus and positioned next to Natalie. Lilly and Natalie were locked in a hypnotic gaze as Lilly caressed her womb almost invasively. Father Lazarus stepped towards them and grabbed Lilly's arm and said, "That's enough, young lady."

"Take your hands off me, you whiskey priest. I can smell it in your pores." She adjusted her dress. "I'm sorry, Natalie, it's just that when I was younger I swore I would never let another priest touch me again."

She turned and walked to the casket.

"You should leave for home," Father Lazarus said. "The funeral will be more of the same. Take my prayer book and pray all the canons for the dead and guardian angels. They are necessary for good passage. I'll see her out."

Natalie looked back at Milo's body one last time for the night then left. Kallistos followed.

I shifted over to watch Lilly. She did not look down at Milo but stared straight ahead, looking at something and nothing at the same time. Milo's soul moved from her gaze, as did Savlo. I looked to Savlo for permission to engage and he nodded. I put my face right in her view. "I know you are demon-possessed. Who is in you? I demand you tell me your true name."

Her vision was fixed, looking through me.

"Father," she said loudly, "What's your name?"

"Father Lazarus. What's yours?"

"Lilly. My name is Lilly." She turned around to face the priest. "Does God still hear your prayers, or are you just giving the dead false hope?"

He cocked his head. "What'd you say?"

"You think that helping the girl will somehow save you?"

"Do I know you, young lady?"

She smiled and said, "Well, you don't know me in the Biblical way, if that's what you mean."

"You should leave, and do not come to the funeral. You are not invited."

She walked down the aisle, stopped right next to the priest, sniffed and shook her head, "Vodka—such a stereotype. I have no need to attend the funeral. I know who keeps the dead. Funerals are for the living." She walked out of the funeral parlor. Father Lazarus walked to make sure she left.

Savlo sent me to Kallistos.

— • —

I caught up with Natalie and told Kallistos of the encounter.

When we reached her home, Helen met us at the door. "Sasha's asleep," she told Natalie.

"Thank you, Helen, for all you're doing."

Helen put both her hands on Natalie's face, pulled it close, and kissed her. "You're my only child, now."

Natalie embraced her and they wept.

"Get some rest and something to eat. I'll be over in the morning," Helen said.

"Okay."

Helen left. Natalie put some hot water on the stove and then sank, exhausted, into the chaise lounge.

Kallistos instructed me to go to the temple of the Holy Resurrection for the night and wait for the funeral directors to bring the body there and guard it.

I traveled alone to the church and stood in front of the altar doors. I adored the tabernacle, holding the Host, illuminated by candles on the altar. I felt a presence of great might and looked about.

"Present yourself," I demanded.

A voice filled my being. "You are our only hope. Fail not. When you have proven your loyalty, entreat the Ancient of Days to release us and we will fight with you when the time comes."

I recognized the voice as my old friend, Azazel, imprisoned deep within the canyon of Duadel. I ached with him. In him I could feel true contrition.

"My heart pains with you, brother. You know I will forever beg for mercy on your behalf, but I can promise nothing. Look at all you have done to the image bearers. The spirits of the Nephilim still ravage the spirits of men. Your secret knowledge deludes them. Why didn't you listen to me Azazel?" He did not respond.

ENTRY 14

Late in the lunar light, Savlo and Milo entered through the closed temple doors and stationed by the chanter's stand in the nave. Milo's body had arrived early in the morning and was in a side chapel, to be brought in after the Divine Liturgy. Milo wanted to be close to his body, telling us it didn't feel right to be separated from it but we stayed in the nave. I took my place behind Savlo's right wing and watched everything.

Due to the many visitors attending, hushed questions and explanations seemed to add a distractive spirit to the Divine Liturgy. The priest and acolytes were more deliberate with their duties, slowing it down.

After the benediction, many people left and many new came, including real estate agents, lenders, and past clients, some I recognized. The congregation of people filled the nave and overflowed into the vestibule. Hundreds of beeswax candles bowed down in the sand as if paying homage. Tears stained the eyes of the faithful. Guardians filled the building to the very top of the dome, heaven and earth met. Most of those attending were sad for Natalie and whispered about her status as a pregnant widow.

Milo sulked, regretting the course of his life, and now he begged Savlo, like the rich man of old to tell everyone that the myths are not myths.

Father Luke and the pall bearers processed into the nave, down the center isle with Milo's casket. Natalie, her Baba, her brother's family, and Milo's family sat in the front pew. She was strong in posture and kept her focus on Father Lazarus, who now stood in the back of the altar wearing his new cassock. The funeral service commenced. Over and over the "Lord have mercy's" sang out into the air. Father Luke, with the protopsalti, chanted the ancient hymns with great emotion. The funeral service prayers cried for absolution of Milo's sins, voluntary and involuntary, of word and of deed, of knowledge and of ignorance. The angels joined in and a beautiful plea on Milo's behalf rose to the heavens, carried by the incense and Father Luke's voice;

"Glory to the Father and to the Son and to the Holy Spirit.

"Looking on me as I lie here prone before you, voiceless and unbreathing, mourn for me, everyone; brethren and friends, kindred, and you who knew me well; for but yesterday with you I was talking, and suddenly there came upon me the fearful hour of death: therefore come, all you that long for me, and kiss me with the last kiss of parting. For no longer shall I walk with you, nor talk with you henceforth: for to the Judge I go, where no person is valued for his earthly station: Yea, slave and master together stand before Him, king and soldier, rich man and poor man, all accounted of equal rank: for each one, according to his own deeds shall be glorified, or shall be put to shame. Therefore I beg you all, and implore you, to offer prayer unceasingly for me to Christ our God, that I be not assigned for my sins to the place of torment; but that He assign me to the place where there is Light of Life.

"Both now and ever and to the ages of ages. Amen."

Many image bearers wept. The body processed out of the nave just as it had processed at Milo's baptism, during feast days growing up, and at his wedding when he was sacramentally joined with Natalie. This was his last procession out from the presence of the community of believers. We watched from a distance, and I focused on Natalie.

Natalie, Sasha, Milo's family, and her family stood in line, thanking and kissing all who came to witness the event. Natalie remained tearless and filled with what could be called resolve. She understood that death was just the beginning of her holy work.

As the line of mourners dwindled, through a hallway door leading to the banquet hall, in walked Milo's hindering angel, disheveled, unshaven and seemingly disoriented, asking the mourners for money. Pastor Daniel was late due to his Sunday duties and was standing in the back next to the funeral directors when they were alerted about the disturbance and escorted him out.

Just past the hearse, in a moment of rage, the hindering angel pointed at Milo uttered a most disturbing curse in an angelic tongue. Pastor Daniel then spent some time talking with him and sharing verses from the Bible, which aggravated the demon more.

"Who was that and what did he say?" Milo asked Savlo.

"He has been your personal foe. He is one of the left hands of Lucifer. Sent at your baptism to hinder you, frustrate you, and orchestrate a constant flow of angst in your life. It's the reason you straddled the rumble strip, willing to throw your life away. He is the reason you thought everyone was against you. He was very effective and a strong adversary. He has had great success deceiving you and has left his mark on your life. He now will sit back and watch the fruit of his labor as we travel on."

The commotion settled down and Milo's body was loaded into the hearse. A train of vehicles marked with orange flags slowly drove along; an angelic train hovered above them, to Garfield Park Cemetery, where the body was to be interred until the final day of resurrection.

— • —

Natalie did her formal duties with regal emotional control. Father Lazarus, who had been silent the whole day, stood by her side as they lowered the casket into the ground with a thud. Image bearers threw flowers into the grave as Natalie watched. Helen left and took Sasha with her to the family limousine. Natalie and Father Lazarus remained. Kallistos, Savlo, Milo, and myself also stood around the hole in the earth for several moments, while the planet continued to spin. The breeze picked up and tears fell from Natalie's eyes for the first time that day.

"Well, Natalie Christopoulos, are you ready to get to work? Lent starts tonight. You should go to the Forgiveness service," Father Lazarus said.

"Tell me, Father, do you see him?"

He paused and looked directly at Milo. "This is a good cemetery to be in. The dead are quiet here."

"Father, please tell me."

"The righteous shall live by faith, not by sight, my dear. Seeing the dead is a curse, a special kind of burden that should not be spoken about to souls such as yours." He threw his rose into the pit and left her looking at the casket of the one to whom she was united.

The breeze grew steady and small demon creatures appearing as children could be seen hiding behind the trees dashing closer to the grave. They called out Milo's name. The world of this dimension lost focus for Milo. All sound was now muffled as we were pulled from behind, through the overgrown thicket of brush, to where a white marbled doorway, cracked across the top, represented an entry gate to our dimension. The last vision Milo saw on earth was Natalie's face mouthing the words, "Goodbye for now, my love."

ENTRY 15

Sins of the Tongue: Toll Houses 1, 2 & 3

Waiting at the white marbled portal was another angel who took Milo and led him through the portal, into the vast desert of the aerial demons. Milo had use of all of his mental senses, now transformed and more suited for him to understand and engage the realm between heaven and hell. He looked to and fro, up and down, and back and forth.

"I'm so small. I'm going to be swallowed up into the great gulf of space." He looked at Savlo and begged, "Don't let go of me."

Savlo pulled Milo closer to his side as a mother hen wings her chick. The other angel appeared larger than Savlo by several feet and held a shepherd's crook. His wings and face were covered by his black cloak. He was inattentive, as a guide who has traveled this path too many times. He constantly recited the psalms, as well as other angelic psalms not known to the children of the Resurrection.

"We're going so fast. I can't tell where I am. Where are we? There's no ground, no sky, just darkness, but I can see. Where are we going? Heaven? Hell? Answer me, someone!" Milo yelled.

The gatekeeper angel, as he was called, said, "We are traveling to the valley of the shadow of death, conceptualized as the aerial toll houses to image bearers. There are twenty toll houses clustered in seven hives. The first three judge the sins of the tongue."

Milo tried to look at his face, but found it covered by his hood.

"It is precisely twenty two psalms away from where the image bearers live."

Milo was fearful. As the gatekeeper angel recited, 'Though I should walk in the midst of the shadow of death...' we arrived at the first hive of toll houses. As we approached, the darkness gave way like a clearing of the fog. We waited in an open space, appearing as gray dirt with a large stone fence separating us from three limestone towers—toll houses. Milo's mouth opened wide and he silently screamed at the vision of the terrible beings and the sounds of rowdy laughter and taunts coming at him in all directions.

He tried to go backward, but the gatekeeper angel did not flinch from his guiding grip. "There is no escape from them. The only way past is through," he said. We came to a closed iron gate with a white-washed tombstone above it. It read, "Sins of the Tongue."

Many demons came rushing to the iron gate. Their mouths oozed with open sores and their ears were large and pointed. They reached for Milo. "He is ours!" They pushed against the gate, but it held.

"Thank God for solid gates," Milo said fearful of them. The demons laughed.

"So witty, this one is. His tongue is so sharp, truly a double edged sword," one retorted. "Good one, Milo! Keep on talking," another said.

Then a demon came from the west, riding a large beast, a bicephalous hound of hell with dog heads and the body of a horse. No hair covered its gray and pink-spotted skin. The demon was impressive in size. His wings were burned off and several deformed ears that moved independently of each other angled towards every sound. He spoke with one voice through two mouths bearing jagged teeth.

"Who comes to find passage through our toll houses? Don't be quiet now, declare your names," the demon said.

The other demons were making demands as well, singing mocking songs and cursing. There was no silence in this place.

Melting with fear, Milo tried to speak. All the demons laughed when they saw he was trying to answer. "Has the cat got your tongue? You were so quick-witted and now, no words?" They continued to jeer and mock him.

"It is I, Savlo-El, guardian of Miletus Emmanuel Christopoulos of the Great Lakes region."

The hellish concierge hopped off his beast and walked to the gate. It was then apparent that he had no eyes. "I know all guardians by voice. Answer me again by name and tell me the name of the silent guardian I hear flapping behind you."

"I am Savlo-El, the angel endowed with His graciousness and protection, and you will not know any other name."

"Oh, that Savlo, are you still sending us souls? You lose every soul you bring us," he said and laughed.

Milo's eyes widened as open as fear could permit.

"Well then, stay here a moment, say ten psalms or so if you please, you babbling fowl of heaven. I have grown to hate the sound of your voice," he said to the gatekeeper angel. "I've been instructed to make notice whenever you come, Savlo. An old friend wants to say some words to you."

He mounted the hell hound, jumped the stone fence, and galloped back behind the three toll houses that flanked a granite amphitheater filled with burning lava. All the aerial demons danced around the amphitheater. Apparitions could be seen standing in the fire pulling their ears off their heads to quell the sounds, only to find them grown back once they burned up.

Savlo stood tall, his gray wings spread to full extent. He looked like a great warrior full of the kind of wisdom that comes from fighting valiantly but losing battles. I feared for Milo that the demon spoke some truth about Savlo, but trusting in demonic words is never something to be done. The gatekeeper angel recited psalms in a minor tone, as we waited.

Savlo turned to me and said, "Once we enter the gate and hear the main accusation, you are to go to Kallistos and tell him." He turned to face the dancing demons again.

Milo looked up at Savlo and mouthed the words, "What am I looking at? This looks familiar."

"The demons have scrolls of all the unconfessed sins you have committed with your tongue; all the lies, idle speech, angry words, rumors, mockeries and using His name carelessly. They know the places you have said these things, and they share their sin scrolls with all the toll house demons. Once they have read all your unconfessed sins they use those details to transform what you see and hear and even perceive to feel. But not simply visions as you understand visions. They are spiritual realities. They use your mental representations to attack your soul. They are constructing a particular judgment of your life. They will make a case that you owe them something, a taxation of sorts. All the words you hear now are words that you have said over your whole life. They repeat them to each other. This is the place you first cursed another person, your parents. Do you remember?" Milo nodded and tried to speak, but couldn't.

"When you were a child, your parents brought you to Greece and you were separated from them. You called out to them but they didn't hear you. You were scared and then you cursed them and cried because you thought they abandoned you. It was the first time you cursed another image bearer and doubted your parents' love."

Milo dropped his head.

"Hey Milo, do you know why your father limps? It's because he hurt himself looking for you while you cursed him. You caused the limp," a filthy little demon said as he watched us, head pressed through the gate bars. Milo looked at Savlo.

"They keep detailed lists. Nothing is hid from them," Savlo said.

The demons started reciting conversations from Milo's life. "Marriage is the constant renegotiation of double standards...My wife is like a Corvette...Why don't you get a fucking job...God dammit, Nat..." They started to sing haunting rhymes with his words. On and on they echoed conversations and words he had said. Milo stared, silent and wide eyed, with his mouth agape.

Then thunder clapped so loudly that everything was silenced. Milo grabbed where his heart would be with one hand and started to sink, his stance giving way. From behind the lava pond of the amphitheater, riding a white unicorn, came a young man gentle and meek in appearance. He was dressed in all white garments and his face was beautifully symmetrical, yet strong. As he drew closer his eyes glistened and his mouth held a slight grin. Milo was instantly eased by his presence.

"Savlo, my old friend, it's good to see you again. I'll make sure to tell your other resident monkeys that you're here again to add to their company," he said with mockery in his tone.

Savlo was silent, undaunted by his words.

"Do you ever wonder what it would have been like if you would have come with us? You've sent so many of their kind to our houses that we actually enjoy seeing you. We consider you one of us, just without the benefits. What do you get for your obedience? Eternal sadness for the monkeys? All the lower heavens talk about you. Do you not care what they say? Do you not want the respect you deserve for the work you do? Why won't you come join me? I will put you in charge right under me as a duke over all the twenty toll houses."

"Join you? You should join me, for I remember you as you were truly created even though you have forgotten. I know who I am. Let me tell you who you really are," Savlo replied.

"Yes, we all know who you are, a failure with no accomplishments, no rank of honor worthy of your greatness, and a fumbling mockery with no one for you to control. I won't listen to your tired old message, servant of the seraphim."

He looked with growing anger at Savlo for seven psalms.

"Who's the watcher?" His gaze switched to me. "I do not recognize you. Have you escaped from the prison of watchers? No, that's impossible. You've been demoted to understudy a guardian? And under Savlo, no less." His laugh reverberated through the whole hive, shaking the stones. All the demons joined in.

"You must be the last watcher left to roam free. You are a forgotten kind, message-less and not trusted around the females." Another demon ran up to him and whispered in his ear. "Yes, you're correct, I recognize him now. You're the old watcher of Laodicea, but you are different. The Egotistical One has renamed you. What is your name and why are you here?"

"Silence, Dumah. Let us pass through, for this child of the Resurrection is true at heart," Savlo said.

Dumah laughed and said, "I beg to differ, and so do the sin scrolls. I have seen them. Many of our toll houses have much invested in him. He is more a part of our rebellion than even the watchers of old." He looked at Milo now. "Yes, you, Milo. I read you just wanted to have fun fucking another woman while your wife laid pregnant—insatiable lust. You're just like a watcher." Milo could not look at the powerful demon of old.

Dumah laughed again, snapped his hood over his head, and reared the unicorn. "I give you Miletus Emmanuel Christopoulos. Test him, tax him, feast on him, and take him for he is ours!"

His announcement thundered through the cosmos of the under-heavens. Cheers erupted deep in the distance from the dark unseen toll houses that lay ahead. Then Dumah rode off into the vastness beyond the amphitheater. The gate swung open, we entered, cir-cumventing the amphitheater, facing the three toll houses. The demons cleared space.

The swarm of dancing demons around the amphitheater began to chant the name of the hive general; Veltas, Veltas, in rhythm with drums. A light turned on in the top of the middle toll house, the tallest one. It resembled the monasteries built into the mountains of Greece on the coast of the Aegean Sea. Milo was gripped by fear as we led him to the edge of the amphitheater.

"Salesmen are the best liars," hissed the crowding demons. They pressed in against us and the constant murmuring of Milo's past words flowed like a filthy river of the most disgusting words in Eng-lish. Flies swarmed over Milo's head. The demons worked them-selves into a frenzy when the huge wooden door of the toll house swung open with a crash against the door well. The demons quieted to whispers. Out stepped Veltas.

He appeared light-skinned, taller than Milo by a foot, and had a gothic beauty to him. He wore the same gray formal wear familiar to highly successful men of Milo's time. His hair was long and black, draping around his face due to a severe widow's peak. His irises were deep purple and held a captivating gaze. His voice was smooth and assuring. "May I call you Milo?" he asked.

Milo nodded.

"Milo, I know how you must feel. You are a man possessing highly evolved verbal skills, like me." He pointed to himself, emphasizing the last two words, and smiled. "I would like to talk with you. If I grant you speech, will you accept? I mean, you want to talk, right?" Veltas nodded his head.

Milo nodded with him, bent over and seemed to dry heave for a moment. Then he said, "Thank you." Savlo dropped his head because Milo had failed to recognize his own sales tactics.

"Veltas, you have no large investment in him. He has told the truth more than he has lied. Let us pass," Savlo said.

The demon did not break his gaze with Milo but smiled at him. "Savlo, I think Milo wants to speak for himself. As far as having only a minor investment in his soul, I beg to differ. Milo, as you can see from my associates—we have the goods on you, right? I mean, look at these sin scrolls, they go on and on." He pointed to the sin scroll scribe, who was constantly trying to keep his arms around the scrolls fumbling out of his grasp.

The sin scroll scribe appeared as a human with no hair or discernable features except two black eyes and four hands, holding magnifying glasses and writing utensils. He seemed to be always trying to point to the words on the scroll.

Milo was more at ease as long as he kept eye contact with Veltas.

The demon came close to Milo and tried to put his arm around him, as if to comfort him and take him home. Savlo's wings flared open, the tips were like red fired razor metal, and severed Veltas's arm off. His whole appearance rippled deformity and from his facial expression, he felt pain. Veltas hissed at Savlo, stepped back, shook the stub of his severed limb and instantly replaced it. I had never seen Savlo's weapon before.

"He has spoken only blessings to his wife and daughter. Blessings from a pure heart," Savlo said.

"Yes, that is true, fowl, but it is easy to love those who love you."

The scribe pointed to an accusation.

Veltas spoke with the enthusiasm of a motivational speaker. "Except his mother, Helen—you were not very kind to her recently, and you were even angry with her, last you spoke. Looks like you cursed her, tsk, tsk, tsk. Milo, you've cursed, spoken idle words, and mocked people, like Rob the newly married and the homeless man, honestly, wanting some money. There is so much to celebrate here, and I say 'celebrate', because I agree with everything you have said and done."

"Milo, my boy, I think it was all justified. Especially the housing scheme you developed, the negotiations—not really lies, but half-truths. Right? It's all about perspective. 'At play in the gray,' I think you put it." He laughed. "That's my favorite line of all time." He looked at Savlo's gray wings and winked.

He continued, "It was part of your job. You had to provide for your family and exploit those people, right?" Veltas grew in size and a dry hot wind started to blow. "I admire you, really. You're a product of capitalistic evolution and have spoken so convincingly and skillfully in your life, I think that you would find a high-ranking place here," Veltas said.

Milo looked at all the demons, and fear silenced him again.

"Don't mind them. You're a great competitor and would do just fine in competition with them. Yes, trust your own words. With your wit and sharp double-talking ways, a valuable virtue here, you'll do just fine." He leaned to Milo and said, "Listen to me and I will sweeten you with a secret. Savlo has a list committed to memory, and you haven't been that bad of a guy in your life, so I'm going to cut to the chase, bottom-line it for you. You can appreciate that, being a successful real estate agent and all, right?"

Milo was confused and remained silent. Veltas became visibly angry. "I gave you the right to speak on your own behalf. You can at least give me the fucking respect to answer me with that sweet mouth of yours. Do you want me to bottom-line it for you?"

"Ye-yes," Milo answered.

"Good. See, that wasn't so hard. I have one question for you. You can lie or tell the truth; I'll be able to tell either way. I'm interested in what you have to say about Pastor Dan and the treasurer incident. Remember sheep number one forty three? Tell me your thoughts about that whole group of Bible thumpers, 'fucking scammers', as you so astutely called them."

Veltas motioned for the scribe to find the sin scroll with the unconfessed sins committed against this group of people. Savlo motioned me to make haste, speaking to my mind to tell Kallistos. I departed unnoticed by Veltas, or so I thought.

— • —

I found Kallistos watching over Natalie nap, as she was exhausted from the interment.

"Greetings, Kallistos. Milo is already at the first hive and in need of help." I told him all the events that had taken place so far.

"Take the tears of repentance and go back to Savlo. Be mindful of the different time streams. A day may be likened unto a thousand years to them."

I departed and reflected on the wisdom and foresight needed to match the experience of Kallistos and Savlo as I readied my will to guard the infant.

— • —

When I arrived, Veltas was winning a debate with Milo. Savlo helped and defended him against all his claims, except the speaking of evil against Pastor Daniel and the treasurer.

"Savlo, you blind bird, can you not see what the scribe has pointed out? This stupid lying monkey of yours—no offense, Milo, is on record saying the most anger filled words, twisting the events in such a way that even I'm impressed. My murder of crows outside the building reported everything."

Milo looked dejected, almost limp. I repositioned behind Savlo's right wing and slid the angelic vial of tears next to his hip. He reached back and took it.

"Let me see again exactly what was said. Do you have such records, or not?" Savlo said.

"Pfft, show him the last twenty-four hours of his words, scribe."

As the scribe laid out the scroll, Savlo sprinkled the tears of repentance over the surface. The ink was blotted out. The mute scribe pointed vigorously, throwing his four arms into the air, Savlo tossed the remains of the tears over the other scrolls. Veltas snapped his head around and grabbed a scroll from the scribe. It was blank. He furiously ripped open all the scrolls and the demons in the background began to gnash their teeth.

"What trickery is this, Savlo?" Veltas said.

"Tears of repentance and forgiveness from those offended," Savlo said.

Milo's hinderer appeared in his ragged garb, standing confused at the event that had just taken place. Milo recognized him this time, from his own funeral. The demon looked at Milo with such hatred that Milo drew close to me.

The gatekeeper angel appeared beyond the lava pool at the hive's exit gate and waved us over. Savlo escorted Milo past the first three toll houses. Milo looked back at the confused frenzy of demons and watched Veltas go back to his tower room. He turned off the light. The demons wailed.

Milo gathered enough courage and awareness to ask Savlo, "How did I get past them? I was guilty."

"You are guilty of many unconfessed sins. This will be the case with all the toll houses we will travel to," Savlo said.

"Well, I'll confess and repent of all my sins now. I'm guilty. You've watched me my whole life. There are greater sins than the ones I'm guilty of here." He was full of despair. "I am condemned to hell, aren't I, Savlo? I'll repent now. Don't take me to another toll house or hive or whatever—I've learned my lesson."

"Your time to repent is over. We will have to rely on the works of faith of those who love you to help you, now."

"How can they help me in such a place as this? They don't even know it exists. Send me back to tell them—to tell my wife."

"There is no going back for you, only going forward," Savlo said.

"I can't do this. I'm going to be alone in hell forever," he said and went limp as we travelled.

"Beloved image bearer, why do you not understand all that has been shown to you your whole life? You cannot do anything by yourself. You are never alone. Were you birthed by yourself? Were you raised alone? Were you baptized by your own doing? Did you feed yourself the Holy Eucharist? Your marriage was a co-mingling work of God with Natalie. Did you live alone? Did your sin involve others? Did you die alone?"

Milo listened but did not answer. The gatekeeper angel recited ten psalms.

"It's true, Milo, we will see whether you'll be held in the prison of your sins in these awful toll houses until the Last Day or be granted entrance into Paradise. My precious image bearer, to whom I've been yoked to since your baptism, you've never been alone but always cosmically connected to others beyond your understanding. Did your life keep rhythm with heaven or hell? That is what is being tested here."

He was quiet for a moment and started to ask another question. He was interrupted by Savlo, "One question per hive."

I smiled.

"Great Lent is about to start on earth. We will wait here for your return. Go," Savlo said to me.

ENTRY 16

"The Lord said, I and my Son will be united with them forever
in the paths of uprightness in their lives."

- Enoch 105:2

I arrived in Natalie's bedroom just moments after I left Savlo and Milo moving to the second hive. I have lived in creation's time stream for so many centuries I forgot how slowly it moved. Natalie was decorating herself in the bathroom mirror. Her face looked weary from crying. She was obeying Father Lazarus's instruction to go to the service that began Great Lent. Kallistos said nothing to me at first.

"As we approached the second hive, holding the fourth and fifth toll houses, Savlo said Great Lent must be starting, and then he sent me to you," I said.

"He is progressing quickly. We'll have to be quick too. Prepare yourself for when the sun sets, the bittersweet season of repentance begins with Forgiveness Sunday and every demon awakens," Kallistos explained.

I remembered monks would come in from the desert to the local gathering in Laodicea. They listened to hymns of the Resurrection one last time in case they did not live through Lent. At the end of the vesperal prayers, the children of the Resurrection would bow down to one another and ask for mutual forgiveness of the sins they had committed against each other through the previous year; merchants, embittered relatives, naughty children, slaves, masters, Romans and even their conquered foes would beg forgiveness from each other. It was something powerful to behold.

Natalie had gathered her things to leave and readied Sasha for their journey to Holy Resurrection when Kallistos halted me. "I am instructing you to keep guard at the nave's entry. Ready your weapon, for no demon is to prevent her from attending. Also, mind the separate side entry to the choir loft. Specialized devils enter through the choir loft every Sunday."

Kallistos hovered over the car, his wings almost swooping it up. I followed behind. As we traveled down Straight Street towards the parish temple, I saw a legion of demons taking form in a military regiment in front of the large wooden doors of the temple. Kallistos motioned me to disappear and take my post between the legion and the doors as Natalie parked the vehicle.

"A watcher, ha! So the rumors are true." Their leader came forward to address me when I appeared. He was dressed like his fighters, in black military gear. They all had smoking swords and boots dusting soot from the bowels of some lower level of hell. Their leader was muscled. His eyes glowed red and his face was that of a ferocious wolverine.

"They sent us here for a she-monkey, and she is guarded by a simple guardian and the last free watcher, brethren," he said.

The legion laughed with one guttural voice and they stamped their spears once with thundering unity.

"Did you hear that, Sasha? Thunder, it's gonna storm," Natalie said.

As she proceeded down the walkway, behind me appeared thirty one guardians from inside the nave, fiery swords drawn. I smiled at the leader.

"It won't be enough, bird man," he said.

Then from behind the Byzantine dome appeared the Principality of Grand Rapids. He took form as a giant grappler, at least one-hundred-and fifty feet high. He was bald, with a long jeweled black braid of hair falling from the back of his head to his waist. He towered over the dome of the temple. He radiated a bluish hue, had no wings and crouched in a pre-engagement stance. The legion of demon warriors all looked up at his immense presence and dared not make a move towards Natalie or Sasha and they began to pass through the center of the legion's formation.

I quickly left to check the side choir loft door. I returned to my post and saw the leader of the legion launch his fiery spear at Natalie's head.

Kallistos wrapped his wings around her as the smoldering spear hit; it pierced the shoulder base of his wing. He winced and was thrust to the ground.

As Kallistos fell, he discharged dozens of white lighted shards from the interior of his other wing. They stuck in the leg of the legion's leader. He bent to one knee. Both of the angels' spirit energy were damaged and were in pain.

The legion sprawled into attack posture when the Principality swung his great arm down and with one swipe flung the first three rows of them a great distance away. He stepped forward, crouched down face-to-face with their leader. The energy between them cracked thunder and flashed lightening as he said with cosmic authority that reverberated through the lower heavens, "Stand down, demon; the King of Glory sends me."

"Who is the King of Glory?" he hissed back.

"The Lord mighty in battle, destroyer of hades and Incarnate for all time, demands you stand down."

The legion went screaming with insane fury and disbanded at his response. Their leader backed away ailing, for his spirit energy was severely damaged by Kallistos' darts of light.

Natalie walked into the candlelit stone nave. A votive candle box flickering light caught Sasha's gaze and the smell of incense wafted around them. Father Luke stood in front of the altar, vested in purple, arms raised in prayer to the Most High. Natalie was safe under the wings of many protectors. With Kallistos's permission, I took my place next to him at the back door inside of the temple.

"Are you badly injured?"

He did not answer me.

"Who was that demon?"

"I do not know his true name, but he is known in this realm as Aneurism and he kills many image bearers."

"Kallistos, a Principality fought for us. This is rare," I said intrigued at this development.

"Stay vigilant; your watcher skills are required of you now."

Natalie was greeted by Helen, who swallowed up Sasha and whisked her away to join her husband. She smiled at Natalie, giving her permission to roam free and worship. Helen was sensitive to when Natalie needed space as a wife, mother, and now a widow.

The Vesper service hymns were chanted in Greek, observing the proper tones set forth by the angels of old. The prayers were read in English. Father Luke was a good and pious man, who had spent time on the Holy Mount Athos, and executed his liturgical duties with vigilance. As was their custom at the end of the service, the small gathering of thirty-three image bearers began to line up and down the center aisle. They were surrounded by lit brass candle-stands, icons, and angels in the domed nave.

The priest faced the front of the line, bowed his head, extended his hand, and then embraced the first parishioner, kissed him on one side of the cheek and said, "Forgive me, brother, of all my offenses."

The parishioner replied, "I forgive you."

Then they switched to the other cheek, giving a holy kiss, and the parishioner said, "Forgive me Father, of all my offenses." The priest shrived, "I forgive you, as God forgives us all." The first parishioner then took his place next to the priest, and the next person greeted the priest in the same manner. Then she stepped to the left, and with the same exchange of forgiving words greeted their fellow parishioner. The beautiful line continued to bind their souls in love and loosen the chains of sins which shackled them.

I heard shrieks outside, and drifted to the side window and peered out. The angels inside were rejoicing and the aerial demons outside were beside themselves with anger; seeing all their year's work dissipate with simple tears and kisses of image bearers forgiving one another.

I resumed my position by Kallistos' side and saw Natalie take her place at the end of the line. She approached Father Luke, who had saved some tears for her. She bowed down on one knee on the hard marble floor of the solea, prevented only by her pregnancy from falling in full prostration and said, "Forgive me, Father, and my husband, for all our sins against you and all the other members of this community."

The priest bent down and helped her up. "Child, you don't have to kneel down. Any gesture of humility is acceptable."

She looked at him with the gift of tears in her eyes.

"Of course, I forgive you and Milo of any and all your sins. Forgive me, sister, for not being the 'good shepherd' to you or Milo; leaving the ninety-nine to go after you."

She grabbed his hand and kissed it. "May God forgive us all," she said and stepped to the left and knelt again. She knelt to every person in line, including Helen, Nico, and Sasha. Each person helped her up and forgave her and Milo.

The service ended with the protopsalti chanting resurrection hymns as the parishioners left the nave in prayerful silence to their homes. Natalie went to the bathroom and Kallistos motioned for me to follow. She entered the stall, unfastened her maternity pants, and sat down. Her one knee was bruised and bloodied from her kneeling, as the skin had been bruised and given way to a slight tear. She took some toilet paper and dabbed the blood until the wound had dried. She exited the stall, washed her hands, and leaned in close to the mirror to wipe her eyes. She turned and accidently missed the waste basket leaving the blood stained tissue on the floor. I turned to follow her but Kallistos stood in my way, pointed to the tissue. Do you know how to transport it?"

"Yes."

"Then take the tissue and go to Savlo. Natalie and the child will be fine." He saw hesitation in my eyes, to which he replied, "We had a Principality here tonight. They will be safe."

I left the stratosphere with great trans-dimensional speed.

ENTRY 17

Sins of the Stomach: Toll Houses 4 & 5

I rejoined Savlo at the second hive standing with Milo starring at the hive gate. Beyond the gate we saw an abandoned city street; full of broken windows, trash littered gutters, and street lights blinked on and off with power surges. At the end of the street was a dilapidated Catholic cathedral with inverted crosses and two smaller lit toll houses, one on each side.

A sign read "Sins of the Stomach," and was hanging by one nail, affixed to a half-opened gate. The gatekeeper angel opened the gate all the way and we walked through, down the middle of the street.

"Looks like the French Quarter in New Orleans. I won a contest once and went during Mardi Gras," Milo said, and his face saddened as he remembered his time of debauchery there.

"I know, five years ago. It's how you started Lent that year," Savlo said.

An old woman figure, half naked, with bruised gray flesh, stumbled out of one of the bars about a psalm's distance ahead of us. She stopped in the middle of the street, took a slurk from an elongated green plastic bottle and recognized us. She spat the liquid out and screamed, "Milo's home!"

The street enlivened, lights turned on, music began to play in a bar. Hideous looking demons, bloated and fat, in revealing clothing, with reddened, bulbous facial features, populated the sidewalks. They were all eating, drinking, belching and acting like rowdy sexually aroused drunkards. They closed in behind us, pushing us forward toward the end of the street. As we got closer to the street's end, we saw a lamb being roasted alive, bleating in pain. A sign fastened to the grill read, "Wednesday's Special." The other side had an omelet chef carving slices off a live pig tied to a pole, standing in its own urine and blood. Its sign read, "Friday's Special."

"Can I take your order, Milo? There's always room for dessert later, remember—to fill in the gaps?" the chef said, mockingly, as his belly burst open, spilling entrails onto the sizzling grill in front of him.

"The Nautilus," is all Milo said.

From behind the left toll house, "Gluttony" scratched on the wall, came a raised platform carried by four Nordic men. Reclining on the platform was a demon who looked exactly like Milo, but engorged by several hundred pounds. He wore a bathrobe that covered nothing. He leaked urine and had no shame.

"Milo, welcome home, don't worry about the piss, I'll clean that up later," he said.

"This is not my home," Milo replied.

"Oh, really? We have your favorite foods and you can eat until you stomach bursts." He laughed, his drink bubbling out of his mouth, and pointing to the omelet chef. "Literally, as you can see. Say, are ya hungry? Ah, doesn't matter, we eat all the time here."

Milo doubled over, dry heaving. "Oh, I have stomach pangs," was all he could muster. The surrounding demons all laughed at him.

"Yes, you've never felt hunger like this before. Set me down, you bastards, and get the hive general," he ordered.

The other toll house door slowly creaked open. On its mantle was the word, "Sloth." Soon, out stepped an emaciated figure that looked like Milo with no muscle tone at all, a skeleton with loose flesh draped over him. He snapped his fingers and a lion bounded to him. He sat on the lion's back and it sauntered down towards us.

"Greetings, Milo. Sorry I'm late in welcoming you. I can see you have traveled far and probably need some rest. We can find someone to do something for you—well, really to do everything for you here. 'Eat, drink, and be merry, for tomorrow you die,' is our motto here. Wait, you're already dead, so I guess the hard part's over, right?" he said.

"Let us pass," Savlo demanded.

Everyone laughed. "What's your hurry?" A voice asked from the darkened cathedral doorway in front of us. Out stepped the hive general. "Milo, my name is Mr. Nisroc, and my two friends are showing you true versions of yourself, Milo. Our sin scroll is long because of your habits and your profession."

He came into the street light's ray, appearing again as a petite balding man with black lifeless eyes. He wore a three-piece suit with several pocket watches and carried a food menu and a golden calculating machine.

"I constantly calculate time by your monkey standards, and I have figures that prove you have spent the sum of your life wallowing in gluttony and slothfulness. So this is home for you. This is the reward of your indolent life. I assure you my calculations are precise." He grew indignant.

Milo looked confused and mumbled, "I worked hard in my profession."

Mr. Nisroc grinned and said, "Oh, benefiting from financial maneuvering at the hard labor of others is not work, but a very sophisticated form of slothfulness. And as for your recent habit, you didn't even have enough gusto to bend to your knees in prayer on Sundays. Remember, you laid on the sofa watching football, golf and food shows. I love the sports of the monkeys, so distracting and delusional." He made a note on a menu and handed it to the scribe, who now was present with one long scroll.

"You mean, church? I went to church. Tell him, Savlo," Milo said.

"Yes, you baboon, we know you went to a service or two, but you had no time for the cultivation of virtues in the soul, the real work of so-called 'Christians.' I don't blame you, though. Fasting, praying, bowing down, giving alms, it's all very tiresome. Why not follow your stomach? Do what you want to do. Let your stomach be your mistress and sloth be your spouse—you can relax here with us."

"I don't understand," Milo said.

Mr. Nisroc's forehead furrowed and the veins in his skull were visible as he raged, "Look, you poor fat slob, this is what your soul looks like." He pointed to each of the versions of Milo. "This is who you really are, on the inside. Time after time you exhibited wastefulness, laziness, opportunistic exploitation of others, and selfishness, with no semblance of self-control. You epitomized gluttony with every lunch buffet you frequented, and slothfulness with every yawn while others prayed. Welcome home, you fat, lazy monkey."

I handed Savlo the tissue with Natalie's blood. He stepped over to the scribe and wiped away the sins of the stomach. Then he turned to the demon, Nisroc and said, "Every transaction Milo closed, a portion went to either a homeless shelter or a soup kitchen in town."

"True, but he still doesn't even know that. He was too lazy to read his broker contract. The company did that for him. I checked for his initials on that section of the contract myself, remember, at the office, when you snubbed me?"

"It's still a good work untainted by pride, and most valuable. The Incarnate One said to not let the left hand know what the right hand was doing," Savlo said.

"Oh, shut the hell up and don't preach to me with all that 'incarnate one' talk. This one's still a slothful, sinful monkey lacking any effort in virtues, so he will rest with us. It is settled and we are finished with you mighty Savlo and company," he said looking at me.

"His wife bled asking for forgiveness with prostrations for him at his parish. She and his unborn son fast for him. Now, let us pass," Savlo retorted.

The demon spun around and looked at the cathedral behind him, then faced us again. He seized the sin scroll from the scribe. The scroll was clean and Nisroc's time pieces were twirling out of time. Nisroc's lips tightened and he back-handed the sin scroll scribe across the face and yelled, "This is all fucked up. Can't you bastards do anything right?"

We were given passage, and as we passed by the cathedral, Milo looked in. He saw Natalie prostrating in the line of image bearers and looked at Savlo and asked, "How can this be?"

"Both good and bad deeds echo into eternity, Milo."

Milo stood at the window of the temple building, outside of time and space, remote viewing the events, unwilling to leave. Savlo instructed me mentally to depart for Kallistos. I went by way of the street.

The demons all watched me as I sped past. I could hear them whispering, "A watcher…look at him." I approached the gate and Mr. Nisroc stepped out from the shadows, still fiddling with his spinning pocket watches.

"So you must be a busy little bird—flying back and forth helping this monkey out. I'm curious, why are you so involved?"

I stopped in front of him and was silent, hand on my staff, ready to strike.

"No need for that, watcher. I have nothing against you. What did you say your name was again?"

"I didn't say."

"Oh, so you can talk? I wonder who sent you? Was it Gabriel, Uriel? You are quick to brandish your weapon. Was it Michael? Hmm, you are under the command of Savlo, and you go back and forth to Kallistos. It was Raphael who has you involved; way over your head, don't you think? I mean, having to watch all the dirty little sins of the monkeys, especially the sex," he said and giggled. "Can you at least tell me why, Milo, is worthy of your watchfulness? There's such a buzz around here about you. People are dying to know—no pun intended."

Savlo appeared directly behind Mr. Nisroc. He jumped, dropping his pocket watch. "Oh shit, Savlo you startled me." He bent down and picked up his watch. "I was just talking to your friend, harmless idle talk, you know, he's a watcher and I like watches—so you know, just some casual conversation."

I stepped around him and made my way to Kallistos and Natalie.

ENTRY 18

"Love and doubt have never been on speaking terms."

- Kahlil Girbran

It was the next morning and the baby's restlessness woke Natalie early. For an hour she watched the ceiling fan spin while Sasha lay nestled beside her. We could not detect any prayers, and her thoughts did not appear to wander. She just lay still.

The phone rang. It startled her and stirred Sasha.

"Hello?" she said.

"Natalie Christopoulos, this is Father Lazarus." We could hear his loud voice as she held the phone away from her ear.

She sat up. "Yes, Father, what is it?"

"Are you still in bed?"

"Um—yes, Father. Why do you ask?"

"There is no rest for the wicked."

She smiled at her joke turned against her.

"Did you go to the Forgiveness service?"

"Yes, it was really powerful, and I—"

"Good. I have some more work for you to do to help your husband. It will require us to meet for more explanation."

"Father, I'm so tired and still trying to work through everything. I need some time. Can it wait?" she asked.

"No. Meet me in one hour at the Eagle and—no, it's called the Rabbit Room Café now—on Wealthy Street. Do you know it?"

"I think so. But in an hour, Father?"

"Yes, one hour."

She sniffed and steeled her resolve. "I guess I'll rest when I'm dead, hey?"

"No you won't, dear, there's no time for idle talk. Forty days, that's all we have." He hung up.

Natalie got out of bed and readied herself to meet Father Lazarus.

— • —

Natalie and Sasha arrived at the coffee shop and saw Father Lazarus sitting at the table by the front window, coffee in hand.

"Are you meeting with that older homeless guy?" the barista asked.

"Oh, yes. He's not homeless, though, but then again maybe he is in a way." She smiled and asked, "Why?"

"He pre-paid for your drink, but it's not enough to cover the little girl's muffin."

Natalie laughed, and looked at Father Lazarus, who did not return the affection. Instead he just stared wild-eyed at Sasha as she took much too big of a bite out of her muffin. They walked to his table.

"Good morning, Father. Are you alright?" Natalie asked.

"We've talked about the inconsequential state of my being before. Is she baptized?"

Natalie took her seat and Sasha sat next to her, mouth already stained with chocolate from the muffin, and answered, "No, not yet."

"Not yet is too late. Now listen to me, dear. The next forty days are crucial. Have you seen any angels?"

"No. Am I supposed to? You keep asking me that. I did find a book by Billy Graham about them at home. I could read it—maybe I don't recognize the angels."

"Do you still feel the 'energy,' as you call it?"

"Oh yes, it's almost constant."

"Good, good. Stay attuned to that. I have a very special pilgrimage for you to go on as soon as you can."

"Pilgrimage?"

He looked at Sasha and smiled at the mess she was making now. "Bring her with you. It will be good for the nuns to meet her."

"Where?"

"There is a convent of nuns and a priest near Detroit. It's called Holy Transfiguration monastery. I want you to call ahead and then go and request an audience with Father Arseny," he said.

"And say what?"

"Tell him I sent you and that you're requesting him to pray for your husband and offer a commemoration for him—by name, very important—by his given and baptismal name. Ask him to mention it every time a liturgy is prayed there."

"That's it?"

"That's all you will need to say. He is a very holy man—clairvoyant, so he will know all that he needs to know by this request."

"This seems a little odd, Father."

"Stay and pray with them for whatever service they offer that day, and give them a large amount of money on Milo's behalf. You have money, right?"

"Seriously? So I pay them to pray?"

"No. They'll pray anyway. They always pray. The giving of the money benefits you and Milo more than them. They will use it to benefit others without you taking credit."

They sipped their drinks and both watched Sasha for a moment.

I said, "Kallistos, I know this monk, he was very active during the Second World War and traveled through my region. He was imprisoned for many years for being strong and vocal about his faith. I didn't know he was still alive."

"He is alive and well. Thank God Almighty for living saints," Kallistos said.

"Oh yes, one more thing. Go to every service offered by Father Job during Lent," Father Lazarus said with a stern look.

"Every service? That guy is a little intense about services, Father, and they're long."

"As much as you physically can endure—it's important work. Be strong, Natalie. And go pray for your guardian angel today. It's their day in the cycle of prayers."

"Okay, Father—Father, will you go with me to some of the services?"

He looked at her for several moments and said, "I must be going." He stood up, put his hand on Sasha's head and blessed her, then headed out the door with his staggering gait.

When he was outside, standing in the window, he turned and made eye contact with Natalie and waved his finger at her. "No rest for the wicked," he mouthed, then half smiled and walked away.

Kallistos sent me to check on Savlo and Milo and tell him about the pilgrimage.

ENTRY 19

Sins of the Hand: Toll Houses 6, 7 & 8

'Good' was all Savlo said concerning the news from Kallistos. We left the remote viewing, and progressed to what seemed higher and higher to Milo, towards the third hive. Milo looked at the gate-keeper angel and tried to discern his appearance again, as he listened to the psalms being murmured. "Why am I getting hotter the farther up we go?" he dared to ask the gatekeeper angel.

"The Ancient of Days is the same to all. His love is either experienced as light or a fiery heat," he replied.

"I want His light, not His heat," Milo said.

"God is the same to all, a light that illumines the saints and a heat that purifies the sinners." Milo dropped his head and he lost even more sense of time and space.

In the distance we heard music playing. Milo perked up. It was upbeat, rhythmic music. "I used to listen to this music. It pumped me up before sales appointments," Milo said.

As we drew closer, the blackness shielding the view now turned to gray smoke and a bright sunny day in a great neighborhood appeared before us. It was an upscale gated community with a sign that read, "Sins of the Hand." The demons all appeared as humans doing human activities. We stopped at the gate and waited.

"Hey, these are all the houses that I've sold. There's my bank. There's my real estate office. Yes, there's the first house I sold and there's the last house I sold over there. There's Karen Ludlow with her three kids playing in the front yard. Is this where all my good deeds are remembered? I mean I'm not all bad, am I?" he asked Savlo.

Off to the right three toll houses stood, resembling tall bank buildings. They were named "Stealing," "Avarice," and "Usury." Out of the revolving doors emerged three enormous wolves, two gray and the center one black. They walked towards Milo as he sidled up to Savlo. They all shape-shifted, at once, into two women and a man, dressed in business attire, all with pale white skin. His head was webbed all over with dark veins. The sin scribe lagged in the rear, holding only one scroll and a sheet of paper.

The demon spoke, "Greetings Milo. My name is Mammon. My associates are, well, let's just call them 'Left Hand' and 'Right Hand.' We see you're here to fulfill your promissory note. This is most honorable of you."

"What promissory note?" Milo asked.

"You signed a pact with us seven years ago, at the seminar."

He pointed down the road to the hotel where the Secrets of Success banner hung. "You said, and I quote—" he grabbed the note from the scribe and snapped it crisply. "I would give anything to have this kind of success."

"Yes, but I said that to myself," Milo said.

"We heard you and we delivered. It's a bona fide contract."

"How?" he asked and looked to Savlo for a defense.

Mammon looked to Left Hand and gave consent for her to answer, "There are certain things that make a pact binding, and you have not only fulfilled them but incorporated them into your life quite habitually. What is the secret of your success in real estate, Milo? How would you really answer that question? Would you write it down on a piece of paper and in the morning thank your subconscious?"

Milo was silent.

"Who do you think was answering you? I'll tell you; we were." They all smiled with such smugness.

"I wish to review the terms of the pact. Give me that promissory note," Savlo said.

"Fuck you. We heard what you did at the other toll houses when you got your filthy feathers on the scrolls," Mammon said, turning a shade darker. His eyes glowed a dim red.

"Where's your baptismal cross, Milo?" Mammon took a step closer to Milo.

Milo dropped his head. "I sold it."

"Actually, you pawned it. I have the receipt in my pocket, yes, you exchanged the symbol of your faith for the great and mysterious secrets of success."

Savlo pointed to Mammon's face, which angered him. "Mammon, there are certain criteria required for pacts. You know the burden of proof is on you, demon."

Mammon straightened his suit coat and gained his composure. "I see, Savlo, you've developed a shrewdness to your thinking. You have an edge, Longsuffering One. Well, shrewdness is a fine vice to practice here; at least it served Milo well in his life. I also sense a negotiation forthcoming. We've made deals here before, Savlo, and if I remember correctly, it didn't go so well for your souls." He then looked at Milo and said, "I can appreciate the fact that you didn't get to choose your guardian angel, so I'll ask you; are you sure you want this bird negotiating for you? Is he the best representation for you in this transaction? I mean, this isn't some house you're flipping to resell, Milo. This is your eternal home. You need a good agent. Hell is a buyer's market," Mammon said.

Milo remained silent.

Mammon motioned to Left Hand to search the sin scroll for a particular transaction. "There are so many sins, but find something really incriminating, a love of money, stealing and usury. Those are the sins of the hand that we judge here, Milo, my boy."

"Proof of pact, Mammon," Savlo demanded.

"Well, pacts are not an exact science anymore, but let's see what we have here as far as terms and conditions are concerned. We need a denial of the Great Ego of Old—that's what we call him here, Milo." He winked at him. "We need the mocking of the symbols—others call them sacraments, but let's not start a debate of terms. We also need a rebaptism and a declaration to the King of Hell and—oh, let's see, a worshipful self-deluding daily devotion to our ways."

He smiled at Milo and said, "It's all here in the fine print of your morning ritual, my man. 'The renegotiation of double standards.' Ah, what a beautiful expression, Milo."

"This is double-talk. He still had faith and participated in Bible study assemblies," Savlo said.

"Everything is double-talk in negotiations, Savlo. But to appease your forensic interest, we do have in our records that he pawned his baptismal cross—ouch."

Right Hand hissed, "Judas."

Mammon continued, "It had been years since he gagged down the wafer and wine. No confession to a priest and a wonderful history of cursing and keeping oaths in that Name. Oh, and sexual relations with that woman, Ms. Maneyu. So that's a monumental denial by actions and its own problem in itself, but there you have it, the basic requirements of a modern-day pact with a Devil." Mammon licked his lips with his wolf tongue.

"The image bearers often lose their way. It's a journey that ebbs and flows with faith and doubt. The Almighty One is longsuffering and forgiving, even for you, Mammon."

Mammon growled with arms raised and the music stopped. The sky turned dark and the demons appearing as humans all stopped and looked at us.

Mammon clenched his jaw and said, "Savlo, you're a witness to this, and so are you, watcher. After denying he who is not named, and forsaking his practices and sacramental protections, he rejected the advice and concerns voiced by his wife, parents, priests, preachers and the promptings of his own guardian angel. He willfully accepted the mentorship of the self-help, subconscious manipulators we sent to him. He stood in the mirror worshipping his own image with knowledge of good and evil and every day declared Lucifer's great revolutionary proclamation, 'I want to be like the Most High.'"

There was silence for a moment as he calmed down and stretched his neck. "Although he was more poetic, 'captain of my own soul.'" He winked at Milo again.

Milo cowered in fear.

"What's the matter, Cap'n?"

"I thought I was doing some good by helping people buy houses," Milo said.

"Like any good businessman, I gotta call bullshit on that. What were your true intentions, Milo, to help people?"

Left Hand whispered, "Thievery."

Right Hand whispered, "Fraudulent Usury."

Mammon pointed to the aerial demon projecting itself as Karen Ludlow in the front lawn of her house. She now looked gaunt and starved. She picked up her baby, tore its ear off with her teeth, and ate it. The other children ran in fear, screaming, "She's going to eat us too." Milo covered his eyes.

"You call that helping people? She bit off more than she could chew with that mortgage, and you knew it. Telling her to go without a pizza once a month—shame on you Milo. But you got paid, along with the lender, and it was win-win for you and him. I for one thought it showed astute business acumen, but I am partial to predatory lending."

"He donated a little bit of money from every closing to a charity, or bought his clients gifts," Savlo said, trying to confuse Mammon.

"Ha! Business referral fodder. He did that to get more business and make himself look good. Twenty-five dollar gift certificates for every thirty two thousand dollars in commission—that really helps people out, Savlo—oh, such compassion."

"Still, it's proof of almsgiving, and the Just Judge is the only one who judges the intent of the heart, just like he will judge you, my fallen friend."

Mammon gnashed his teeth at Savlo. "It doesn't matter. We have a pact. He denied the divine bastard in word and deed and placed all faith in himself, just like his marketing material illustrates." He pointed to a billboard showing Milo appearing to stand on water— a marketing campaign he used. "Every morning he proclaimed his self-actualizing faith and baptized himself ritualistically in that shower, repeating his mantras. He then put his faith into action by calling on the universal law of attraction to serve him the secrets of success. Intention, consent, and action. That is a bona fide pact any way you look at it, and I'm frankly tired of this negotiation, fowl," Mammon said and came close to Milo's face. His skin turned black with coarse hair, his nose became a snout, and the Wolf of Souls revealed himself, snarling and drooling foul smelling foam.

"Mammon, heel," Savlo commanded. "Let's review his transactions to see if there are any actions of thievery and fraudulent usury. I'm familiar with your double talk and I think you're trying to sell us a contract that has no validity."

Mammon moved back, keeping his wolf head, and led us down the street towards the houses. He snapped his fingers in the air and several demons, hideous black bat creatures, flew out from the toll house roof tops holding files. They had copies of all Milo's transactions, and we walked through the neighborhood starting with the very first house Milo had sold. Savlo refuted Mammon's accusations. His memory and skill was phenomenal. Milo watched silently as the two angels argued the most detailed points of human law with great negotiating prowess.

Savlo then spoke to my mind, "Go tell Kallistos what has transpired at the third hive. Tell him of the meeting with the lender at the bank concerning Milo's last transaction, the Ludlow file. He will know what to do."

I could sense the faith Savlo was placing in me. I bowed and left.

Right Hand made note of my departure. I was gaining popularity in these wicked and depraved toll houses and growing more uncomfortable with the attention.

ENTRY 20

"Alms doth deliver from death, and shall purge away all sin."

- Tobit 12:9

I arrived at the Christopoulos home, during a thunder storm. It was morning and Kallistos was on high alert. The demonic attention around the house was elevated. Demons were trying to infest and oppress every aspect of Natalie's life. Whenever love is shone, evil seeks to distort its reception and frustrate the image bearers. It has always been this way, and was so especially now.

Kallistos and I positioned very close to her and I told him of Milo and the Ludlow file. Natalie was busy with domestic duties and Sasha was watching television. The phone rang.

"Hello," Natalie answered.

"Hello, Natalie. This is John from Open Door Realty."

"Hi, John."

"Natalie, once again, I'm so sorry for your loss. I didn't get a chance to tell you at the funeral, but it was always a joy working with Milo. How are you doing?"

"Oh, it's been trying. Thanks for asking. I haven't cleared his desk yet, have I? I'm sorry."

"Please don't apologize. We've not touched a thing and won't until you're ready. I hate to bother you so soon, but the reason I'm calling actually has to do with a transaction Milo was involved in. We're missing the file from his desk and were wondering if he kept some files at home. It's a client named Karen Ludlow who bought a house on Silver Street."

"I can check his desk, John. Is there a problem?"

"Well, it's nothing you have to be concerned with, just some final details we have to wrap up with an audit."

"An audit? That can't be good."

"Like I said, it's really nothing to worry about. We can handle it here at the company."

Kallistos leaned in and spoke to her.

"John, Milo always spoke very highly of you, especially about your sincerity and honesty. So, I need to know something about him."

There was a long pause before Natalie continued, "Was my husband an honest agent? John, don't be quiet now. I need to know this." Her voice was firm.

"Natalie, to my knowledge, Milo was above board on all his deals. They were technically complicated but legal, except this last one. There are some questions about it, which if we had his file, I'm sure would be cleared up. I'm positive it would be."

"Listen to me carefully. You're not showing any disrespect to my husband by sugar-coating anything. I'm making you tell me. It's important for me to know the whole truth about Milo."

There was another long pause.

"Come on, John. You know me. What's the problem?"

"Okay, but again, I'm sure this will be cleared up once we see the file. We're not sure how or if it involved Milo, but there is a predatory fraudulent lending accusation against us from Hillside Bank."

"Well, that's our personal bank, so we should be able to find out whatever we want," she said.

"Oh, your personal bank—that's one thing we had hoped it didn't involve."

"Why?"

"Well, there are certain rules that we have to follow and one major one is we cannot be involved in the financing of the buyers we represent. For example, we can't give the buyer money to buy the home. This is what is being questioned."

"Okay. Well, let me see if I can find the file, and how about I drop by after lunch and you can fill me in more?" she said.

"Natalie, there is no reason for you to be involved. It's a company issue now."

"That's where you're wrong. It is deeply personal to me. Please don't deny a widow the opportunity to know the last decisions her husband made."

"I feel horrible, now that I called," John said.

"Don't. I'll see you soon."

— • —

Natalie dropped Sasha off at Helen's then after a quick check in a cemetery for Father Lazarus, traveled to Open Door Realty. She walked into an office full of pointing and whispering.

As she passed the title office, Lilly jumped up to greet her. "Natalie?" she said and leaned out her office door.

"Yes?"

"Hi again. I'm Lilly, remember me? We met at the wake but that was such a hectic day, I don't blame you for forgetting."

"I know who you are, Lilly." Natalie was stern-faced.

"I see you're *still* pregnant?" She reached to touch Natalie's stomach again. Natalie stepped back.

"What can I do for you, Lilly?"

"Well, how about you stop by my office before you leave? I have something to tell you."

Natalie and Lilly's eyes locked in a stare, and neither blinked. Natalie turned and walked away to find John's office. Kallistos was prompting aggressively, but Natalie's gait was energized with anger.

John stepped out of his office and greeted her with a delicate embrace.

"Natalie, so good to see you—please come in. Sit down." John shut the door behind her.

"I have the file for you. It looked pretty typical to me," she said. "But maybe your eye is better than mine."

He took the folder and paged through it. With Kallistos' hand on her shoulder she was able to concentrate on this issue.

"Milo always said that agents were bottom-line kind of people, so what's the bottom line here? I can take it, John."

He smiled, looked at the file again and then said, "Well, the loan officer for this last transaction was abruptly fired. Apparently, this Karen Ludlow is a single mother, and due to the nature of her employment it was a challenge to document her income. She needed to have a certain amount of money in a bank account as a reserve before the lender would clear the file for a closing. The day before the closing, her name showed up on a bank account with enough money to meet the qualifications."

"Okay. So what's the problem?"

John could not read her mood. He looked down, stalling the conversation. His guardian then appeared and prompted him. Kallistos stood behind Natalie and put his hand on her back. It was the confrontation with Lilly that caused her to speak tersely with John.

"The problem is that she was named on a joint account with you and Milo."

Natalie processed this information for a moment.

"Was he having an affair with her?"

"No, of course not. I'm not saying anything like that, Natalie. Milo loved pay days. This particular week would have been his fourth closing and I think he just got a little too creative."

"So what's going to happen?" Natalie asked. Kallistos stepped back from her.

"Well, since the house was owned by Milo on paper, legally, for that day and now he is—I think the bank is going to disqualify her from the loan and take the house back. It's all very confusing and what Milo was doing is even more complicated," John explained.

"Can they do that? I mean, I'm the inheritor for everything of Milo's."

"Who knows what the banks can do nowadays, but I wouldn't doubt it."

"She was a single mother, you said, right?"

"Yep."

"John, who are you working with on the bank's end?"

"The branch manager."

"Give him a call and see if we can drive over and meet him," Natalie said.

"Why?"

"I'd like to discuss a solution."

"Natalie, you don't have to do that."

"Just call him and see what you can do. I'll be right back, I need to visit the ladies room."

She walked out and went to the restroom. She stood in front of the mirror looking at herself, taking several deep breaths. "Milo, what have you done?" she whispered.

"I know one more thing he's done that you can't fix. I'm late," said a voice from a closed stall.

"I'm sorry?" Natalie said.

"I'm late, and you said you knew who I was, so I assume you're a smart girl and can figure it out."

Tears rolled down Natalie's face and her lips quivered.

"Child support from any life insurance policy is expected. I'm told you're an honorable woman, and that's an honorable request considering the shame your husband has brought to me and now my bastard orphaned child."

Natalie stormed out.

Kallistos and I stood in front of the mirror. He shone, filling the room with angelic splendor, and instructed me to look at her only in the mirror.

"Lilleth, come forth!" he demanded.

The door of the stall slammed open without being touched and there behind us, reflected in the mirror, stood the ancient succubus, rubbing her lower stomach. Her voluptuous cleavage mounded up toward her serpentine face.

"Greetings Kallistos, you beautiful bird," she hissed.

"What evil have you done here?"

She looked at me, laughing. "Ooh, the watcher, I've been dying to ask you if she is carrying yours."

"Silence, succubus—by threat of Archangel Raphael, I establish a hedge of protection around her and forbid you contact with her from this day forward," Kallistos said.

She recoiled and hissed at us. I stamped my staff and the blade appeared and Kallistos's wings shimmered. She walked out of the stall, shape-shifted back into her womanly form of Lilly, and then stood right between us. She slathered her lips with bright red paint, and looked at both of us in the reflection. She puckered and kissed the air. "Don't get all hot and bothered, my little birdies, it's all in good fun," she said, then sauntered out.

We left, found Natalie and hovered above her vehicle as she followed John to the bank.

"I witnessed her and Milo conjugate. I sensed her evil then, but Savlo didn't recognize her," I said.

"Her presence is hard to discern now. She was seen by all in the Garden and with the other watchers—but now, in secret, she possesses and transforms host bodies of image bearers with traces of Nephilim ancestry. She has mastered the dark deceptive wiles of seduction and illusion. I didn't know for sure until she opened the door."

"Will she stay away? Do we really have the power to bind her?" I asked.

"No, not by ourselves, but she got what she wanted, so I suspect we will not see her again in this dimension for quite some time. But she is most devious and will remember you. She has a history with your kind, and that is why I suspect she chose to take Milo's seed."

"Divine intrigue?" I asked.

"Worse, demonic intrigue," he answered. Kallistos then positioned inside the car and helped Natalie regain her peace. She was distraught with emotion, but Kallistos's connection with her was strong.

— • —

Natalie pulled into the parking lot. John waited for her and held the door for her and they were escorted to the office of Jeff Vanderhoef, the branch manager.

"Hello, Mrs. Christopoulos—John, finally nice to meet you face to face," he said, sitting down across from them at his large glass desk. "Mrs. Christopoulos, I'm sorry for your loss, and John has told me you are aware of our situation. I must tell you, we have remedies for this type of problem, and really don't need to involve you any further."

"I appreciate the gesture, I really do, but I am here to offer you a business proposition."

"Okay."

"You sell mortgages all the time, right?"

"Yes," he said.

"Well, I would like to buy this particular mortgage from your bank."

John looked at Natalie and said, "Nat, what are you doing? This is rash. What's done is done."

"John, don't be emotional. 'It's just business,' isn't that what you preach to your agents?"

"Yes, but—"

Natalie took control of the conversation and said, "Jeff, I would like to buy the mortgage from your bank. Now, if you look at my accounts you will see enough money to buy it. In fact, there should be enough money to cover it plus any fees the bank may assess."

"Well, there's a prepayment penalty of one percent—"

"Jeff!" John sternly interjected.

Jeff thought for a very long time as he looked at Natalie and her file, trying to assess her motives.

"Mr. Vanderhoef, I know this may be out of the ordinary, but I simply want to buy the promissory note. It's not that difficult of a transaction, is it? I mean, cash is king, right?"

He smiled and said, "Well, in banking, 'paper' is king, but to answer your original question, no, it's not a difficult transaction, since the underwriting was done in-house."

"John told me Milo was involved in a more complicated paper trail, but actually owned the house for a day. Well, as Milo's beneficiary, I'm here to make it right, and you have already dealt with the problem of your lender, so let's save everyone a whole lot of headache and do the best possible thing for everyone right now."

Jeff thought again for several moments, staring at the file and said, "Okay, it is highly unusual, but I can see you are determined, and it saves the bank money and hassle. We will want indemnification for everything."

"Fine," Natalie said.

"I'll pay all the bank fees, Natalie will only pay the note off," John said. Then he looked at her and said, "I will not take 'no' for an answer on this one, Natalie."

She smiled and gave a concessionary nod then said, "Can we do it today, Jeff?"

"Well, yes, I can have my assistant draft the payoff and make the transfer of funds. You will have to tell Ms. Ludlow of the resolution. She is aware her loan was under investigation and was cooperating but she'll be glad to hear of this, I'm sure."

Natalie stood up extending her hand to shake, and Jeff obliged. "Please excuse me; I need to use the restroom again. This baby is something else, I tell you." She smiled at him. "Thank you, Jeff," she said, and left the room.

Jeff instructed his assistant to create the necessary paperwork. The process took about thirty psalms worth of reading. Natalie signed for the transfer of funds, the payoff to the bank, and other litigious protections and indemnification forms. John read all the forms, witnessed them and wrote a personal check for the bank fees. The assistant took the forms to make copies for all the parties.

Kallistos and I followed the assistant to the copy room, and as the forms were being copied he touched the machine and created a paper jam. The assistant cleared the paper tray. The signed promissory note was crumpled so she threw it in a 'to shred' basket. She finished making copies and left. Kallistos picked up the crumpled form and said, "Take this alms gift to Savlo. Tell him about Lilleth."

Before we parted I heard John giving Natalie directions to the house on Silver Street.

— • —

I arrived back at the hive gate, and both Left Hand and Right Hand growled as I took my place next to Savlo. Mammon and Savlo were standing in front of the house on Silver Street, in heated debate.

"This transaction alone," Mammon pointed to the demonic Karen Ludlow, who was still eating her children, "is enough to prove that his heart is calculating benefit for his own sinful intent and exercising the full validity of our pact."

"Since we are bound to wait until the Ancient of Days judges the true intent of his heart, a point I have fully debated and defended this whole time, are you willing to wager his soul on the validity of this one transaction?"

"Yes, it's obvious what's going on here," Mammon said, and the hoard of demons surrounding him collectively winced.

I handed Savlo the copy of the promissory note. The wolves growled, arching the hair on their manes.

"What the hell is that?" Mammon asked.

"This is what you call a technicality. It's the actual promissory note to Karen Ludlow's property and it shows that Milo's estate owns the loan. You have different signers on your copy. So the validity of your contract is void, and the end result of this transaction has been transformed into a great alms gift."

"Give that to me," Mammon said; snatching the note.

He held it up and compared it to the paper the sin scribe had, which had lost its signatures. Then he threw it down. "You think you can come here with the help of a sneaky watcher and manipulate the emotions of his simple widow and save his soul? Your trickery is worse than his, Savlo. He still committed the sin," he said and transformed back into the Wolf of Souls, frothing with anger, and the two she wolf demons flanked our sides.

"A deal is a deal, Mammon, the validity of the Ludlow transaction for his soul. Is there no honor among thieves?" Savlo asked.

Mammon backed down and barked out a command. All the demons who had mounted behind him, eager to tear us apart, scattered.

"Savlo the shrewd, this defense cannot hold up through all the toll houses. Milo is thoroughly deluded and has defiled his wedding garment. Look at him, fearful and despairing, because he knows he's among the chief of sinners. The next toll house will test more personal, deeply rooted sins, and everyone will know of your tricks with the watcher's help," Mammon said, bowing his head in defeat. He let us pass through to the other side where the gatekeeper angel was waiting. We sped away from that toll house.

"He is greatly helped by his wife," the gatekeeper angel said to Savlo.

"Yes, he is," Savlo said. As we travelled on, I was given instructions to travel back to Kallistos once we approached the next hive of toll houses.

ENTRY 21

Sins of the Eyes: Toll Houses 9, 10, 11 & 12

When we arrived at the next hive, we found long lines leading to the ninth, tenth, eleventh and twelfth toll houses, where the sins of the eyes were judged. The lines snaked back and forth many times down a sloping parking lot and then were roped off to make space for a great throne draped with lizards and reptiles whose eyes rolled in all directions. Seated high on the throne was the hive general.

He looked fierce, black and muscular with the lower torso of a snake and the head of a man whose hair was on fire. Next to his throne boiled pots of eye balls. He constantly perspired, his face glared with raging anger. He coiled on his throne and cursed the souls with evil stares.

"The Evil Eye," I whispered.

Savlo nodded.

"The light of the body is the eye: if therefore thine eye be single, thy whole body shall be full of light. But if thine eye be evil, thy whole body shall be full of darkness..." the gatekeeper angel broke from his psalmody to quote an evangelist.

The gate read, "Sins of the Eyes: If you have ever looked over your life and thought you deserved more, then you are one of us."

Milo looked over the lines and said, "They're so long."

"We will have to wait in this line," Savlo said.

"Dear God, I don't want to leave this line," Milo whispered.

Just then the Evil Eye rose up on his mighty tail, squinted in our direction and screamed ferociously, "Milo!"

We did nothing. He coiled and sprang up and down in a fit of rage. "Bring him forward, now! I want to look deep into his soul." He revealed sharp, jagged teeth and his forked tongue flicked out. He was slithering back and forth as a woman beckoned us to come and skip to the front of the line.

Milo's head was lowered and his conscience exhausted by shame from the other toll house accusations. When he looked up, he winced at the apparition of the woman from his grocery store line, bleeding from her eyes and ears. She smiled at him, revealing her sheared teeth and said, "Looks like you're first in line here, mister high and mighty."

Milo started to drift backward but the throne of anger had an attraction that drew him closer. Milo was instantly angry, for this sin rested in his heart like a serpent in hibernation easily awakened.

As we made our way to the throne through the weeping souls, they lashed out at us from all directions. "Cutters! Who are you to be in front of me? Asshole! Back of the line, pal." Again and again the insults continued until we reached the front of the line.

"Milo, let me be up front with you," the Evil Eye said. Milo cowered at his intimidating gaze; the fire on his head flamed up and he yelled right to Milo's face, "I hate you!"

Milo mustered the courage to speak. "Why?"

"Because you lacked the courage to act as you truly believed."

He motioned for the sin scroll scribe to present the record.

"Judging from your record, you saw yourself better than other people, but joked with self-deprecation. You were envious of others' success but insincerely complimented their achievements. You reveled in 'transforming' the grossly exploitative capitalistic system—calling yourself a real estate god. And finally, my little rube, you were full of anger but waited until you were alone, driving down the rumble-stripped highways to express your true views of others. You shared my perspective of the monkeys but did not let it shine. "

"So you admit virtue—self-control," Savlo was quick to point out.

"Shut your mouth, fowl. This is my toll house. I don't have time to deal with you."

He fixed his cursing eyes on Milo and started to slither back and forth.

"I acted out of low self-esteem," Milo whispered.

The demon general laughed a guttural laugh so loud it echoed to the four corners of his kingdom. Signs reading, "Injustice," "Envy," "Pride" and "Anger" lit up on the tall stone toll houses. Thousands of blackbird devils flew out of the windows, swarming and circling around us. "He has low self-esteem," yelled the hive general, and more laughter clattered around us. The flying devils swooped down, hovered in front of his face, and cawed the very words Milo had said throughout his life, and then vanished, leaving a stench-filled vapor.

Milo looked at Savlo and said, "They know all my fits of rage, and exactly what I said in them."

He turned away from the devils, and then recognized the apparitions in line behind him as the people he had said all these things to. They began to voice their complaints which were his memories. "You told others I was a fool to buy that house, but pressured me to do it anyway," one person said. A demon looking exactly like Bob, the church treasurer stood a couple apparitions back with a dagger lodged in his heart. "I didn't deserve your anger. I just counted the money and wanted to make sure you received the total tax deductible amount."

"I know, Bob. I'm sorry," Milo said.

The woman from the grocery store, farther back in the line, yelled, "I was a poor person, widowed. Every dollar counts to me. I was just trying to save a little for my grandbaby's diapers; food stamps don't cover that. You were the meanest person ever to speak to me. I was humiliated."

The demons belligerently assaulted Milo, on and on with jeers and accusations about his memories. Then the Evil Eye raised his hands and silence fell on them all. "Milo, I would like to bring out 'gimme a buck Bill' before us as the ultimate example of who you really are on the inside."

Savlo spoke to my mind, "Tell Kallistos he'll have to arrange an encounter with the diabetic William Washington, who lives under the S-curve that runs through the city."

As I slowly receded into the line, Milo closed his eyes and covered his ears. "It's all true. I'm a horrible person," he yelled, and fell down. "I'm sorry. I'm sorry!" He wept bitterly.

"You are horrible with your tongue, that two edged sword slicing up your fellow primates every day for seven glorious years. Listen to the lines some more. This is their day to be heard, and you must listen." The accounts of his sins continued to be voiced and he continued to weep as I sped to Kallistos.

— • —

I arrived, informed Kallistos of Milo's current hive trial and told him about William Washington. He thought for a moment. "You'll have to guard Natalie. Arranging an encounter can be a difficult task. I hope he's drunk," Kallistos said.

"Really?"

"Oh yes, the inebriated often do the work of angels. She's decided to clean out Milo's office today and is almost done readying herself. I need to find William Washington," he said and disappeared. Natalie immediately got chilled and put on a sweater.

I watched her get ready and attend to Sasha with the greatest of care. Sasha had stopped talking as the reality of her father's death scarred her psyche deeper and deeper every day. Natalie walked her over to a neighbor's house in hopes of getting her to talk and play with one of her friends.

On the way back from the neighbors, Natalie noticed the rain clouds forming and stepped back inside to get an umbrella. I looked up and saw a host of flying demons weaving in and out of the clouds and clapping thunderously as they planned an attack. Natalie grabbed some empty boxes she had saved and was off to Open Door Realty. We drove without encountering demonic activity.

While pulling into the parking lot, Natalie noticed Lilly walking to her car. Lilly noticed her too and immediately started to rub her belly, but did not look Natalie's way. She got into her Porsche and sped off. Natalie parked close to the door in a reserved parking spot, took a deep breath, and said, "Lord bless her and change me."

She walked into the office and made pleasant formal greetings to everyone. She stepped into Milo's cubicle and Ricky spun around on his chair. "Natalie, I'm Ricky Osborne. I'm sorry I couldn't make it to the funeral and I'm so sorry for your loss. I've sat across from Milo for a couple years now. I liked him a lot; he was always making people laugh."

"Thank you, Ricky."

"He was a good man," he said.

Natalie smiled at him until it became an awkward silence.

"Well, if you need a hand carrying out those boxes, I'd be glad to help."

"Yes, I think I would like some help with the heavier ones."

"No problem." He stood up, shook his empty coffee mug to her and walked off.

She turned to face Milo's cubicle, standing in silence for many moments, shedding only a few tears.

I looked over the symmetrical alignment of cubicles and saw demons popping their vermin heads up, looking at me. They were lesser demons and easily banished if I wished to expel them temporarily, but they would come back due to their deep infestation here. They hissed at me, and then ducked down again. Then a demon with the head of a toad popped up in the cubicle next to Milo's and spoke, "Why are you here, watcher? It's not like Kallistos to leave her."

"What concern of that is yours? What is your name, toad?"

It croaked a curse word at me.

I made my eyes glow white with light. "Name?" I demanded.

"They call my kind 'Innuendo,' for that is our work here. You want a peep show into our work?"

"Silence." I pulled out my walking staff and held it high; the flaming blade shone forth. "She does the work of the Blessed Virgin," I declared to them all.

They all hid and hissed away. The toad demon closest to me snickered, "She doesn't look like a virgin, probably thanks to you."

I swung my staff and sliced off the demon's mouth, leaving its energy speechless for a time. "Vile words have no place around her," I said. They all sunk out of view and I heard Lilly's name from several different places.

Natalie put two boxes on Milo's desk and loaded the files, trophies and office tools into one of them. She asked Ricky to take one out to the beige Volvo. Then she lifted the upper desk cabinet and saw his books. She looked through all of them, for Milo had marked passages in each with yellow sticky notes. She pondered the sayings as she piled the books in the second box. Ricky had come back, and she asked him to take that box.

"Natalie, is there anything else I can do for you? Aside from this, I mean. Anything at all? Just name it."

"That's sweet, Ricky. Thanks, but I'm making do, for now."

He smiled and carried the box away.

She sat down in Milo's chair and looked at the bulletin board, which was spattered with various phrases, incantations, affirmations, and positive self-help statements.

One picture was turned backside out. When she flipped it around she saw it was a family picture. "What kind of private life did you lead, my love?" she whispered. I heard all the amphibian demons laugh. She sat in his chair for several moments, taking down each paper and tossing it into the lined trash can under the desk. She pocketed the photograph in her sweater.

Soon Ricky was back. He looked over at her and said, "So are you just going to throw all that stuff away?"

She smiled, wiping her tears away. "It's all lies, Ricky—the beliefs of demons and charlatans."

"Well, I don't know about demons, but they sure help with the grind of the real estate biz. I mean, it's hard on a person's mind and every little bit of motivation helps," he said.

She stood up, grabbed the trash bag and said, "Thank you again for all your help." Then she smiled at Ricky.

"You can leave that here. We'll have someone take care of it."

"No, I need to take out Milo's trash."

She walked towards the door, and through the window, I noticed William stumbling along the building sidewalk across the street. Kallistos had done it.

She was walking out of the building when she heard, "Ma'am, excuse me, ma'am. Can I acks you an honest question?"

She stopped and faced him.

"Oh, God bless you, you're pregnant. God bless you," he turned around looking for someone else. Kallistos whispered to her mind.

"Hey, hey, sir," she said.

"Yes?"

"What's your name?"

"My name is William Oscar Washington, but most people call me Wow."

"Or 'gimme a buck Bill'," a young woman yelled from three cars back behind Natalie. "Hey Bill, she's pregnant and just lost her husband. Why don't you leave her alone?"

William looked back at her. "Oh I'm sorry ma'am; I didn't know you was a widow, too. I'm sorry, I'm outta here."

"That's okay William. My name is Natalie Christopoulos," she said and extended her hand.

"You can call me Bill. Nobody really calls me William anymore, not since I was——." He stopped mid-sentence.

"Well, I like the name William. It's a good strong name and someone very wise told me names are important."

He beamed with a smile.

The woman who yelled walked up to them and gave William five dollars. "Here, Bill. Now leave her alone."

He stood there and did not leave, but quickly put the five dollars in his pocket.

The woman turned to Natalie and said, "Hi. I'm Amber, and I knew your husband. In fact, we competed quite often for Agent of the Month. I could never beat him." She forced a smile.

"Amber, I know your name. Milo had mentioned it a couple of times."

"Milo?"William barked.

"You knew my husband too?" she asked him.

He lowered his head. "I'm sorry, ma'am, that your husband died, but the last time I talked to him was the worst day of my life." Kallistos placed his hand on her shoulder and encouraged her.

"Bill, shut up,"Amber interjected.

"No, Amber. Please, William, tell me about it."

"Bill, don't,"Amber said.

"Yes. Tell me what happened," Natalie insisted.

"Well, ma'am, the short of it is, he was on his way to lunch with a very pretty red-head, driving an expensive SUV and dressed in some fine clothes. I needed some money for a diabetes testing kit and acksed him if he could spare ten dollars and seventy fi-cents," he said as he swallowed hard and lost focus in the conversation.

"He's drunk. Come on, Natalie. Let's go. I'll buy you a cup of coffee and tell you all about Bill. He's a scammer,"Amber said.

"Not yet, Amber. William, please. Did he give you the money?"

He wiped his running nose with his sleeve and continued, "No, ma'am, he didn't. He got angry with me, insulted me, bragged about how he worked for everything he got and then mocked me by offering to help me get a job, if I cleaned up and got a life."

Amber shook her head in disapproval. "This is such a scam. How can you spit on the memory of him to his wife. Shame on you, Bill."

"William, what Amber said is true; I am a widow. Milo died in a car accident several days ago now. I'm still putting the pieces together of his life. I loved him very much, but I can tell you knew a very different person than I did. I must ask a very important favor of both of you." She held both of their attentions now.

"Come to lunch with me and tell me more about Milo, the good and the bad." She looked at them both with deep, warm eyes. "Do you have the courage to honor me with the truth?" she asked.

Amber shot William an angry glance, but agreed.

"There's a hot dog place by the Amway Hotel. Do you know it?" Amber nodded.

"Good. William can you get there?" Natalie asked.

He nodded. They all left.

— • —

When William entered the restaurant, the manager hopped from behind the counter and said, "Bill, you can't be asking my customers for money."

"No, it's fine, sir. He's my guest. We're having lunch here and I'll pay for everything."

The manager conceded and returned to his station behind the counter.

They sat down. "So, William Oscar Washington, tell me your story," she said.

William told his life story to the two women. They laughed, were saddened, and for the first time in a long time, William was treated like an image bearer who had been fighting and losing a battle his whole adult life. He had wisdom and had been a successful merchant at one time according to worldly standards. His guardian did not talk to Kallistos or me. He simply meditated next to William.

Amber shared about her often heated competition with Milo and confessed the bitter grudge and anger she held toward him. She was especially repentant about her last conversation with Milo. Her guardian did not speak to us either, but smiled approvingly with this interaction. She knew of Milo and Lilly; she said it was office gossip.

Natalie listened, but her eyes were focused on the pain in Amber's soul.

Natalie shared stories of Milo that were very different from theirs. She explained some of her thoughts about what Milo had been doing and how she was dealing with her loss of him. They spent the afternoon together and talked as friends, sharing their life burdens together. Demons howled outside as Kallistos stood guard.

"Thank you both for sharing with me your lives and some of the stories of Milo. My life will never be the same, and I wish Milo could have been here to really know who you both were. Perhaps you would've seen a different side of him if he were here too." She swallowed hard and said, "My life is still connected to Milo."

They smiled and nodded at her. Kallistos gently prompted Natalie, and then stepped back.

"I have one final request, and this is solely to benefit Milo's soul. You may not understand or agree with it, but William, I want to take the commissions from Milo's final deals that are going to close, rent you a furnished apartment for six months, and buy you the medical equipment you need," Natalie said.

Amber's eyes opened wide.

"William, when you asked my husband that 'honest question,' was it really honest?"

"Yes, ma'am, it was."

"Let my husband reach out to you through me and accept this, as one child of God helping another," Natalie said and squeezed his hand three times.

William lowered his head with humility and accepted.

"Look up at me, William. This is not pity. This is love in action. Please forgive my husband."

He lifted his teary eyes to her and said, "I do."

She looked to Amber and said, "Will you please make sure this happens?"

"I will, Natalie."

"I would also like you to take over my husband's business. I will give you his database of clients. I think he has twenty or so listings."

"Natalie, I'm fine, I don't need your husband's business."

"I know. I mean no disrespect to your abilities. I don't know how else to apologize and make right Milo's behavior towards you and his clients. But I trust you to treat them well."

Amber started to weep from a place deep inside her soul and dropped her head into her hands. Her guardian came closer to her.

Natalie leaned forward, grasped her hands when Amber said, "His behavior towards me was the same as mine towards him." Amber continued to cry and whispered, "I'm so sorry, too."

Natalie pulled out the family picture she had pocketed and gave it to Amber and said, "Pin this in your cubicle and never forget what has happened here today."

Amber wiped her eyes, nodded profusely and said, "I won't. I won't."

"Finish out Milo's business and give all the money away as you see fit."

"Are you sure?"

"Yes, I'm fine financially," Natalie answered.

They exchanged kind words and left the eatery.

William Washington's guardian broke his mediation at Kallistos's request. He had suffered much sadness at the hands of William's hindering angel, but now flickered with light. "Please," Kallistos told him, "go with the watcher to the toll houses and testify to the Evil Eye what has taken place here. I will watch William while he is with her."

— • —

William's Guardian and I travelled quickly, trans-dimensionally.

"Have you been to this hive before?" I asked him.

"Many times."

We were making our way through the lines and could see Milo and Savlo still standing before the throne of rage. A demonic apparition of William Washington was yelling his vile case against Milo when William's guardian stepped forward and announced, "I have testimony relevant for this trial."

The general spun around and asked, "Who are you?"

"I am Ambriel, Guardian for William Oscar Washington the third."

The Evil Eye looked at the apparition of William, who transformed his appearance, revealing a sinister bearded face with one crazed eye. It was William's hindering angel. He said, "I was there when Milo cursed him, as were you, Ambriel. There is no debate here. Even Milo agrees with us."

Ambriel stood tall, raised his arms and multicolored wings, shimmering colored light and said, "I've seen a great and wondrous display of humility, contentment, forgiveness, love, and justice." All the demons present violently shook their heads and shrieked in pain at the mere mention of these virtues. Ambriel detailed the conversation and events that had just taken place in the earthly dimension. With every new detail of the testimony, the sin scroll scribe saw Milo's account fade.

"Where two or three are gathered in His name…," the demons scattered into the toll houses and the evil-eyed demon general slithered back to his throne, hands pressed against his ears, "…there He is also!" Ambriel shouted. Thunder clapped, lightning exploded throughout the hive and the ground shook at the mere mention of His name.

Savlo bowed to Ambriel, who disappeared, and then led Milo to the edge of this hive where the gatekeeper angel was waiting to continue on. I was sent back to Kallistos.

ENTRY 22

"The angels are the dispensers and administrators
of the divine beneficence toward us."

- *John Calvin*

Natalie had made the prior preparations necessary to go on her pilgrimage to the monastery and meet with Father Arseny. The drive was over two hours and Sasha slept for most of the journey. She pulled into the guest house parking lot and walked around a bit, observing the cemetery. It was a quiet place with large tombstones. She and Sasha entered the greeting area and walked into the gift shop. A very young woman introduced herself as Sister Rachel and offered her assistance.

"Oh, you are much too young to be a nun," Natalie said.

"I'm not a full nun. I haven't taken my vows yet, but God's will be done," she said.

"Yes, that's a good way to look at it. I'm here to meet Father Arseny with a request. I called ahead."

"Oh, you called the other day. Yes, let me get Mother Alexandria for you," Sister Rachel said.

Natalie watched Sasha look over Pascha eggs and Russian nesting dolls. This was a holy place. No demonic activity could be detected. The guardians of the nuns followed behind them, elevated and in a constant state of deep focused meditation. Kallistos had told me they fight many regional demons at night here.

Sister Rachel returned with a disappointed look on her face and said, "I'm so sorry but Father Arseny is not feeling well today and is not taking visitors."

"But I called ahead. Can I just see him for a quick moment?"

"It won't be possible. I'm sorry."

Sister Rachel's guardian opened his eyes and spoke to both of us telepathically, "Go in peace, I will have her make a note of your visit and request."

Kallistos prompted Natalie to not insist on a visit, but accept this.

"God's will be done, right?" Natalie replied.

Sister Rachel beamed with a smile and said, "That's a good way to look at it. I can write your name down and record a prayer request if you like?"

"That would be nice. Thank you."

She gave Natalie a pen and paper and then spoke playfully with Sasha as Natalie wrote. Sister Rachel took the request and humbly retreated back to her work of cataloguing the gift shop books.

Natalie sat down in the greeting area on a chair and rested her eyes, for it was a long drive back. Sasha was looking out a window at a cat in a sitting garden. She let the peace of this place, which was beyond human understanding, seep into her soul.

Moments passed before she heard a higher pitched older man's voice say, "Hello, Natalie," as if he knew her.

She opened her eyes and before her stood a portly old man in a black cassock with a beard as white as wool. His eyes were a deep dark warm brown. She had seen the same eyes with St. John Maximovitch, and they engaged her full attention.

"Father Arseny?" she asked.

"Yes, I can tell you suffer for him. Just like our Lord on the cross looked down on the people and granted them forgiveness, for they knew not what they were doing—you have the same forgiveness for him."

"Father, I'm tired."

"But your faith is so strong and you are beloved by God. You know this love, yes?"

She nodded and looked down at the ground.

"Find encouragement in Christ's sufferings. I will pray for him by name until Pascha."

Natalie stood up to thank him, but he was gone. She looked around, and then saw Sasha run into the gift shop. She walked over to the library and approached Sister Rachel. "Sister, did you see where Father Arseny went?" she asked.

"I'm sorry? Father Arseny isn't here. He's in his cell on the other side of the monastery."

"No, I was just talking to him," Natalie said.

The young novice looked confused. "That's physically impossible. He is sick and walks very slowly these days. You must have been dreaming."

Natalie fell silent for a moment. Then she handed the sister a check for a large amount of money.

"This is for the memorial of my husband, Miletus Emmanuel Christopoulos. Please make sure it's recorded in his name."

"Of course, of course, I'll make sure he is named on Saturdays when we pray for the souls of the dead. Thank you, Mrs. Christopoulos."

Natalie walked hand-in-hand with Sasha out of the guest house and left for Grand Rapids.

"Kallistos, will this help Milo?" I asked.

"Yes, but this helps her more than him. Her acts of faith, hope, and love flow effortlessly from her, for she now trusts the Kingdom of God in the world."

— • —

After the long drive back, the duties of the pregnant widow had weakened her body but not her emotional resolve. She laid down and napped as Sasha watched television. We stayed close. She was faithful to the directive of Father Lazarus, attending almost every service during Lent and praying prayers of the heart in deep silence several times a day. She longed to talk with Father Lazarus again and spent time every day looking for him in the cemeteries, but was unsuccessful. Kallistos told me Satanial was hunting him, and Father Lazarus was wisely hiding.

— • —

At the beginning of the next lunar phase, after her visit to the monastery, Natalie was organizing her home when the doorbell rang. At the door were Brooke and Pastor Daniel, dinner in hand.

"Hi, Brooke, Pastor, come on in," Natalie said, maneuvering around boxes of Milo's clothes waiting to be picked up by the Salvation Army. "I'm sorry for the mess, but it's a slow process. Oh, it's so good to see you both. Please come sit with me for a while."

They came into the house, walked to the back family room and Pastor Daniel noticed the lit candles in the corner.

"What's going on over there?" he asked.

"Oh Pastor, that's my makeshift icon corner. I sit and pray there."

"Hmm, and what's with all the pictures, looks like a shrine?"

"They're icons and they help me stay focused. I find great comfort with them around."

Brooke put the dinner on the dining table and said, "It's just a casserole, but it's my grandma's secret recipe and it heats up well for leftovers."

"It'll be great. Thanks so much, Brooke."

Pastor Daniel was studying the prayer corner.

"So, how are you feeling? It's got to be getting pretty close?" Brooke asked.

"Yeah, pretty much any time, really."

"Natalie, this is so much to deal with. How are you really holding up? How can we help you?" Brooke asked.

"Can we sit down for a little bit?" Natalie asked.

They all reclined in the adjacent family room and Natalie shared with them all she had learned about the toll houses, from Father Lazarus, the encounter with Father Arseny and the angel promptings. She also shared how she had grown close to Mary and thought about her life as a role model. They did not fully understand, nor could she describe it in a way they could.

"Wow, Natalie. I don't even know what to say to all that. I really just wanted to know how you and Sasha were doing," Brooke said.

"Oh, I'm sorry, Brooke. There's just so much going on and no one to talk to. Sasha is at Helen's again tonight. She stopped talking after Milo's death and I thought moving Milo's stuff out would upset her. But I'm doing okay, surprisingly. Helen's been great and, well, of course my guardian angel has been a great comfort."

Brooke was scandalized into silence.

"Natalie, I've always been a straight shooter. I was with your husband and I'll be one now. I think you're on the short road to having a mental and spiritual breakdown. You've got to come to grips with the reality of your situation and get some help, some good Biblical grief counseling," Pastor Daniel said, sounding almost confrontational.

Brooke nodded and said, "I know someone who helped my sister-in-law last year, very kind and very knowledgeable about the Bible."

"Listen to Brooke if you refuse to listen to me. We're really concerned about your mental state and your physical health with the baby. I mean, Natalie, toll houses and angels and a drunk who see ghosts. You have to admit this sounds pretty crazy."

Kallistos drew close to her.

"Pastor, do you believe in spiritual warfare and angels?" she asked.

"Of course, it's biblical."

"Well, you know when the Devil tempted Jesus in the wilderness?"

"Yes, it's in Matthew, Luke and Mark mentions it."

"Well, the Devil took Jesus to a high mountain where He could see all the kingdoms. Now the words 'toll houses' aren't used but the Devil is transporting Jesus through the air and tempting him, then a bunch of angels ministered to Him. Something is going on."

Pastor Daniel leaned back and was silent in thought and said, "Jesus, wasn't dead yet."

"No, but it happened in a spiritual realm?" She leveraged herself up from her chair and retrieved a book about angels in her icon corner and said, "Pastor, this is a book by Reverend Graham, I've marked a passage. Please read the part I have underlined?"

Pastor Daniel took the book and looked it over, "I haven't read this one," he said and cleared his throat. He mumbled through the words describing 'the Prince of the power of the air.' He paused and skipped down the page, "hmm."

He closed the book and looked at the cover.

"Pastor, I don't have a direct verse from the Bible but I believe something like this is going on with Milo. If Jesus was flying around in the air with the Devil tempting him—I believe there is a lot going on in the spiritual realm."

Brooke looked at the floor and Pastor Daniel at the icon corner again, their angels prompting them aggressively.

"Pastor, I only have a short time left to help Milo, and I'm trusting that I can make a difference in his battle."

The room grew awkwardly silent now.

"May I take this book for a spell?" Pastor Daniel said.

"Of course."

"I'll get it back to you pretty quick."

"No hurry, I've read it already."

"Well, we should be on our way then, and sure would like to see you Sunday," he said.

Natalie smiled and tightly embraced Brooke around the neck.

As they departed from the porch, I saw a most angry demon in the front yard. He was seething spittle and fury was on his face. Kallistos advanced to the front porch and they locked eyes, both their wings spread and weapons poised to strike.

"The last time I saw you was on that mountain over-looking those kingdoms, Kallistos. Now you use that story to unsettle my work with him?" the demon said.

"Sometimes, it takes an angel's perspective of Scripture to get a preacher like him thinking," Kallistos said.

"I hate you, Kallistos, and I will tear your image bearer apart through the very people she loves at that assembly. You just wait," he said and melted as wax from a candle into the earth.

ENTRY 23

Sins of the Mind: Toll Houses 13, 14 & 15

Natalie spent the next couple days going through Milo's library and home office collecting papers, note cards, quotations, and all sorts of sales sorcery the demons use to promote the lust of the flesh, the lust of the eyes, and the pride of life.

She had been attending most morning services and Wednesday's Presanctified Liturgy at St. Mary's with her Baba, who had not stopped praying for Milo since he died. Natalie had taken great interest in the special prayers she had heard during Lent. She would pray them for Milo, inserting his name all throughout the services. As she redeemed her time here it strengthened her and gave her eyes to see that which most do not.

This morning, she stayed after and Father Job came from behind the iconostasis through Archangel Gabriel's icon-clad door.

"Good morning, Natalie. How are you today?"

"I'm fine, Father. How about you?"

"Thank God. Where's Sasha today?"

"Helen's."

"What do you have there?"

"I cleaned out Milo's office the other day and went through his home office and took these down from our bathroom mirror. Look at them—what do you think?"

Father Job pulled out several of the cards and papers and put them back in the plastic trash bag.

"Seems like motivational sales slogans and such."

"Yes, that's true, but I kind of look at them as pieces of Milo's inner thoughts."

Father Job remained silent and looked quizzically at her.

"I'm not sure, Father, but everyone pretty much has conversations with themselves on the inside, and fill their heads with all kinds of thoughts, some good and some bad. I think these are things that Milo thought about, and I know he recited some of them into the mirror every morning. I really thought nothing of it. He was just hyping himself up, you know? But for some reason, they disturb me now."

"Okay. I can't say I am following you totally on this one, but real estate can be a brutal business and I imagine it takes encouragement from time to time."

"Exactly, it can be brutal—brutally destructive to someone's soul. Have you ever thought about a salesmen's job much, not just real estate but the whole idea of aggressive sales?"

He raised his eyebrows and quickly nodded, indicating he had not.

"Well, I have, and my husband was in a terrible grind and it ripped his soul apart. This is what he lived on, mentally and spiritually. There's a terrible evil in this stuff, I know it, but I can't explain it. Please Father; don't look at me like that. Most everyone now treats me, well—you know what they say about my behavior, lately."

"Rather dismissive of your thoughts as superstitious and in need of grief therapy?" he asked.

She smiled at him and said, "Don't we all need a little grief therapy?"

He smiled back at her. "So what would you like me to do?"

"Burn them, bless me, and give me penance to do for Milo."

"Natalie, really?" he asked.

"Yes, I'm very serious." She became very animated and intense with him, the same way Father Lazarus talked with her.

"Penance has been minimized to the monastics in our tradition and is done very little in the parishes, especially in this country."

"Father, I'm not asking anything of you that you would not consider if I confessed these sins myself."

"I'm not sure finding encouragement in quotes and slogans is sinful, Natalie."

"What if it was more than encouragement? What if it was a creed? What if I was confessing another creed?"

He thought for some moments, walked over to the chanters' stand, turned out the lamp and closed the Triodion book. His guardian angel nodded to Kallistos and followed him behind the iconostasis through Archangel Michael's door. He returned to Natalie with a smoking censer and a metal trash can. He censed her three times as she crossed herself and bowed.

He then took the metal trash can, the bag of papers, and the censer out of the church to the front porch. Natalie followed him. He dumped the papers into the trash can and then, using tongs, took the coal from the censer, held it up and said, "As the coal from God's altar cleansed the unclean lips of Isaiah, so cleanse now this family from any demonic influence, whether it be incantations, curses, magical thinking, or other creeds of any kind."

He tossed the coal into the trash can and the papers caught fire, billowing an unusual black smoke that wafted high into the air. They both stepped back. He turned to Natalie and said, "Depart in peace, handmaiden of God—read as much of the Psalter as you can before you go to sleep tonight, and profess the Nicene Creed every day of your life. That's what I would have told Milo." He turned, walked into the church, and waited for her to leave. She soon did.

Kallistos sent me to Savlo and Milo, for he knew this was an unusual but zealous act of repentance.

— • —

I arrived to hear Milo and Savlo in an animated discussion. They had not left for the next toll houses. They stood at the exit, gatekeeper angel waiting; reciting psalms.

"I don't understand why this is all happening to me. I thought Jesus died for my sins on the cross, paid my debt and all that. This was a done deal. I was going to be saved from all this," Milo said.

"Where is the justice in having the Son of God, innocent of all sins, be killed for your free will trespasses?" Savlo asked.

"I thought that's what the whole 'saved' thing was all about. I believe all this—I'm saved. That was in the last sermon I heard. I thought I was going to heaven, and here I am going through these hell hives or whatever they're called—toll houses? I said the prayer several times and accepted the Lord as my savior. Did it take? I don't get it. Am I saved or not?"

"We will see, but salvation happens by greater means than you speak of," Savlo said.

"Greater means? Why can't you speak plainly to me?" Milo asked.

Savlo was silent.

We ascended higher and higher into the dark, when Savlo spoke, again, "Milo, trust in the Lord with all your heart and lean not on your own understanding because it is incomplete. You do not yet understand the great mystery of salvation because you are clouded by vice and lack virtuous eyes." Milo looked disagreeable at him. Savlo continued, "Who are you to claim such a grace with certitude? Who are you to make transactional demands of the Almighty One? You are an image bearer and you only exist because of the love the Holy One has for you. You're not an individual striking a deal with God. Salvation is a mode of existence, energized by who you love and who loves you. Love God and love your neighbor; that is the currency of salvation."

Milo did not argue back.

We stopped abruptly at the fifth hive's wooden gate. Before us the sign read, "Sins of the Mind: Begrudging, Murderous Words and all Magical Incantations of Harm."

The gatekeeper angel raised his voice as he recited a psalm, "Create in me a clean heart, O God, and renew a right spirit within me. Cast me not away from thy presence and take not thy Holy Spirit from me."

We looked through the gate and saw an evening carnival of sorts in a farmer's field. Music blared, the air smelled of candy confections, and lights were blinking everywhere, distracting our gaze so as to not look at one attraction too long. The gatekeeper angel swung open the gate and we stepped inside. There were three toll houses that appeared as red and white striped tents, before us. One was named "Evil for Evil," the second was "Sticks and Stones," and the third was "Eye See Me."

There were no demons present and no greeting by a hive general. We walked up to the entrance of the first toll house and looked inside. We saw two demons, human in form, dressed in business attire, standing in the middle of the tent, yelling angrily at one another.

"I will never forgive you for that."

"Well, whenever I look at one of your kind, I get sick to my stomach."

"You deserve to get sick to your stomach, because you're a repulsive backstabbing son of a bitch."

"Me? Let me tell you all the times you've lied to me." He slapped the other in the face, who immediately reciprocated.

One of them looked over at us and said, "That stupid pregnant monkey has already foiled us, and it's this son of a bitch's fault."

They continued to exchange evil for evil, hitting and cursing each other, so we went to the middle toll house, "Sticks and Stones," and looked in. The walls were filled with white wooden plaques hung by nails and stained by black smoke. Each of the plaques pictured moving holograms of people Milo knew. The people were grossly mutilated or in agony due to violent means: decapitated, disemboweled, and eaten alive by insects.

From the back of the toll house came a demon appearing as a meat butcher. He held in one hand a sharp stick and in the other an axe of sharpened stone. His steps thudded as he approached us. He stopped six paces from us, eyes yellow and squinting in fury.

"Penance! She dedicated every fucking psalm to someone or some group of people you murdered with your words, you foul-mouthed monkey," he said.

He then stabbed himself in the eye with the stick and cut off his ear with his axe, blood glugging out of his head. Milo covered his mouth with both hands. He turned and walked away, disappearing before he reached the tent's rear exit flap.

We quickly went to the third toll house, "Eye See Me," wondering what Natalie had done to destroy this one.

It was dark, with one spotlight shining on a pink, hairless, fleshy creature sitting naked on a stool with its head lowered. A smoldering metal trash can was at its feet.

"The way I see it—the success or failure of your life, that is—depends on the way you look at it," the creature said.

It raised its bald head. It was a Cyclops. Its one eye shared the same brown pigmented iris as Milo's.

"The real magic—the real secret to success, true happiness—is to keep your eye on yourself." It blinked. "If I remain the center of all thought and attention, then I can attract the gaze of others to look at the world the way I see it. It's supposed to be a universal law in your dimension," it said as it kicked the trash can over.

It stood up and looked directly at Milo and said, "I thought we saw things eye-to-eye, but you kept a secret from my view. I thought you loved her for the benefits she gave you, like a clean house, children, and sex. She met your check-list when you married her. You remember—marriage is the constant renegotiations of double standards. It's all about getting your way. But she was the forbidden fruit you kept from me, hidden in your sincerity. I look back at it now and should have seen it."

We said nothing.

It turned and walked back to the rear of the tent and said, "She may have saved you from our carnival, where your inner thoughts wound others, but she cannot save you from when you put your thoughts into action and impregnated the ancient Succubus from Savannah."

"Who?" Milo whispered.

"Lilleth, you sty," it laughed then exited through a slit in the tent.

We walked towards the exit gate.

"Savlo, what are the next toll houses?" Milo asked.

"Toll houses sixteen, seventeen and eighteen form hive six, the Sins of the Bowels. It's where fornications, adultery and all forms of sodomy are revealed to see if you lived for carnal pleasure and self-love."

"I repented of that, in my backyard, remember?" Milo said.

"Unknown to us at the time, you have participated in a most evil plan by a cunning and powerful temptress," Savlo said.

"I was tricked?"

"A deception with cosmic implications, I'm afraid."

"How can I be judged for this, then? You didn't protect me from having sex with a demon!" Milo yelled.

"Fidelity in a blessed marriage offers divine protection and makes folly of all the devils' snares. Your marriage to Natalie had been your greatest protection while you were soul sick in your life. I called to you. I screamed for you to run but you wouldn't hear me. That was a free will choice energized by sinful passions, rather than love."

The gatekeeper angel secured Milo and led him away.

"Go tell Kallistos that we battle Lilleth next," he said and I left.

ENTRY 24

"The task must be made difficult, for only the
difficult inspires the noble-hearted."

- *Søren Kierkegaard*

It had been thirty turns of the planet when Natalie walked into St. Mary's temple at sunset. It was one of those communities, especially during Holy Week, where the piety of old Russia—a lingering nostalgia in this country, still whispered a deep mysticism to the parishioners' souls. Natalie walked into the open nave, covered her head, and stood in the middle to the north side. She had done this many times since Milo's death, but this service was different. She was holding hands with Sasha and Helen was accompanying her for this service.

Father Job started the Bridegroom Matins with the opening blessing that unites this world with the angelic realms, "Blessed is our God, always, now and ever, and unto the ages of ages…" The litanies rang out in antiphonal chorus with the 'Lord have mercy's' sung by the congregation. Candles lit the room and Sasha was quiet. Father Job was fully vested and seemed to be floating around the nave, swinging his censer, filling the temple with smoke.

Father Job processed with the Bridegroom icon and placed it on a stand in the center of the nave. Angels and image bearers all bowed their heads. He chanted a hymn slowly, in a deep minor tone, and read the Gospel. Then with solemnity the people responded with contrite hearts and one resounding voice the ancient chant;

"I behold Thy Bridal chamber richly adorned, O my Savior; but I have no wedding garment to worthily enter. Make radiant the garment of my soul, O Giver of Light, and save me."

Natalie looked up and saw heavenly bodies, choirs of angels chanting in concert with them on earth. Her eyes were opened further as the spiral of angels sang. Her mouth gaped open and she looked as if she might faint.

Sasha looked up at her mother but didn't speak.

Natalie bent down to her daughter's ear, "Do you see anything in the air?"

She shook her head, indicating, no.

Helen looked at both of them, then to the dome and back at them.

"I see real angels," Natalie told her precious little girl.

Kallistos and the rest of the guardians remained out of her line of vision, but we all knew she was experiencing a great vision.

She spent the rest of the service quietly describing her vision of the angels to her daughter.

The service ended with great solemnity and image bearers dispersed quietly and quickly.

Father Job looked at Natalie's face and saw it glowing like that of Moses. He knew not to ruin it with questions and speculations about divine visions. She walked out of the building, and there standing on the sidewalk across the street was Father Lazarus, waiting for her.

"Father!" she cried. She looked to Helen and asked if she would sit in the car with Sasha.

"Can you meet me at the bus station, downtown, tomorrow morning?" he asked.

"Um, yes, of course, but where have you been?"

"Hiding."

"From what?"

"Not what, who."

"Who then?"

"Have you been faithful in the little I have told you to do so far?"

"Yes, Father." Her face held a serious expression and she asked, "Why?"

"You didn't tell me Milo was unfaithful to you before his death."

"I told you none of his sins. How did you know that?"

"The dead are horrible at keeping secrets from me." He exhaled. "Meet me tomorrow, please. I must talk to you about the woman. This is a sin unto death," he said and looked around quickly then walked away.

"Father!" she yelled.

He raised his hand and waved it in the air, but did not look back.

She went home, put Sasha to bed, and sat at Milo's desk. A bug-eyed demon with an almond-shaped head stared through the window at Natalie. Before I left to aid Savlo and Milo, I observed Natalie for some time. She logged into his online accounts and researched all she could about Lilly before she deactivated his accounts and pondered many things in her heart.

"Go," Kallistos ordered me.

Natalie was crying and had grown weak as I left. I knew Kallistos would pray all night for her to the Queen of Heaven.

ENTRY 25

Sins of the Bowels: Toll Houses 16, 17 & 18

We approached the sixth hive's brazen golden gate, ribbons of silk flowing in an unfelt wind. The gate sign read, "Sins of the Bowels." Beyond the gate, across curving hills wet with dew, were the three toll houses of the sixth hive. A large turret appeared as a phallus with two smaller domes bid us to enter its open gate.

A young prince walked from the domed toll house on the left, below the door mantel marked "Fornication." Curly black locks of hair jostled to his shoulders. He was dressed in a garment befouled with bodily stains. Behind him followed a harem of she-devils, all scantily dressed and speaking in foreign tongues. Their eyelids were painted heavily and they all looked lustfully at Milo, licking their over-plump lips and whispering of how they would violate him.

"Now, now, my delicious ones, he has been claimed," said the Prince of Passion.

"He is protected by the seal of a sacramentally blessed marriage and you have no claim to his soul," Savlo said.

The Prince laughed and said, "We have every claim on him, for he defiled his marriage bed."

One of the she-devils spoke with Milo's voice, "Married sex is like a B minus, never bad but not always your best work."

Another said, "My wife is like a Corvette, but Lilly is like a Porsche."

Another said, "I can't order, but I sure can look at the menu."

"And quite a menu you fingered over with your dirty little mind, Milo," The Prince said and pointed to the many groups within the harem displaying parodies of all his sexual thoughts, lustful looks, passionate strokes and dark desired fantasies.

"There are thousands of unconfessed sins, both voluntary, knowledgeable and willful defilements in word and deed which this naughty boy has committed. 'Have no claim,' Savlo? I expected more of a defense than everything but sexual penetration is excusable," the Prince said as the she-devils laughed and started rubbing each other.

From the other domed toll house, named "Sodomy," came that disgusting, hobbled hermaphroditic toad-like creature, full of oozing sores. He hopped closer and closer to Milo until he was inches away from his face. Milo tried to look away from this putrid apparition. He gargled the most horrible accusations of incestuous thoughts about Sasha and Helen.

"Silence—you speak lies and I will not allow it!" Savlo thundered, shielding Milo from Pharzuph.

Then in the doorway of the tall center toll house stood Lilleth, auburn hair cascaded down her shoulders, one hand tangled it. She wore a long black leather jacket, which pleated over her hips and covered very little. Black boots came up over her knees, leaving her white smooth thighs exposed. She smiled at Milo and emanated powerful waves of magnetic seductive energy.

"He's all mine, girls. I'm his baby's mama," she said and opened her jacket, exposing her rounded stomach.

Milo looked at her, then to Savlo and said, "She doesn't look like a demon. I mean, that really looks like Lilly."

The Prince, his harem, and Pharzuph made an aisle way but stayed close to listen.

"Milo, she is an ancient succubus with unique powers to possess and physically transform a soulless host. Her name is Lilleth. She deceived even me. Now she has complicated things on a cosmic level beyond my powers and rank." Savlo then looked to me and said, "Zazriel, I thought she was lying. Gabriel must know of this pregnancy, immediately."

Lilleth, the Prince, and Pharzuph all gasped at once. "Zazriel!" Lilleth said and smirked. Immediately the Prince, his harem, and Pharzuph fled away, shrieking in delight at having learned my name.

Lilleth walked towards us, glaring down, for her secret plan was now sweetened with this information.

"Hello, Zazriel. Mmm, a big strapping watcher, the last of your kind, an ethical slut able to run loose and gobble up the daughters of men." She laughed and continued, "Is Natalie's child yours? Will we have more Nephilim to play with? Oh, I hope so. My child will have great fun with them."

She turned to Milo and said, "Honey, if I have a son, I might name him Solomon, because he was a lust-child like ours is. I told King David to watch Bathsheba bathe, just like I knew you were watching me every time I bent over. Oh, that was so much fun. You were really yummy," Lilleth said as she swayed her hips in front of us.

"Lilleth, you admit, that you deceived him, so his sin was involuntary, for who can resist you?" Savlo said.

"Your defense is so thin Savlo, and you're a bore. I must admit though, Zazriel makes this very interesting. The whole thing just turns me on," she said and looked me over from head to foot. My energy flickered as she walked around me and stroked my deep peacock-like feathers. "I just like saying your name. Zazriel, ooh-la-la. So your son and my son are coming into the world, brothers from different mothers," she said then laughed.

I said nothing to her.

"Milo, baby, we had some fun, didn't we?"

"I repented and confessed to my wife and she forgave me," Milo said.

"Oh, really? Milo, do you know what your wife did last night? She was crying about us, looking over all our conversations in your internet chats. Forgot to delete those, didn't ya?"

She turned to me and said, "Zazriel, did you witness this great act of forgiveness? My sources tell me, she only started to forgive him."

I stared into her mesmerizing dark green eyes, filled with enough deviancies of a thousand adulteresses. "Zaz baby, let's go ask Natalie how she feels now," she said and disappeared from before us.

"Quickly, go, but engage her not. Milo's soul is in the balance here, not hers or your image bearers," Savlo said.

I fled as the harem came to tempt Milo with offers of endless pleasure.

— • —

Natalie was on her way back from meeting with Father Lazarus at the bus station when she pulled into the parking lot of Open Door Realty. I explained all that had happened at the hive and Kallistos was discernibly concerned about another encounter with Lilleth. In turn, Kallistos told me of Father Lazarus's instructions to Natalie.

"Lilleth is a most powerful foe, involved in corrupting their race throughout history. Only seraphim around the Throne and the mighty cherub who guards the Garden, who first cast her out with a flaming sword, can exorcise her," Kallistos said.

"What will you do?" I asked.

"Me? We will trust in the Lord with all our hearts and lean not on our understanding, for this is beyond us," he said.

I could discern Natalie was hesitant about the hard advice Father Lazarus had just given her at the bus station. She entered the office back door, for she wanted to secretly meet with Lilly. She tried Lilly's office door handle, but the door was locked and the lights were off. Natalie walked a few paces down the hall to the closing room and there Lilly stood, wrapped in a long, dark overcoat, her arms crossed. The anger on her face startled Natalie.

"What do you want?" Lilleth asked.

"Oh Lilly, I'm glad I caught you. Listen, I have been thinking about you."

"Good, because your husband sure didn't—he got me pregnant and then killed himself."

"What?" Natalie asked looking shocked at Lilly's tenor.

"Just get to it. What the hell do you want?"

"Lilly, I'm coming to you because I want to help you."

"Let me ask you, Natalie. Are you sure that child is Milo's? I mean, he knocked me up, maybe y'all had some kind of open marriage thing." Natalie momentarily dropped her head. Lilleth glanced at me and winked. Kallistos stood behind her with both hands on her shoulders.

"What—no. What are you talking about? Lilly, I know what you must be feeling because I am feeling some of the very same things."

Lilly laughed and said, "You think so? You know what I'm thinking and feeling?"

"Yes. I mean, we're both pregnant, alone, angry, confused about a lot of different things. It's tough to go through this alone, so I want to offer you my friendship."

Lilleth continued to glare at her.

Natalie spoke rapidly and did not look away from her, "I want to help you—pay you child support from the insurance money and we'll help with daycare and private schooling and stuff like that. But more than that, I want you to meet Milo's mother, Helen. She is a wonderful and loving woman. You can be part of our family as much as you want. We can talk about it more later, but I wanted to come here and offer you this, my friendship from my heart."

Lilleth blinked slowly, momentarily closing her eyes, and then said, "Do you realize your husband seduced me and shit on your marriage? I mean, you're pregnant and he made passionate, aggressive love to me. Right here on this table. How can you look past that? Screw him for leaving us with his mess to live with, right?"

Natalie took a deep breath and exhaled. She remained silent for a moment then said, "Lilly, I don't know anything about you, so you may not understand this, but when Milo told me of the affair, he wounded me deeply—to the core of my being, and I was mad as hell at you and him."

Lilleth smiled a thin evil grin, making sure I would notice.

"Then he died. And I can't explain it, but my love for him deepened or something, and all those feelings seemed to—I don't know. I guess love has a way of covering all those sins and changing how you feel about someone. It has to—you have to forgive, or how else do people live and move on?"

Lilleth squinted, started to look gaunt and said, "So he gets a pass? No way, sweetie—not from me. And you think I need your forgiveness? You bitch. You think I need your money? How self-righteous of you. I refuse to be insulted by your pity. You have some sick notions going on. Screw Milo and screw you for trying to work out some grieving pathology on me. Milo was a selfish prick. And to hell with you—I don't ever want to see you again. You are a self-deluded woman and you will have no role in my child's life."

Lilleth stormed past Natalie, pushing her against the wall, and went into the bathroom. Natalie stood in the hallway just outside the door to the bathroom, confused, but waiting for her to come out.

John stepped out of his office and said, "Natalie, what brings you here?"

"Hi John, I stopped by to see Lilly."

"Oh, I'm sorry you missed her."

"I didn't miss her. I just talked to her. She's in the bathroom—rather upset with me."

"Natalie, are you feeling alright?"

"Of course. Why?"

"Lilly just up and quit. She left a week ago. She said she was moving back to Savannah."

"Huh? No, I just talked to her."

Natalie walked into the bathroom and called, "Lilly?"

Silence. She checked each stall, and then walked out.

"John, I just saw her, I swear. We had it out right here in the conference room and she stormed into the bathroom."

"Natalie, listen to me. You're a very sweet woman, but I think the stress is getting to you, as it would anyone. I'm telling you this as someone that cares for you. Go get some help. I'll help you find someone if you want. Sheesh, I'll pay for it. You need some help, though," John said.

Natalie shook her head and walked down the hallway. She stopped at Lilly's office, cupped her hands to look in the door window. The room was empty. She looked back at John who looked sympathetically at her, then she walked out the back door.

"Go quickly to Savlo. Lilleth has a head start on you," Kallistos said, and stood close to Natalie with his wing around her.

— • —

I stepped out of the earth's time stream and went as quickly as I could back to the sixth hive. When I arrived, Lilleth shape shifted her lower half into her serpentine form, but maintained her now bulbous womb and mounding cleavage. Her head snapped to look at me and her forked tongue flicked out.

"So that's how Savlo has gotten Milo this far through the toll houses. You sneaky little bird man," Lilleth said.

Her eyes filled with rage and she refocused her attention back to Milo and said, "I'm going to let you pass. Not because I have to let you go." She shot Savlo an evil-eyed glance. "But because I, too, carry your child, and it will be a thorn in the flesh of your other son born by that bitch of a woman. She really is quite disgustingly deluded, and not very pretty. You could have done better," she said and laughed. "Well, come to think of it, you did do better, you did me better than I've had in hundreds of years. My little Milo, maybe I'll seduce your son. You know, the sins of the father are the sins of the son." She slithered close to Milo and whispered in his ear, "We can have a most unholy family now. Maybe I'll have a girl and then she can offer your son a ride in her Porsche of a body." She pushed him back. "So many choices but as for you, I'll let you pass, not because you are forgiven by me; no, because you really fucked up the cosmos on this one." She closed her eyes, shooed us back away from her and said, "Go away, little birds, for his ultimate demise is in the final two toll houses."

She then looked at Savlo and said, "Sorry ol' bore, but looks like you'll lose another one. I can tell, this guy just doesn't get it."

Then she looked at me, licked her lips and said, "Zazriel, it was so nice to meet you and discover your name. By now it's known throughout the lower heavens and all the bowels of hades. I do hope to see you again. Maybe our children can play together?"

She turned and slithered away, then stopped and turned her body around and said, "Milo, I should offer to let you be my sex slave for all eternity, but I'm just not that into you. I am far more interested in the mess you've left behind. Bye-bye, sweetie pie." She turned and left for the toll house door.

We slowly exited the hive while many of the she-devils baited him to stay with them, offering more sexual pleasures. He didn't acknowledge them. The gatekeeper angel was waiting for us. We ascended for the final two toll houses.

ENTRY 26

Sins of the Heart: Toll Houses 19 & 20

We'd been travelling upwards for many psalms into the dark expanse around us. Milo showed a little optimism, for he had made it through eighteen of the twenty toll houses. It was not of his own accord, but he was beginning to see, hear, and feel the power of his wife's love. Far in the distance, off to the right, a place was discernable through a narrow rocky valley. It emanated a great light.

As we passed by the dwelling of light, Milo noticed a great white gate which walled off a most lush garden. Before the gate stood the ancient cherub; holding his flaming sword. He was a formidable creature; his face was attractive but serious, watchful in expression, with white eyes, white hair, wings of gold, and garments translucent with a jeweled breast-plate. He held his flaming sword on guard against us as we passed by.

"Is that heaven?" Milo asked.

The gatekeeper bowed his head to the great Guardian of the Garden and said, "The entrance to this heaven starts in Paradise, the Garden where God and man walked in the cool of the evening, where image bearers were clothed in a glorious robe of light."

"I see people there. Are they real? Who are they?" Milo asked.

"Those are the holy ones purified by martyrdom and those who have made it through the toll houses," the gatekeeper said.

"The beggar in the parable I heard Pastor Dan preach about, is he there?"

"It is a parable that contains real and terrible truths as you now know, and yes, he's there among others. They intercede for the children of the Resurrection—offering their prayers as incense to the Ancient of Days."

"Am I going there?"

"Do you wish to approach and challenge the flaming sword of fire for entry?"

"No, I'm not worthy."

The gatekeeper looked to Savlo and acknowledged the purifying effect of His holy fire had begun to heal his spiritual blindness. "Enough talk, old friend," Savlo said to the gatekeeper, who continued reciting the psalms in an angelic tongue.

"Milo, you've seen much on your journey. Your wife has sanctified you as Saint Paul teaches a holy wife can do. However, the last two toll houses discern your faith and test your heart for compassion. We cannot go with you."

"What? You have to go with me," he said and clutched at Savlo.

"The gatekeeper will have done his job and has other souls to escort. I will soon send Zazriel away, for he has almost completed his mission. Milo, listen to me. I will stand at the gate as long as allowed—until He sends me to another."

"So you're going to abandon me, too?" Milo interrupted.

"Silence, before your words condemn you, right here and now."

Milo tried to get free from the angel's grasp and flee into the darkness but he could not.

We approached the black wrought iron gate standing well above our statures. Engraved in the cold obsidian mantle were the words, "Sins of the Heart." We stood in front of the gate a long time staring at a darkened, foggy, brick city square, street lights flickering on and off randomly. The gatekeeper had finished the Psalter and we listened to him as he joined chorus with the imprisoned watchers, who were not far away. My heart was saddened for it was such a sad plea for forgiveness to hear. Onoskelis took form in the obsidian pillar and asked, "Zazriel, do you think Milo is more deserving of forgiveness than your watcher brethren? Is it fair he's gotten off so easy, committing the same sins they did?" I sensed she had taken personal interest in me. I did not answer my new foe.

We heard an echoed rattling of keys and a series of doors being opened. We couldn't see anything but the creaking of the doors made us all cringe. The fog we had been staring at wafted away.

"The sins are all laid bare and seen by all now. The hive generals made true accusations and feel tricked. Why do they feel tricked?" The voice was heard with a raspy tone and reverberated from different locations.

"I don't know anything anymore. I've misunderstood my whole life," Milo said.

"They had good cause, but they were somehow cheated by the angel and her," we all heard the voice say.

"Natalie, my wife," he wept the words.

"Yes. She must be powerful. She must be dangerous. She fights with love."

"She's a saint," Milo said most assuredly.

"A saint? Could it be true?" the voice echoed all around him.

"Yes," Milo said, and grabbed the gate to look in.

"What about the sins? The way she was treated?"

Milo was silent and shamed, again.

"Ahh, what can we say? She is full of virtue and love. Deep down you—we detest her," the voice whispered.

"I don't detest her," Milo said.

"Remember she said, 'your actions have spoken more than your words ever could.' Remember now, all the sins of your heart and your disdain for holy things, like baptism, Eucharist and even marriage," the voice grew louder.

The iron gate swung open. "You belong here. You do not deserve her love or to live in the light of the heavens. You should roam these dark, cold streets, alone, faithless, regretting the lies that you lived."

"Don't listen to the voice, Milo. Reflect back on what you have witnessed so far," Savlo said.

"What good is a guardian angel anyway? You were supposed to be saved from all this, remember? He's a liar. It's just spiritual mumbo jumbo. No one ever really understands it. Stay here. It's not so bad, being the captain of your soul. This is your world. You deserve it. Relax and embrace your myopia," the voice now thundered.

"Milo, you are the object of love and life, not the source thereof," Savlo said.

"What the hell does that even mean? I'll show you plainly that life is the constant renegotiations of double standards. You have done well for yourself in the afterlife. I'll show you your treasures and where your heart really is. Turn your thoughts and energy inward and come and see for yourself," the voice said.

"These are ancient temptations, Milo. Don't listen," Savlo said.

Milo clawed at his mind and said, "I can only hear one voice. It sounds familiar. I know it."

"Forget all the other toll houses and despicable things you saw. You got away with all those sins. Come and see all the possessions you have amassed. Remember how they praised your name. Feel way down deep that you actually did something good with your work." The voice moved, and whispered in his ear, "Sure, you have sinned, but who hasn't? Come and see eternal life as you have secretly created it in your heart of hearts. Indulge in your own self-love. You are a self-made man."

Savlo said, "You don't have to stay here, Milo."

"I deserve this, I created this afterlife. The voice is right, Savlo," Milo said.

"Milo, this is a deception. The voice is you. These are your inner thoughts heard aloud. All the demons are speaking through your heart of hearts. They are using your thoughts against you. Trying to get you to believe lies," Savlo said.

"No Savlo. The voice is right," Milo said.

The voice was joined by a legion of demons. It thundered, "I have sown the wind, now I'll reap the whirlwind!" A great whirlwind swept Milo through the gate. The gate slammed shut and Savlo stood looking through the bars.

Before our eyes appeared a great city square, a domed Eastern Orthodox temple was at the far end, abandoned. His wrecked SUV was parked in the street. Billboards with his sales awards and statements of his prideful marketing slogans were visible on some of the buildings. The square was lined with vacant businesses offering satisfaction for the passions of his life. The center of the square rippled and was steaming where he walked, as if a river of fire flowed underneath. Milo was the only visible creature; we could not hear the voice anymore. He was shaking and his energy was deforming its appearance as he walked in the heat of the evening, alone, reiterating all his words, regrets and thoughts that revealed a lack of compassion for others, self-love and denials of faith about His eternal love. He was the captain of his own soul, shipwrecked in a mental prison, with no community to tell him he was loved, and no one to love but himself.

I knew then, watching Milo, that toll houses and even hell would not be empty if the image bearers believed the demonic lies that they were alone in the world, unloved by others and forgotten by the Almighty One.

"Zazriel, I will answer all your final questions now. For your apprenticeship is finished," Savlo said.

He did not face me, but kept his gaze on the tortured soul-sick image bearer.

"Oh mighty Savlo-El, I have only one question for you." I respectfully bowed to one knee. My heart was so broken I could not voice the question. All I could stutter was, "How…"

He looked at me and said, "Rise, Zazriel, forget not what you have seen and learned." He opened his wings and drew me close to his breast, igniting a light between us. He wrapped his wings and arms tightly around me and said, "Love what He loves, that's how."

He loosened his embrace and said, "Now go and wait with Kallistos for the babe is to be born, soon."

I left Savlo watching Milo suffer in the loneliness of his self-delusional personal hell.

ENTRY 27

"My beloved spoke and said to me, 'Arise, my darling,
my beautiful one, come with me.'"

- Song of Songs 2:10

I arrived on the night of Great and Holy Pascha and shared all with
Kallistos. Natalie had persuaded Father Lazarus to come to the
Greek temple with Milo's family for the Rush Hour service and the
midnight Resurrection Liturgy. This being the Feast of Feasts and
the only time he partook of the Eucharist all year, he obliged.

This night the demons were silent, hiding in the woods and
shadows near the temple. The faithful processed around the outside
of the building carrying candles, chanting;

"Come ye, take light from the Light, that is never overtaken by
night. Come, glorify the Christ, risen from the dead."

Over and over the song was sung and Natalie and Father Lazarus walked arm in arm, holding each other up. I was not sure how
either of them found the strength to do anything.

After the proclamation of the Resurrection Gospel in English
and Greek, the faithful heard, together with the myriads of angels

flying above in the lunar light, the great truth that shakes the foundation of the universe, as it was proclaimed by the priest, "Christ is risen!" And the faithful shouted, "Truly He is risen!" They proclaimed it again in Greek and in Arabic and in Slavonic.

Then the choir with the celestial choir sang the Resurrection hymn, forty times in several languages so the world would know;

"Christ is risen from the dead, Oh Christ is risen from the dead, trampling down death by death and upon those in the tombs, bestowing life."

Natalie appeared to be wrapped in a faint garment of light. Father Lazarus smiled, Helen wiped her tears and Nico held Sasha's hand, singing to her in Greek. They entered the nave again to commence the Divine Liturgy proclaiming the Great and Holy Resurrection of the Lord.

Natalie was in the front pew. She could see Father Lazarus behind the altar, standing like one of the icons. Suddenly she buckled over in pain. She looked down and saw watered blood dripping on the floor. She collapsed down on the pew and fainted.

Commotion ensued. Father Lazarus took off his stole and threw it at an altar boy. In a controlled stumble he staggered to her from the side door of the iconostasis.

"Natalie, Natalie!" he shouted, and shook her trying to revive her. He looked at Nico and commanded him to get a car.

He moved swiftly around the side of the pew and lifted Natalie up into his arms. He found strength and rushed her out of the temple. Helen and Sasha followed.

— • —

As they pulled up to the same hospital where Milo died, Natalie came to consciousness and whispered, "Call Pastor Dan. Tell him to come, quickly. God wants him here." Helen retrieved her cell phone from her purse and made the call.

Father Lazarus lifted her from the car and gave her to the medical staff. He stood in the entry way, blood on his cassock.

"You killed her, Priest, you know that? Oh, and I know someone who is hunting for you," the hunched-over figure said as he stood in the doorway of the waiting room. It was Natalie's hindering angel.

The priest was struck silent.

Natalie's hindering angel then looked at us. Defeated and crippled by the love she possessed in her heart, he cursed all guardians and limped off into the night.

"Zazriel, it's time for Milo and Savlo to witness this," Kallistos said as he bowed his saddened head and followed after Natalie. I went to go inform Savlo.

— • —

Savlo had not left the gate when I arrived. It had only been a half a turn of the planet but for Milo, in this horrible tormenting toll house, it had been a thousand years.

"Savlo, Kallistos said it is time for you to witness," I said.

Savlo spread his gray fire-red tipped wings, emanated a great light, and called to Milo with great authority, "Miletus Emmanuel Christopoulos, attend!"

For the first time Milo looked over at Savlo and walked to the gate, jittery and weary from inner torment.

"There's a great gulf fixed between you and her, but you must behold all of this," Savlo said.

Milo held the bars of the gate to his own prison and beheld the landscape of his aerial toll houses in ruins due to the acts of her violent love.

In the far distance, through a portal, he saw the hospital room where Natalie was being prepared for surgery.

"Natalie, my love," he whispered. "I remember her. My son is about to be born. There's my Sasha, my mother. There they all are, so beautiful. I remember them," Milo said.

The voice began to whisper to him again. "Shut up! Stop!" Milo screamed to his tortured inner voice. The demons were silenced and he was now open to Savlo's words.

"What's wrong, Savlo? Why are there so many people there? What's going on?" Milo asked.

Savlo and I left Milo at the gate and joined Kallistos and the others in the hospital room through the portal.

— • —

Several nurses were preparing Natalie for an emergency caesarean section. She was semi-conscious, feverish, and starting to swell. Pastor Daniel had just arrived and joined Helen and Father Lazarus standing off to the side in the preparatory room. Nico and Sasha were in another room. The doctor had a three-dimensional ultrasound machine ready to scope over Natalie's womb, while several nurses were about their duties. One nurse came into the room and showed the doctor some blood and urine test results.

"We have to move this up. Tell the OR to get ready. Let me take a look, then we'll go. Natalie, I'm Dr. Vandenberg, Dr. Bowne's partner. Do you know where you are and what day it is?" he asked.

"Yes. I'm in the hospital and it's Easter for the Orthodox."

"Okay. Do you know these people here?"

"My mother-in-law, Helen, Pastor Dan and Father Lazarus and my daughter should be around here with my father-in-law. They're all my family, now."

He looked over at them and they all nodded their heads.

"And who's going to make medical decisions for you once you're under anesthesia?" he asked.

"Helen?"

"Of course, honey. Yes, of course," Helen said.

"Well, Natalie, I have some concerns about what's going on with you, so I'm going to take a look real quick at the baby and then I'm going to ask you some more questions."

"Okay, doctor," she said.

The machine was turned so that everyone could see except Natalie.

Helen gasped.

"What is it?" Natalie said, alerted.

"Looks like a snake coiled up around him," Pastor Daniel whispered to Father Lazarus.

The doctor turned the machine so only he could see.

"Is my baby okay?" Natalie asked.

"Yes, right now your baby is okay but his heart-beat is slowing and he appears to be struggling. The umbilical cord has been shortened and has entangled with his body. There's been a placental abruption and a decompression of the uterus," the doctor said.

"Lilleth has done this," I said to Kallistos.

"What's going to happen, doctor?" Natalie asked.

"Natalie, listen to me very carefully. We're going to have to move very fast. Do I have your full attention?" he asked.

She looked at her new family and then Kallistos made himself visible to her. She recognized him through her spirit and said,

"Yes, I'm aware of everything going on in this room right now, Dr. Vandenberg."

"Good." He moved the machine away and held her hand with tenderness. "Listen to me, dear. I don't know why this wasn't diagnosed earlier or what may have happened to you, but there are several serious concerns I have and you have a very serious decision to make." He looked into her eyes and continued, "You have what's called severe pre-eclampsia. Your liver and kidneys are shutting down, you're bleeding a bit internally and your baby is under a lot of stress."

"But my baby is okay, right?" she asked.

"Yes, for now, but we have to act quickly. There are some risks to both of you. You have a possible life-and-death choice to make. Are you able to make this choice with a clear mind?" the doctor asked.

"Yes, of course, what choice?" Natalie asked.

"We could abort the pregnancy and that would stabilize you, or we could do the emergency C-section, but your life could be at risk. Either way we need to act quickly," he said, holding her hand with both his hands now.

The doctor looked over to Helen, Pastor Daniel and Father Lazarus for them to consult with the decision.

"Doctor, you don't need to look to them. I will take any risk— even lay down my life for my child. The choice is very clear. Do the C-section, save my baby. I know I will make it through the surgery," Natalie spoke with the peace of soul that passes all understanding, and Kallistos nodded affirmably concerning her living beyond the delivery.

The doctor spun around and walked out, and the nurses quickly rolled Natalie to the operating room. Savlo stood in the portal answering Milo as he rapidly asked questions concerning all that had happened. I went with Kallistos and Natalie.

— • —

It had been three hours and Natalie's body was damaged. The doctors had done everything they could to heal her, but could not. They were able to stabilize her and moved her to a recovery room. She had been in and out of consciousness for several minutes at a time. She was able to hold her son during this time and spoke the most beautiful words to him. The baby was in good health, due largely to Kallistos advising me on how to intervene with the other guardians and the doctor's hands in the operating room. While she was holding him, she had a seizure and they took my image bearer away. Then she lay wrapped in blankets as Milo had been, with machines and tubes administering medications in both her arms.

A short while later, Natalie roused awake to the amazement of the nurses and asked if her family could join her in the recovery room.

"Mommy," Sasha said as she ran to her bedside. Natalie put her hand on Sasha's head and looked into her eyes for a moment, connecting deeply with her soul.

"Did you see your baby brother?" she asked.

"Yes, he's cute and his hair is curly, like Daddy's."

Natalie smiled and then closed her eyes and pulled Sasha close to her.

"Mommy, are you going to go to sleep forever like Daddy? You look the same,' Sasha said.

"Sasha, Mommy loves you. Mommy loves…"

"Uh-huh," she said.

Natalie was fighting a seizure when Nico scooped up Sasha and took her out of the room.

A few moments later, Natalie came back to consciousness and her eyes were fully opened. She now saw all of us, as well as the trans-dimensional portal in the room. Kallistos pointed to the portal where the aerial toll houses lay destroyed and Milo stood at the gate.

Her head slowly turned to see him. "Milo, my love," she said with tears welling up in her eyes.

Pastor Daniel asked, "What is it, Natalie? What do you see?"

Natalie did not have enough strength to look at Pastor Daniel. The doctor entered the room and said, "She's probably hallucinating. She's in terrible pain and heavily medicated. I don't know how she's even conscious. She's incredibly strong."

"Or she's seeing a vision," Father Lazarus said to the discomfort of everyone in the room except Helen who sat down in the chair overcome with emotions.

Natalie lifted her head and looked across the great divide at Milo again.

"I can see our boy. He's fine. He's kicking at the nurses," Milo said.

She smiled and laid her head back. Milo then pointed to the ruined toll houses, "Look, you did all this. You destroyed the toll houses and paid for my sins."

"Milo, how could I do that…toll houses…just love Milo" she whispered.

There were several moments of silence with Natalie smiling, full of peace, then losing all expression. Her eyes then opened wide and she said, "It's not what you thought, Milo. It's not easy. It's a victory won," she said as another seizure shook her body.

"What is she talking about? Toll houses? Who is she really talking to?" Pastor Daniel asked with frustration.

No one answered; the doctor mouthed the word, 'hallucination' to him.

"How did we fight—or win?" Milo asked.

Her eyes opened with his question and said, "Milo, I connected to God...Father Lazarus told me how..." She fought to stay awake, then continued, "I, I loved everyone in my way...Amber...William wow...Lilly...You...this is how love wins. You must fight every part of yourself to love Him and others...fight...love...win," she gasped out each phrase then closed her eyes again.

Milo was drawn to her and shook the gates and screamed her name, but they remained locked.

She heard him and had a burst of energy and said, "Milo, just love what He loves, for love is as strong as death," she said.

We angels now illuminated the room. Milo gazed over the ruined toll houses again and his whole appearance changed. "Yes, love what He loves. His love is everywhere, in everything, in you, in me. He's always saving us. I see it now. Natalie, I see what He loves now," he said.

Father Lazarus watched in total amazement as he was given full view of Milo, the toll houses, and us angels. He walked over to her and absolved her quietly in Russian, then stepped back. Several moments passed as we all watched her body fight for breath.

Pastor Daniel's eyes welled with tears as he watched her writhe with pain but could not understand her visions. He bowed his head and held his Bible tightly. He looked at the doctor, shaking his head perplexed.

More nurses hurried in but the doctor knew there was nothing they could do, so he had them stand next to him.

Natalie's eyes opened slowly and she was energized with divine peace. She focused her gaze on Kallistos for several moments, and then asked, "What should I name him?" Kallistos deferred to me.

"Baptize him Tobias, for we will sojourn together," I said.

Natalie looked over at Father Lazarus standing next to Helen sobbing into his arm and said, "Name him Emmanuel Tobias. Baptize my children. Helen, Father, write about this day…tell my children…how much their father and mother loved them."

Helen could only nod her head, affirming the request.

She looked at Savlo and Milo in the portal and said, "We are the Beloved of God, together, as one."

He nodded.

"Christ is risen," she said.

We all replied in unison, "Truly He is risen."

There was a pause, she blinked a long blink and said, "Love is stronger than death or hell or any toll house."

Savlo smiled and bowed his head to the saint.

Natalie looked at Kallistos and smiled, "Thank you, my Good Energy."

He bowed deeply.

Father Lazarus shook his head and smiled for the first time in many years, restored with the joy of His salvation. His guardian then appeared behind him.

Natalie looked at me and asked, "So, you're the one? My son's guardian?"

I nodded and was energized by her approving smile.

She looked at everyone in the room one last time, pausing, smiling, tears rolling down her cheeks, and then her soul rose from her body. She extended her hand to Milo and said, "Come away with me, my love."

The gate of the last toll house fell off its hinge, and their souls were joined as one, in the cosmic mystery of His communal love.

The room filled with the fragrance of sweet-smelling flowers.

Then we disappeared.

ENTRY 28

"Precious in the sight of the LORD is the
death of his saints."

- Psalm 116:15

The Divine Liturgy had concluded. Father Luke came from the altar through the holy doors, jeweled cross in hand and said, "Dear brothers and sisters in Christ remain standing for a moment. We have the forty day memorial service for Natalie Christopoulos and then following coffee hour, we'll baptize her two children, the grandchildren of Nico and Helen Christopoulos."

The deacon and protopsalti chanted the short memorial service with the proper Byzantine tones. Guardian angels filled the nave of the temple, swirling and singing with the choir and laity. Kallistos's testimony of how love must fight to win and the way for some to make safe passage through the toll houses had circulated among the ranks of the guardians. It brought about a renewed fervor to the angelic rank.

"May her memory be eternal…" the closing hymn reverberated and filled the air as the faithful readied to exit the nave. After the third refrain, Nico yelled, "Axios!" The angels responded back, "Axios! She is worthy."

Natalie's soul was not present but all of her family was, as well as Father Lazarus who was to be the boy's godfather. Some of the older parishioners shuffled to the coffee hour, but most stayed for the baptisms, especially the mothers of young children. It was noisy; much like Noah's ark, but the mothers would not leave to the glassed cry rooms in the back. They did their best to quiet their children, as did their guardians.

The acolyte prepared the baptismal font, the holy oil for sealing and the scissors for shearing the children's hair. Father Luke and Father Job led the people to the back of the church for the exorcism and the beginning of the baptismal service.

Father Lazarus held Emmanuel Tobias and an image bearer named Nicole Thoma stood next to Sasha as her godmother.

Father Luke instructed those present to spit on the Devil, denounce him and all his kind, as he read the baptismal service book. Moans and screams coming from outside the temple could be heard by us angels. I looked out the window and recognized Emmanuel Tobias's hindering angel from the doctor's office looking at us. She held her solid black-eyed gaze, empty of any emotion. Then she revealed a crocus and affixed it in her hair and smiled at me. I looked away.

The service progressed and as Emmanuel Tobias was being dunked under the water for the third time, I illuminated and was sacramentally yoked to him as his guardian angel. Father Lazarus patted him dry and was trying to swaddle him in a white linen robe when Helen bumped Father Lazarus and said, "Let me dress lil' Emo."

He handed the babe to her and I noticed he looked over at me. I smiled at him. Father Lazarus looked too, but could not see me.

He grunted and knew the boy had vision into the angelic realm. He then crossed himself but told no one.

Sasha was next to be baptized. She sat down in the baptismal font, which was undersized for a girl her age. After praying, Father Luke dunked her once, then twice. Her guardian had not yet appeared which drew angelic attention as we looked around. Upon the third awkward dunk of Sasha, Kallistos appeared, radiant in white light, and was yoked to Sasha. I smiled.

As the newly baptized, sealed and illumined image bearers were consuming the Body and Blood of Jesus Christ in the Holy Eucharist for the first time, I turned to Kallistos and bowed my head.

"Natalie had one final request for her daughter and the Lord granted it," Kallistos said.

"Where's Savlo?"

"I don't know."

The people spontaneously sang out, "God grant you many years..." three times to the whole Christopoulos family, and then everyone departed for the celebration in the banquet hall.

I remained in the empty nave for a moment as they escorted Emmanuel Tobias out. Amazing and wonderfully confusing is the relationship between image bearers and The Holy One. I wondered about what Azazel foreknew, offering to fight with me if I could somehow gain leniency from God's punishment for them. I cleared my mind of these thoughts. It smelled like church and I smiled again, thinking of Emmanuel Tobias, now.

As I was leaving, high in the dome above, an icon of an angel moved. Then as if from a window into heaven, the Archangel Raphael manifested himself and floated down to the center of the nave. I bowed to one knee and he addressed me, "Arise, Zazriel. You have done well in His eyes."

"Glory to God in all things."

"Indeed. Was your apprenticeship satisfactory under Savlo?"

"Oh mighty Raphael, it was more than I am worthy to have watched."

He smiled.

"I do have a question, if you would be so willing to grace me with an answer?"

"Just one?"

I smiled, for I now knew he had talked to Savlo. "Yes, just one. The boy looked at me, but did he see me?"

"Ah, yes, he did. The Holy One wants to present him with a special calling, if he should choose it. The end of days is drawing near and the young boy is to wear the angelic schema, after the Seven Holy Ones that walk the earth."

"The Angelic Schema of the Seven? You mean a Navel Gazer? But—"

He disappeared, leaving me with only one question answered.

I left the nave, reminded that I was not a forgotten creature, nor the spat out watcher from Laodicea. Rather, I have always been in the silent presence of the Ancient of Days who holds all creatures in his loving communion since the beginning of the cosmos.

I was a watcher and I watched, but now I am a guardian. Therefore, I guard.